THE GIRL FROM JEPARIT

Carl Spence

Published in Australia in 2018 by Carl Spence

Email: cfspence1@gmail.com

ISBN 9780648334804 (paperback)

A catalogue record for this book is available from the National Library of Australia

This book is a work of fiction. Names, characters and incidents portrayed in it are the product of the author's imagination. Any resemblance to actual persons, living or dead, is entirely coincidental.

For my family

CHAPTER ONE

Norwich, England.

For Paddo, the fact that he came from quite a wealthy family was sometimes embarrassing. It wasn't affluence itself that was a problem, but occasionally he found the attitude that went with it, at least when it came to some people, a little distasteful. He loved his family and never took for granted how they had provided for him. Possessions and materialism itself seemed immaterial to his happiness.

In his late teenage years, he sometimes wondered whether this was all a simple act of rebellion. Was it the left in him that had discarded the right? That did not seem to explain it either, for Patrick (Paddo) Paddington-Smythe had very little interest in politics or money. He had come to the conclusion that sometimes people are the way they are simply because that's the way they are. Born a certain way, for want of a better deduction. A case might always be made, he reasoned, that everyone is, in some way, the product of their environment. Paddo was not closed-minded about this. His education was well delivered and he took most of it in. After all, the Paddington-Smythes spared no expense on their two sons' schooling. But then, it seemed to him, that very similar environments can't explain big differences, even between two brothers, separated in age by a little under two years.

When Roger, Paddo's brother, entered his final year of school, he announced to his parents and anyone else who appeared remotely interested that he had decided to enrol in a professional stockbroking course straight after graduation. He indicated he was planning and indeed expected to achieve the making of his first million pounds by the age of twenty-two. That same year Paddo told his father, Lachlan Paddington-Smythe, that he would journey to India immediately after his last year of school. Lachlan asked why.

Paddo did not dislike his father's ways yet, in truth, there was no adulation. He disliked his parents' materialistic approach to situations and their mild sense of superiority, but that was not enough to say he disrespected them. Some of their values he considered a little superficial. They had no spirit of generosity, for one, but they loved their sons. There was no question about that.

It was never entirely clear to Paddo or Roger how Lachlan had amassed his wealth. Paddo usually never gave it much thought and understood it was something to do with a variety of businesses, many more than one, it seemed, and that some were off-shore. He suspected Roger knew more than he did. His mother, Miriam, had never worked, at least not since marriage. Lachlan never talked much about his work, even with Miriam, as far as Paddo could tell. He was often gone for more than a week at a time on the Continent and sometimes South Africa. Questions were never asked.

Paddo told his father he wanted to experience life in India and wanted to go to a country where the weather was warmer. It was as simple as that.

That same year Roger made his announcement, Paddo decided he would join the theatre group at school. His first play was a comedy that one of his classmates, Joe Constantinides, had written. Miriam had asked if he was serious about this new interest in comedy and theatre and Paddo replied that no, he wasn't – he was merely doing it for a laugh. His mother never asked him any other questions about it and came to all his plays in high school.

Joe Constantinides had been born in England into a Greek family. Paddo tried to suggest to Joe to make some changes to the play and thought it was more like a Greek tragedy than a comedy. Joe had a stubborn sort of a nature and was rather inflexible in his approach to most things.

"You think it is a Greek tragedy? How do you mean?" Joe responded.

"Well, it's more like something Euripides has written. It's got potential to be funny, but it's all a bit conservative and dramatic. I don't think my character is very funny. He meets a sad end, which some of the audience might find cathartic, but I am not sure about it all, Joe."

"I am not changing a thing."

From then on in, Paddo referred to Joe as 'Constant' and Joe thought it was just a shortening of his surname, which was part of it, but missed that it was really a dig at his conservative, set in stone ways.

It turned out that Joe also didn't want to offend his parents by anything radical in the play. Mr Constantinides found the play hilarious, although by that stage, he was suspected of early onset dementia.

Paddo's interest in theatre may have been influenced by the artistic culture of Norwich or that side of Norwich, at least, rather than a true passion for it. The truth was, at this moment in his life, Paddo didn't have a true passion. But he was willing to keep on the lookout for one. They lost contact after their final year at school and Joe went on to a job in banking in London while Paddo kept his focus on that trip to India.

Norwich is a city that Paddo had heard described by some in his theatre group as having 'a touch of affluence about it'. He had even heard that one could smell the 'old' money if you walk through the laneways slowly enough and sniff hard. Yet he felt there was a definite civility about it. And whilst not really religious, he liked the churches. Like much of England, he could not help but notice that atheism, agnosticism and general ecclesiastical indifference were widespread in Norwich, despite one of the greatest, most beautiful cathedrals in the kingdom. Canterbury and York Minster stood among several rivals, but to Paddo, it was a matter of opinion which was the more architecturally stunning. In his view, Norwich was the clear winner. He had pride in his city yet recognised his bias when it came to such comparisons.

To anyone who knew him, it was obvious that Paddo loved Norwich. The air was cleaner than London with far fewer people. Not that he disliked people. It was people that he liked far more than things. India would be something to behold, given how he felt and how many people lived there. He had no intention of going for a long time. Just enough time to experience something that Norwich would not offer him.

"I don't have a travel bug, Mum. I just feel it would be a good idea to see a little of the world before I get too old and maybe get stuck in a job." Paddo said this the day he left for Delhi.

Miriam was worried and felt it was not at all a place for her young son to travel alone. His maturity for his age was noticeable, if not admirable, and he had confidence in his own abilities. But maturity and confidence abroad could lead to trouble, in the eyes of his mother, and she told him there was too much risk for one so young.

By the time he had reached eighteen, he stood just on six feet tall. He was solid but not overweight. He was also handsome, with a sort of boyish charm, wavy brown hair and near on perfect teeth.

Roger had some trouble with his teeth as a child and eventually had to endure corrective surgery and then braces for a few years. For a time, he struggled with a bit of a lisp and wouldn't smile. Paddo was regarded as the lucky one. Roger never displayed jealousy. There wasn't any time for that, when the corporate ladder was there waiting to be scaled. The journey to the top, without looking sideways, dominated his thoughts.

By the time Paddo had left the ground at Heathrow, Roger had made a quarter of his desired million pounds. He had mentioned this to Lachlan and Paddo one afternoon, casually and a little out of context.

Paddo had saved some money by working part-time whilst in the final two years at school, but it was on the surface largely insignificant as he was the beneficiary of a sizeable trust fund, as of course was Roger. The modest amount saved seemed important to Paddo almost as a symbol of his independence and perhaps, more significantly, because it involving cooking and serving tea and coffee.

In those days, he worked at a café downtown but doubled as an assistant cook at a restaurant, roughly splitting his out-of-school time equally between the two. On the whole, he met more people in the café. One person he met was Thomas Greer. Tom was almost the same age as Paddo but, although he too was from Norwich and had grown up there, they had not crossed paths before.

Paddo was not particularly interested in music or the arts, except for the performing arts. He was even less interested in school, but he was not inattentive and put in a moderate effort. The lack of academic ambition did not seem to bother either of his parents much. The money being spent, whilst perhaps wasted to some extent owing to his indifference, was a worthy spend alone in their eyes, if for no other reason than people would know where their boy went to school.

He did not have a lot of close friends at school, yet he was casual and friendly with most. There was Joe of course and whilst he shared the interest in the school plays, he found some odd lack of desire to spend more time with him. Perhaps it was Joe's conservative nature but whatever it was, it didn't bear thinking about too much. Girls seemed to be interested and most would refer to him as Patrick. Some girls said he showed a mild aloofness without arrogance which they found quite appealing, even drawing a sense of fascination, something which Paddo was never aware he might exude. As equally as Roger was consumed by all things financial, Paddo was absorbed by just existing in the moment, with no particular hobby or, it could be said then, interest in dating.

Paddo however liked Tom Greer, almost from the moment he met him one Sunday afternoon just before closing time at the café. It was a meeting that nearly did not happen. He was not meant to work that day but had been called in, owing to someone on the roster calling in sick.

Tom was meant to be playing cricket but it had rained all day and he had wandered around town in the afternoon, stopping for coffee late then intending on walking home.

There was a small village green near the café and as Paddo glanced out the window that afternoon as he was serving, he saw this shortish, curly blond-haired fellow with white trousers, white cricket shirt and a maroon coloured jacket stroll through the green. Something about him took his eye. He had a confident stride and a smile. The steps he took as he walked seemed wide for his height and made him look closer to the ground than need be. He passed some buskers along the way, giving them a sort of nod of approval, before he walked into the café and took a seat at the counter. The rain had stopped and a faint glint of sun tried to shine through the windows. People seemed ready to come out and enjoy the remaining daylight. It was at these times especially that there was something intangible about Norwich that Paddo really liked. A look of happiness on this fellow's face perhaps typified it and Paddo asked him, "What would you like?"

"An Americano would be fine." He paused and then said, "But, if there is a Latina in the kitchen, and please, *please* don't get me wrong, I wouldn't mind her instead, just quietly, as some company on this beautiful afternoon would be tremendous, don't you think? I would like to make her breakfast in the morning. I don't think you serve breakfast, do you?"

Tom was cocky and he often misfired when pointing his odd and sometimes inappropriate sense of humour in the direction of the public. By that stage, he had not got into a fight brought about by his smart mouth. That was only a matter of time, by then.

"What you see on the board is all we offer I'm afraid. There is however an establishment down the road though, that might be different." Paddo was a master of reminding the customer it was all about their choice, even if they chose elsewhere. He didn't say what the 'establishment' was to which he was referring and made a quick guess that it might be obvious.

"That's more than fine, but I am expecting a bit of a hard night, so the biggest cup of black coffee you can give me will be just fine, please."

As Paddo reached for the large cup, he decided that this fellow could not be more than eighteen years old. There appeared to be a sense of maturity there yet it was tinged with immaturity. It seemed that when he spoke he was older than what he looked. It was getting on towards the end of business for the day at a quarter to 5 pm.

"You know we are closing in fifteen minutes?" Paddo offered the information, almost just to see his reaction.

"Oh, I didn't know that. But, I don't think I will be hanging around after the doors close anyway."

Paddo placed a king-size mug containing the Americano in front of him. As only two other customers remained, he decided he would grab a tea towel and chat whilst pretending to look busy.

"You said you are expecting a hard night?"

Tom took a large sip and before he completely swallowed it said, "I meant, it may be hard to go to sleep after this strong coffee."

"And that would make it a hard night?"

"Well yes, in a way. Unless I can find something to do that might be interesting."

Paddo placed some cups away before re-engaging. "No cricket today?" This was an obvious statement, rather than a question. Sometimes if it merely drizzled he had noticed the cricketers still played. Today the rain had been unusually heavy.

"No. That's the thing, and I would be tired if I played of course. We were meant to take on the old boys. We couldn't even get a start. It's such a shame because it's only once a year. Even though they would have been flogged and hopefully, we would have been visiting one of them, at least, in the hospital after the match, it's such a great event."

Paddo could see the jacket was worn with some pride but he could not quite make out the emblem, apart from the embroidery of the cricket stumps.

Tom had a way of engaging a person when he spoke – not so much with what he said, but sometimes the way he said it. There was a sparkle in his eye and an underlying enthusiasm that seemed to radiate. It was almost like he was aware he was cheeky and most times he could get away with it, just with a smile. But there would be a sizeable gap between this very first meeting of minds and their second. In fact, a bit more than four years would pass before their next conversation. Paddo would travel to India and come back to his job in the café. The intervening years would each produce in them a sort of galvanising impact on their forming personalities. The dreams were there, seemingly below the surface, hidden by some more powerful force of living in and for the moment.

"I was never a cricketer," Paddo added, wiping the rim of a saucer with the towel.

"It's never too late for the gentleman's game. Did you play sport at school? Are you still at school?"

Paddo picked up another cloth and ran it over the counter, before placing several cups on the shelving behind him, ready for the morning crowd. He took some change from the tipping bowl and put it in his pocket. "I did the usual. Gym was fun. And wrestling, before we couldn't do it anymore. I am about to finish up this year."

"Me too. What are you thinking of doing?"

He had been asked this question more times in the last six months than he cared to remember. "I don't know."

"Me too."

They both smiled.

The buskers outside by this stage had begun to lift a little and the music could be heard inside. It sounded like folk, with a sort of quirky edge to it.

"They're not bad." Tom looked in their direction as he swivelled on his chair.

Paddo nodded and rested his elbows on the counter. "I like them. They often sit on the lawn, just there. One of their friends often brings a bottle. They don't ask for money. I like that. I just wish they'd sometimes start a little earlier in my shift."

"You have a lot of shifts?"

He stood back upright. "I am here Saturdays at the moment. Sometimes they call me in on a Sunday. And Wednesday afternoons."

Tom was enjoying himself. He looked around the café, as if he had never been in one before, with big eyes that wondered at the world.

A moment or two passed. The buskers had moved onto their next piece. The fellow with the flute was particularly good. They both seemed to be listening and talking at the same time and chatted for longer than they realised, almost a good half an hour after closing. Paddo had a cup of coffee after the doors closed and told Tom he could stay. Each shared a story or two about school. Paddo mentioned he had a brother, not much older, who was into stockbroking and that they weren't particularly close and that he wouldn't be following that route, that much he knew. Tom didn't say a lot about his family and Paddo did most of the talking. He found Tom to be a good listener, despite his cocky nature.

Tom eventually looked at the clock on the wall. "I shall drop in again, if you don't mind."

"That would be great. What's your name?"

"Tom. Tom Greer." They shook hands. Tom walked out onto the lane. He looked left and right as if either way would be just fine. He made his move and wandered away.

Paddo had a funny feeling, unlike one he had experienced before. It was sort of an excited contemplation of something better to come. A friendship, perhaps. It was odd and he was a little bemused by it all. It almost had a romantic notion about it but with a 'b' in front. His sexuality was not 'fluid' he had once politely told a boy who had eyes for him at school. He smiled as he put the last of the dishes away and thought about heading home.

Tom didn't live far away and could walk from town. He crossed the river near Whitefriars and turned right past St James Mill. It seemed he never got tired of admiring the beautiful weeping willows near the Mill. After the river took the bend, he wandered down Gilders Way and to his home. This was a route he often took. Had he continued down Whitefriars, to the corner with St Crispins Road sometime in the course of the next couple of years, there was a chance he would have run into Paddo outside the theatre near the old church. The two paths came so close to crossing again in those years.

Paddo walked to his home in the opposite direction. It was a much longer walk, to a much bigger house. In fact, it was more like an estate, compared with Tom's lodgings.

The list of 'never experienced' items for Paddo and Tom, at this stage of their lives, appeared noteworthy. Neither had been drunk nor been under the influence of an illicit substance, been involved in a fist fight or even a trivial misdemeanour in the eyes of the law. They disliked no one and no one disliked them. They had also never been in love.

When it came to love, Paddo had only peripheral experience. He loved his parents and his brother, no doubt. But sometimes he felt there was some sense of duty about that love. He wondered, at times, whether his parents loved each other. He even wondered, occasionally, whether their marriage was nothing more than an arranged marriage, where the arrangement was based on money. When a rich person marries a poor person, there can be no doubt the marriage is for love, it seemed to him. He tossed these thoughts around in his head, without real contemplation, and felt he just might be already wise enough not to expect perfection in marriage, or indeed anything else.

He enjoyed the company of his peers, without seeking it out. He particularly liked the parties thrown in his final year at school. Not all were as good as they could be. "I can tell you," he would say, "sometimes the difference between a mere party and a really great party, for one person, can simply be one conversation with a person in the kitchen." He would often then add his favourite saying about everything was relative anyway. And that subjectivity was king, in this world.

When Tom went home that night he remained awake, like he expected, for a good deal of time. The caffeine kicked in, as he feared it would. He gave some thought to his future, momentarily, but eventually fell asleep before properly considering a thing.

As he made his way out of town on the walk home that evening, Paddo reached into his pocket and pulled out the change from the tipping bowl. As was his habit, he placed it in the plastic cup sitting at the feet of the last beggar he would pass on his route. He could hear his mother's voice in his head as he did it, saying it was highly irresponsible to do such a thing and only encourages *them* not to get a job. "See the signs on the wall," she would say, pointing to the guidance that it is better to give to a reputable charity that could then give proper care. It made no difference to Paddo and if he was wrong in doing what he did, it didn't bother him at all.

CHAPTER TWO

The quality Kaju Feni, together with too much beer, removed one of the 'never experienced' from Paddo's list. He came close to expelling most of what he consumed on that balmy evening on the west coast of India, just south of Goa and knew it was his own fault for overindulging. After a month in Mumbai, he had decided it was time to escape the masses and make his way south to Kerala. On his way, he was advised to try both the cashew feni and the toddy palm feni.

Someone also told him that the feni liquor selling market is somewhat unorganised. "This is our heritage brew," he was told more than once by Jasthi, a young fellow who acted as his guide for those few days. First, he tried it straight, then with lime juice and eventually in a series of cocktails. By mid-evening, there was nothing straight or organised happening. By the time he arrived in Cochin, several days later, he was just beginning to emerge not merely from a hangover but some kind of malaise. He felt his sharp mind temporarily blunted. But he had fun and enjoyed Jasthi's company. What was it again that he said about not drinking too much of it too quickly and mixing things up way too much? He gave some thought to his self-inflicted wound and the evening he had spent with his guide as he sat on a bench on the waterfront promenade, sipping tea.

Paddo spent a little over three months in India. After Delhi and a trek to Punjab in the north, he turned south. After Rajasthan and a week in Jodhpur, he settled on a route that would keep him west. He always felt safe, except once, when travelling late one night on a rickety old train. The doors were open and could not be closed. But generally, he had felt no less safe than on the Tube in London. He kept in contact with his mother, for he knew she would be worried.

A very good cook for his age or any age, he also loved curry. He made careful note of ingredients and methods whenever the opportunity arose. Not all ingredients of the same freshness would be able to be sourced in the UK so he twice packed a box and shipped it off to Norwich. He included some strong, deep red chilli powder and bowls and utensils, together with packaged spices. In the end, he packed too much and most would go stale before he could use it.

He took in a salutary lesson in Mumbai. Staying in a shared accommodation, with a very good kitchen, it was a prime opportunity to do some cooking. In the morning, he wandered through a market place and purchased all of his selected ingredients. He had fresh chilli, dried whole chilli and red chilli powder. The cooking went very well until he rubbed his eye and a speck of chilli got into it. He made a more embarrassing mistake later by not washing his hands covered in chilli before touching a sensitive part of his skin, on a sensitive part of his anatomy, when he was in the process of relieving himself. "Where did Patrick go?" a girl asked in the accommodation. Someone else replied they had seen him running in the direction of the showers.

Tom, at this time, surprised not only his parents but himself by enrolling in an undergraduate course in photography at the Norwich University of the Arts. His mother said to him she had no idea that he held such an interest, to which he replied that he had just developed it. Besides, he figured, there was nothing else he wanted to do, so it could be used in a way to hold him over for a while. He bought two second-hand SLR cameras, one digital and the other, film. His first set of photographs comprised various scenes around the River Wensum, including the weeping willows and Pulls Ferry from numerous angles and he seemed pleased with his composition.

For Paddo, it would prove a matter of some regret that he did not take many photos in India. Some were stored on his phone but, not long after he returned, he lost the phone. He did not post any photos or back them up, so much of what he saw would have to remain in his mind's eye for as long as it would allow.

Upon Paddo's return to Norwich, the list for both boys started to dwindle at some pace. This was true, with the exception of love.

In fact, Tom knocked three off his list in one night. Not long after he was underway with his course in photography, he went on his first serious pub crawl. It turned out to be somewhat of a blur what happened in between and he was very lucky not to be found floating in the River Wensum the next day. Part of the problem was that well before the evening got underway, a fellow who was in his second year in the same course that he was taking offered him a joint.

"Be sure not to smoke after ten ales." Regrettably, that was the only advice Eric, 'the Viking' offered, delivered in a slow, deep drawl. He was known as 'the Viking' due to his height and that he was from Norway. He didn't say that it was a particularly potent strain of cannabis, and unfortunately, not to *follow it* with ten ales.

By about 10:30 pm, in the small beer garden at the fourth pub, it was a blow to just below the ribs that nearly sent Tom spiralling over the edge with a splash into the river. A one-way dialogue was happening of sorts where Tom was hardly taking a breath. If he had fallen into the river, he may well have continued to talk under water. Earlier in the evening, he had a small crowd laughing and entertained by his wit and charm. But a corner got turned somewhere on the road to intoxication and what started out as something people found funny all began to turn askew. He missed the detours and road signs along the way.

"I can tell you that in my humble view, it can be said that virtually all the best things in life begin with the letter 'B'." By now, he was making it up as he was going along, in the process losing the ear of most. All it seemed, except Darryl Bird.

"What, for example?" Darryl was not particularly interested but wanted to see Tom bury himself in a hole.

"Boobs for one! But then there's breast, bacon, balance, ah yes, let's not forget balance of course, beautiful, bread, brainy, brilliant ..."

"Brilliant is not a thing." Darryl played the first warning card of a three-trick hand.

"Well, Darryl, you would know about that." Tom continued motoring along. "Brave, busy, big, bountiful, best ..." The list was about to expand rapidly but Tom was leaving out bunkum and bombastic.

"I shall cut you off there, Greer, and say you are full of bullshit. And that begins with a 'B'."

Tom was not aware that card two had been played.

Unfortunately, he said, "Well, Darryl, there are a few exceptions, it's true. 'Bird' is one and 'bully' begins with a 'B' and I believe you are a bully."

"Is that right?" Darryl was from Australia. He had met Tom once before and Tom had said something that had annoyed him. He could not recall what but he also had far too many ales under his belt that night.

"Bite me. That begins with a 'B'." Tom should not have said that.

Darryl didn't bite him but he gave him a clip over the ear. It was less than a heavy-handed blow and sort of old-fashioned in a way, designed to sting and to wise up. Tom clenched his fist without thinking, something he had altogether stopped doing, and swung a punch that missed Darryl but caused him to trip back and send a pint flying off the table, crashing to the floor. Darryl didn't delay, regained his composure and efficiently hit Tom in the stomach with a short, sharp punch. Tom immediately doubled over and felt pain like he had never experienced. He dropped to the floor and could not get up for several minutes. Darryl left the pub, almost casually, like he was strolling out of a movie theatre.

Everyone knew that Darryl was not a particularly likeable fellow. Equally, the crowd that was there knew Tom was not trying to offend anyone really and he had accurately labelled Darryl as a bully. When Tom woke up the next day, he realised he had some serious lessons to learn.

He swore off dope for life after that.

It wasn't until the end of that year that Paddo smoked his first joint. It was at a party where he didn't drink. He enjoyed it when having a conversation in the kitchen, his favourite place to be at parties and generally, for that matter.

There would be no fist fight for Paddo for a few years. But about that time, he was caught speeding in his father's Aston Martin and lost his licence.

And it seemed before they noticed, two years passed in the lives of these young men.

Paddo bought an old Volkswagen Beetle nearing the end of its days, mostly on account he didn't feel comfortable continuing to drive his father's cars.

"I am sure your father will allow you to drive the Range Rover, if you would prefer. He doesn't use it that much." His mother had not quite realised he was not into high performance, prestige motoring.

"It's fine, Mum, really. I am happy with the Volkswagen. That car is far too big for me."

If there was ever a status symbol for the British, just one single possession you could nominate, among a few, the top-of-the-range Range Rover may very well have been the item, so Paddo thought. In fact, he had incorporated his views into a play. He was trying to confine himself to parodies, although they were being performed less frequently in town than drama.

"Behold the Range Rover," his character in *The Bard Laid Rare* set in contemporary Canterbury, exclaimed. "The embodiment of refinement, utility, craftsmanship and overall superiority. A simplicity of style that says, 'You've made it.' Thou shall look at me and extend your warm approbation." There was no doubt in his mind it was a very fine vehicle. It just wasn't his cup of tea. It bewildered his mother in particular when he would make fun of their cars and take aim at virtually all luxury or prestige vehicles, be they from the UK, Germany, Japan or Italy, driven by their friends.

When he turned twenty-one, Paddo travelled to the Glastonbury music festival for the first time. He could have borrowed the Range Rover, not only to have more room for his camping gear and two friends who came along but to best deal with the parking and mud. It rained, as he was told to expect. The old Volkswagen leaked and he got bogged.

He had been able to go back to his job in the café after his trip to India. The café served good food and had a decent kitchen and he asked to spend more time there, instead of at the counter. The shifts were close to full-time. Being behind the scenes, it explained why on several occasions he failed to see Tom in the café. Tom gave up on ever seeing Paddo again and eventually stopped going to that café altogether.

Paddo had returned home after his shift and had sat down for a cup of tea with his mother. "I don't know why you keep that job, Patrick." She had said this more than once recently. "Your father could do with some help. I'm sure he would take you on and pay better money."

"Mum, I don't even know what Dad really does. Where is he at the moment, anyway?"

"Patrick, you know where he is. When I spoke to him last night he was in Jo'berg. I mentioned a week ago he would be there. He works very hard, you know that."

"Yes, but what exactly does he do, Mum?"

"He is looking after our business interests there. He manages our investments. You know all of this, Patrick."

"Oh, yes I forgot. Very absent-minded of me."

"Roger said he is doing exceptionally well. I was just telling Anne the other day that he has bought himself a flat in W1 in London. At his age!" Anne was Miriam's sister.

"That's right. I forgot about that too. Remind me to see the doctor who Mr Constantinides is seeing for his dementia. I should check in now, before I forget. Where's his number?" Paddo could see he was frustrating her and knew he was frustrating himself.

"It's just that your father and I would love to see you fulfil your dreams. Your potential."

"I know, Mum. But fulfilment is a way off yet. I'm just twenty-two, you know, and I'm happy cooking for the moment. It's not urgent. It may never happen. Anyway, I don't expect to stay in that job forever, or even Norwich for much longer."

"Are you thinking of London, as well? That would be wonderful, Patrick. A flat near Roger is something we could look at. Lachlan was just saying last week he thought it might be a prime time to invest. Somewhere in West End, even. You could get a job, what with your interest in theatre."

"I wasn't thinking of London. I have never really liked London."

"You might like it when you get there. Roger could introduce you to some of his friends."

"Ah, no Mum. I have met some of Roger's friends before. Roger and I don't share the same tastes, I'm afraid. That fellow that stayed overnight – when he came back last month for the weekend and brought him with him – Henry! I mean, he even asked me would I mind carrying his bag to the taxi when he left, as if I was his personal slave. He was so pompous and a bit rude to you, I thought. Quite rude, in fact."

"He had his hands full with a case of wine he was taking back."

"He was a pompous nob, Mum."

"Don't say that, Patrick. Where would you go? Don't say Manchester. Or Birmingham, like that fellow you went to school with! Oh, what's his name?" His mother was almost distraught. "Tell me you're not thinking of going to Birmingham!"

"Ed Redding. He is quite happy, so I have heard. He has met a girl from there. No, I am not thinking of anywhere in England."

"Italy is lovely. But of course, their economy is down the drain, you know."

"I am actually thinking of Australia."

"Since when?"

"I thought about it ages ago, when I was in India."

"Why would you think about Australia when you were in India?"

"I thought about a lot of things there. That was part of the point of going. Of finding out about things, outside of this city."

"What would you do there?"

"I would work that out when I got there. Probably just travel for a while, I guess."

"Your father's been there, a long time ago."

"It's not going to be tomorrow. I need to build some money up before I go."

"Darling, we can give you some more money now. I would like you to stay in England, though."

"Thank you, Mum. I know that. And I appreciate it. But taking more money is not for me, just at the moment. You and Dad should spend it on what you want to do. I can look after myself. I don't need a lot for what I want to do."

"What *do* you want to do, Patrick? I find this dreadfully hard."

"It's more what I don't want to do, at the present time. You don't need to worry." He got up and put his hand on her shoulder as he walked back into the house and said that he was going for a jog and would be back for dinner.

He ran through town at first, then across the Novi Sad Bridge and out to the football club. He made his way back to Riverside Road and crossed the river at Bishop's Bridge, before turning right at Pulls Ferry and slowing down to a walk on Ferry Lane. By the time he got to Pottergate, he felt clarity of mind and purpose. Australia it would be. But he did not want to go by himself. This time, he wanted company. Who? No one came to mind.

Another birthday would come and go.

He bought a push bike and sold the Volkswagen. He started to save money and rode the bike to work at the café and to the theatre. His confidence grew and he allowed his hair to fall to shoulder length. The thespian good looks continued to charm his female cast members and some friendships and intimacies came his way. He never sought it out, though. And in this time, he broke at least two hearts, of which he was genuinely oblivious.

It was on a Saturday morning in summer, when a turning point arrived. Looking back, it could be said there were actually two moments in the space of one hour. At the time and to him, both were as unexpected as each other.

Paddo's shift started at 12 noon. He had decided to drop by the stalls at the market and get something small but decent to eat before work. The colourful, open-air market was one of his favourite places to eat and people watch.

As he swung around Rampant Horse Street on his bike, heading in the direction of the stalls, he noticed a beggar sitting in a new location. He passed the person, then stopped and glanced back. Not a lot of people were around and this person looked strangely familiar. "It couldn't be," he said.

He got off his bike and slowly wheeled it back in the direction of the man. He could see he was young and better dressed than beggars he usually saw around town, although his clothes were very dirty. As he approached, the beggar did not move his head and was resting his back against the wall. He had a hat in front of him, turned upside down. One leg was extended out next to the hat and he held his hand around his shin of the other. His hair looked like it had not been washed for a month or more.

Paddo stood with the bike in front of the young man.

"I know you," Paddo said, almost involuntarily.

"Hello Patrick." He turned away as he spoke, not meeting Paddo's eye at all.

Paddo shook his head in utter disbelief. For a moment, he could not speak. "Dennis Whitcombe. What are you doing here? I mean, the last time I saw you … I don't quite—"

Dennis looked up at him and interrupted. "Understand? It's a long story, Patrick. I am fucked up. And I am broke. As you might have noticed."

There was something not right about this, Paddo thought. *His posh accent, for one.*

"Are you stopping to tell me something or are you going to put a fiver in the hat?" Paddo could see his teeth had started to turn brown and looked around to see who was watching or hearing this.

"What the fuck, Dennis! What's gone down? I saw you two years ago at Janice's 21st."

"Yeah, well, let's just say my fucking parents booted me out on the street because I wasn't good enough for them, was I? I don't need their shit. They're dead and I'm dead in their eyes, as far as that goes, squire."

"That's no reason to be begging for money." Paddo checked himself a little, after he blurted that out. There is more to this, he realised, but he was still shocked.

"I have been unwell, probably because of the fucked-up shit they put me through." He turned his head, gave a fake smile and said to a passer-by, "Any change, Sir?"

Paddo could see one eye was totally bloodshot. He also had a scar on his cheek that he didn't have before.

The Whitcombes were very wealthy people. Dennis was the youngest of four. All of the others had gone into the family business which had been in operation for generations. Paddo's parents knew the Whitcombes, not well, but they knew them.

"I'm sorry to hear this, Dennis." Paddo was struggling to think of what else to say.

"Not as sorry as I am, squire."

"Look, I have got to go to work. But if …"

"Well, do you just? Better run along, then."

"If there is anything I can do, Dennis, talk to your parents …" He didn't really know what to say but wanted to say something meaningful.

"You fucking stay away from those bastards! I don't need your fucking help! Why don't you take a ride but, oh, give me a note in the hat, before you get back on your bike, kind fucking Sir." Paddo had no cash on him. He was intending on getting some near the markets. Now he was running out of time.

"I would, but …"

Before he could finish, Dennis stood up. "Just fuck off, then, would you! Leave me alone!"

As Paddo got on his bike, Dennis yelled at the top of his voice, "Get the fuck away from me!" He had fury in his eyes now.

Paddo's heart and mind had stopped racing by the time he got to the edge of the markets. But what had just happened bothered him, deeply. He got off his bike, found an ATM, withdrew some money, got a bite to eat and sat on a step above the stalls and tried to process what had just gone down. He felt like a drink – a serious drink. That would have to wait. He might even turn up late to work. It was only a short shift and he had no plans for the evening. The last performance of the last play for the year had been last weekend. He had nothing on the horizon. All sorts of questions started flooding into his mind. What was he doing with his life anyway? He felt a pang of sadness for himself and the world and Dennis.

He was cranky with himself that he hadn't any money to give Dennis. It was now totally out of the question that he would go back there. He could hear his mother's voice again and he tried to push it out of his brain. 'They will only spend it on grog or drugs.' He sat there confused. The whole thing was confusing. How could Dennis have fallen so low? Dennis' parents were quite ruthless in their business dealings and perhaps even dreadful people admittedly. But still, he couldn't make any sense of it.

The time was now 11:50 am. He didn't enjoy his food. It had been relegated to a mere necessity rather than an indulgence. The sun was shining and a reasonable size crowd was now building in town for the afternoon. It was likely to be busy at the café, and perhaps the time would pass quickly, he considered.

As he stood up to leave, he glanced down at a fellow with a tripod, taking photos of the stalls in the market. He was pointing his camera to get a shot of the multi-coloured striped roof tops, it seemed. Not giving it a second thought, he glanced again in that direction as he got on the bike. Did he recognise who that was? He thought for a moment.

He glided down on the bike for a closer look. It was Tom, with the blond curly hair. He was maybe a little portlier but it was him. He surprised himself that he could recall his name. Should he say hello?

"Hello, Tom." Paddo smiled as Tom turned around.

"Well, blow me down, son. I remember you," replied Tom, with a grin as well. They shook hands. "Are you still at the café? I have assumed not, as I haven't seen you there."

"Yes. I am not at front of house. I'm in the kitchen. I don't come out usually, until after my shift. I'm about to go there now."

"My compliments to the chef, then."

"What have you been up to?" asked Paddo.

"This." Tom pointed to his camera. "Last semester I completed a course in photography at the school down the way. It's been unexpectedly fun. I don't think it will translate to any money, though."

"Brilliant," said Paddo. And then he looked at his watch and paused a bit and said five words that would change his life forever, but of course he did not know it at the time. "What are you doing tonight?" It was almost the most spontaneous gesture he had made in his twenty-three years. He had a flash thought that it was an inappropriate thing to say and his confidence had already strangely taken a hit from what he had just been through with Dennis Whitcombe.

"Nothing in particular."

"Well, I finish at five. What about an ale? Can I meet you at the pub near the river, further down by the park?"

"Why not!" Tom sort of stuck out his chin as he said that and gave his trademark smirk with a glint in his eye.

"Brilliant. I shall see you at 5:30 pm, if that's alright."

"Yep."

As he rode off, he felt better and as he pushed the pedals, he looked forward to what the evening might bring.

CHAPTER THREE

In his spontaneity, if not haste, Paddo realised by 5:15 pm that he had somewhat underestimated the time it would take him to go home after work and make his way to the pub. He made a quick change of clothes and decided to call a taxi. Even so, it wasn't until just before 6 pm when he arrived and he expected Tom not to be there, having waited long enough for him to show up.

His fears were immediately validated on a quick scout of the interior and the outside beer garden. He was about to leave when Tom walked in.

"Sorry I'm late," Tom said, with a smile.

Paddo felt some enormous weight had dropped off his shoulders, after a brief moment of despondency.

"Oh, you're not late. I just arrived myself. I was worried you had left, tired of waiting for me."

"Not at all. Let's grab an ale and sit over there for a while." Tom pointed in the direction of seats outside. They both took a seat, without going to the bar. A small crowd inside and outside made for a comfortable atmosphere. The light was starting to fade but the sun was still in the sky.

"You know, it's funny." Tom started the conversation, as if he could sense how Paddo was feeling and wanted immediately to put him at ease. "You look pretty much how I remember you. It's cool to be catching up with you. It's almost like we have known each other for a while. I haven't had an ale in here for ages. I can't remember what beer I drank but I do recall whatever it was, I had far, far too much of it."

"It can be thirsty work, taking photos, I'd imagine," Paddo replied, a tad nervously.

"I was just happy no photos were taken of me that last time I was here." Tom's self-effacing attitude reflected a sense of humour that he directed at himself quite often. He usually left his more powerful darts for others, as a general rule. "At least no photos that I know about, anyway. And if *I* don't know, then …" He shrugged and smiled and suggested they get a beer.

Paddo went to the bar and arrived back at the table with two pints.

"Cheers," Tom said and they touched glasses.

Soon they were chatting like they had spoken on many occasions before. As if they had known each other for years. Before long, one pint turned to two and then three. The sun seemed to be setting slowly and the weather was still warm. Paddo relaxed.

"You have been in Norwich the whole time?" asked Tom.

"Yes. Well, except I went to India for a while."

"Wow! How was that?"

"It was what I expected, but also not what I expected, if that makes sense."

"How so?" Tom enquired.

"I expected it to be very different from England. Not just in the obvious ways. And it was. The culture, the food, just the way of living. But I didn't expect the regional differences, the way things changed across different areas. I loved the people, even more than I figured."

Tom listened with genuine interest to Paddo's stories of India. He laughed about the chilli burning not just his eyes and mouth. They ordered some dinner and chatted well into the evening, as the pub began to fill up, inside and out. Their school days became a topic of conversation for a while. Tom had not gone to an exclusive school, like Paddo, he mentioned.

"Are your parents part of the nouveau rich?" Tom put on a posh accent when he asked that.

"I don't know. I don't think so. They have had their money for a while. Mum was from a wealthy family. Dad wasn't as much, as far as I know."

Tom said his father was a baker and his mother had been a nurse. The conversation got around to Paddo's brother, Roger.

"My brother's job is money. He is very interested in it, like my dad. He's not a bad fellow. But, I am sure he doesn't donate to any charities, put it that way. Although, I don't either and I should. We are not close, really. Just not much in common, I suppose. He has one friend, Henry, I can't think of his surname. He's from London, I think. He visits quite often, a little too often. It seems every time Roger comes home, he brings Henry. Anyway, I can't stand him and I can stand most people."

Paddo was still not over the regret he felt about his bell boy efforts in carrying this fellow's bag. But that wasn't the only reason he had developed a dislike of Henry.

They laughed as they swapped descriptive insults of metaphorical proportions. "He is like the fellow at everyone's school that says in a whiny little annoying voice, 'It wasn't me, it wasn't me, Sir, I swear – it was him, he did it.' The tattletale type, who now drinks wine from Bordeaux, then sips and says it cost him a small fortune but is worth every penny." Paddo had loosened up. He had started to feel that he could only truly be himself among some people and Tom was apparently one of those people.

The Saturday night crowd had begun to roll in and the pub was now close to capacity. It became much harder to hear. The subject of Roger's friend had taken Tom's interest.

"How often does this fellow visit?"

"Too often," Paddo replied, losing interest. He was by now glancing at two girls who were standing at the bar. He thought he knew them.

"What does he do?"

"He is in stocks, like Roger, I think. Maybe a derivatives dealer. Something like that."

"And he stays at your parent's house?"

"Yes, with Roger." Paddo drained his pint and suggested another. By this stage, they had been in the pub for more than three hours.

When he returned to the table with two more, Tom said, "When is he up next?"

"Who, you mean Henry? This coming weekend, I think. Can't we talk about someone else? I shudder to think."

"Of course, I just think maybe we could fix him up, a little." Tom had been thinking between brews. He had improved his tolerance of alcohol considerably and had learned the art of pacing oneself, if a session was to be enjoyed. Switching to lower alcohol pints helped, he had noticed.

"Nothing sinister, right. Just touch him up a bit," Tom said. Paddo had raised his eyebrows. "Nothing physical. Far more subtle. I think it might be worth a go," he added, with a look of mischief in his eye, something Paddo was witnessing in his new friend for the first time.

"What do you mean?" Paddo's interest had been reignited somewhat.

"Well, is he a creature of habit, as far as you could tell?"

Paddo thought about that. "Well, yes. Now that I think about it. I don't know him that well. But, for example, he always has to go down into the town virtually as soon as he arrives. He's fond of Stenmark's Café, near where I work. Thank God he prefers there. I'm sure Roger just wants to hang out at home after the train from London, but no, he always has to skip off to the café immediately."

"Perfect," Tom said.

"I noticed last time, in particular, because my mother wanted to make some tea for them. She'd baked something to go with it and had been waiting for them to arrive. He was rude to her, in his rush to just dump his bag and get out the door and off to the café."

"He's arriving next weekend, you say?"

"As far as I know."

"Can you get his number for me? Mind you, you don't have mine." Tom reached into his pocket and asked for Paddo's number.

"What do you have in mind, Tom?" It occurred to Paddo, as he asked, that of course he didn't know Tom that much at all. But at the same time, he felt he had known him longer than some friends he had known for years. He found it odd.

"Leave it to me, Paddo."

"You are not going to do something silly. Hang on, you don't even know where I live."

Tom looked at him. "No, not at all. And I don't need to know where you live to carry this out. Where do you live?" They smiled.

"That sounds scary, 'carry this out' when you say it like that," Paddo said.

"If you get me his number, I will call him next Saturday morning. I will say, 'Is that Henry?' I will ask permission to call him again, later that morning, and I expect he will give it to me. It will be as simple as that. He will never lay eyes on me. Trust me, Paddo."

"Don't hurt him."

"Of course not! It won't work, if you can't get his number by say, Friday."

"I should be able to get it from Roger. I will try."

It turned out that Tom knew one of the girls at the bar, not Paddo. She came outside and chatted briefly with him.

The dark night sky overhead made its presence felt and the air cooled and by 10:30 pm they had decided to move inside. By then the pub was full. Soon Tom was standing, chatting away to his lady friend and her friend and Paddo was nearby talking with some people from the café who had stopped in for a drink.

Eventually, Tom poked his head around and said to Paddo, "Another ale?" Tom seemed to have plenty left in the tank. In their high heels, the girls were a good several inches taller and Paddo had lost sight of him.

"Look, I must be going, I think," Paddo said. By this stage the bar was so crowded it was even harder to hear. Shouting was the order of things now.

"Righto, son. I will call you. Oh, and get me that number!"

"I will," replied Paddo. He turned to leave and had politely excused himself through the crowd to the door when he heard Tom calling him.

"Paddo. Paddo …"

He turned back.

"Sorry son. I almost forgot to tell you. I am off to Australia in two weeks! I was going to mention it before, but we got sidetracked on something. I'm going for at least three months, I hope!"

Paddo was almost incredulous. It had been a big day and he was tired.

"That's brilliant, Tom. I will call you." And he left.

Paddo went home and straight to sleep, barely processing the last thing Tom had said. This was mainly due to the alcohol but by mid-morning, he had given it a working over, with the rest of the previous day's events.

His first thought was almost sheer envy and that feeling was not what he was accustomed to at all. He was ready to quit his job at the café immediately and ring Tom and say he was coming too. But how could he possibly do that? Home alone and virtually talking to himself, it forced him to think. He hardly knew Tom, he said to himself again. He could be an axe murderer or worse and he would never know. He laughed as he considered what could be worse than an axe murderer. With a mild hangover, he had forgotten about the plot against Henry. But that's right, he realised, they were planning some practical stunt, or Tom was. Was that really a good idea? What will Roger say? Do I care? He tossed all these questions over in his head as he cooked scrambled eggs and black pudding, for what was more like brunch than breakfast.

He had barely finished his coffee when his phone rang. It was his mother, wanting to know if he had found the eggs in the fridge. "Yes, Mum. Thanks for that."

"And did you manage to feed Regal yet?" Regal was the cat.

"No, Mum. I'm not long up. I'll do that straight away." But Paddo thought the cat could wait, at least until his headache had gone.

"Well, I'll be home later this afternoon. I'm playing tennis with Anne. She has booked the grass courts this time!"

"That's good. I probably will be gone by the time you get home."

"Okay, then. Please don't forget to feed Regal. You know where his goodies are kept. Love you, bye."

By the time Paddo left around midday, he hadn't given Regal another thought. He walked to town and browsed in an old LP record store, very happy that he did not have to work. He managed to get Henry's number by contacting his brother, misleading him by saying he was updating his contacts and it was a good idea to add Henry. Giving the number to Tom was another step altogether and he wasn't quite ready to do that.

On Monday, still not having contacted Tom, as if on some mission, Tom contacted him, asking for it. They spoke only briefly on the phone and Paddo gave Tom the number. "I am going to send him on a wild goose chase, if that's okay with you. Just a plain, old-fashioned, wild goose chase. Be sure you are out when they get to your mother's place."

They caught up for a beer, just the one, on Thursday afternoon but Tom wouldn't let on exactly what he had in mind. Chatting mostly about Tom's plans for his trip to Australia, Paddo was very interested to know all about it but didn't let on that he too planned to travel there as soon as he could.

Saturday morning soon arrived. Roger had called his mother the night before and yes, they would be coming, and confirmed they would arrive after catching the early train from Liverpool Street. For some reason never clear to Paddo, Miriam was actually looking forward to the visit, which had become all too regular. Henry was such an arse, in his eyes, it was beyond Paddo to realise his mother was of course simply looking forward to seeing her son.

Like clockwork, as soon as they arrived, Henry wanted to dump his bags and go downtown.

"I so need a latte from Stenmark's, Roger. What do you think?"

Miriam said she had made a cake. She was, like Paddo, a very good cook, when she did cook, and had gone to some trouble to bake one of Roger's favourite Victoria sponge cakes.

"Thank you Mrs P-S, but I'm kind of fond of this exquisite scone-like thing, I don't know what you would call it, Roger, a torte? It's from Stenmark's. Perhaps afternoon tea, if we decide to come back." Henry was almost robotic in his habits. It was close to a replica of his rudeness last visit, except the cake was different.

Just as they were about to leave, with Miriam following them out the door, Henry's phone rang.

"I should have turned the thing off," he said. "Don't people realise I am off duty? Hello."

"Henry, is that you?" came the reply. It was upbeat in its tone, imparting an eagerness for confirmation.

"Yes, speaking."

"Wonderful. I am so glad I caught you."

Henry was expecting it to be a work-related call.

"I'm a friend of Roger's brother, Patrick. I am not interrupting anything, am I?"

A little bemused, Henry looked at Roger and said, "No."

"Oh, that's wonderful. Look, I am very sorry to put this on you, and I will explain it all later. But, it's just that we are planning a little surprise for Roger. It's not his birthday or anything like that, but coming up soon is a little milestone of sorts, as it were, and well, we were thinking of throwing a little surprise party for him to celebrate or commemorate, if you are with me?"

"Yes," Henry said, in a slow, interested way.

"The thing is, we don't want Roger to know anything about it, at this stage of course."

"Ah, huh." They were all standing in the hallway. Roger wasn't paying any particular attention and was quietly telling his mother they would definitely be back for her cake later that day.

"Anyway, something has come up, I'm afraid. I am calling you because, well, Patrick, he's at work this morning. He had to start five minutes ago. He gave me your number, I hope you don't mind me calling you. It's difficult for him to use his phone at work. His boss is a real arsehole."

"No, that's all fine. What's the problem?"

"Thanks, Henry. Look, I suspect Roger is with you and frankly, I can't talk long just at the moment myself. Jenny … please just wait, I think we have a solution to this problem." He moved the phone away slightly and paused for a moment. "Sorry, Henry. I'm juggling a few things here at once. It's been a bit of a funny morning. Anyway, Paddo went shopping downtown before work this morning for the party. The party is a few weeks away but he accidentally left something at the department store. I was wondering if you could go downtown and see if you could pick it up. He left it by accident and now he can't go back."

"Well, I don't see why not. Where did he leave it, exactly?"

"Near the 3rd floor at Geralds. It's a department store, as I said."

"Oh yes, I know where that is."

"Oh, wonderful," Tom replied.

"What am I picking up? If he has left it by accident, is it going to be still there?"

"We can only hope," replied Tom. "Listen, I will have to call you back. The store, its … Jenny, it's alright! Look, I would go down there myself, but something has come up, and this morning I'm stuck out on the coast. Paddo rang me in a panic."

"It's fine," Henry said.

"Listen, if I can call you in half an hour, I will give you precise directions once you are inside the store. Would that be okay? Again, I am sorry about all this. My name is Tom. But don't mention me, as I say, we need to keep mum about all this."

"Of course. I will handle it."

"Thank you so much. I'm looking forward to meeting you at the party. The details will be supplied soon."

And with that, Tom went off the line and Henry put his phone in his pocket with a smile. It was always such a treat to come to Norwich, he silently considered. Once a month was not enough.

"Who was that?" asked Roger.

"Just another client who can't wait. Sorry about that. Let's get that taxi."

Tom got straight on the phone to Paddo and told him to lay low until at least after midday.

Whilst a little distracted, Henry himself was more than upbeat himself, once he arrived at Stenmark's.

"Unfortunately, I am expecting a call again from that pesky client shortly. And I will have to take it in a park or outside or something, I'm afraid, as he wants me to go through some detail with him. I don't want to talk here. Confidential and all and the guy is a bit sensitive. It shouldn't take more than fifteen minutes."

Roger nodded approval as they sat at the counter but he was barely interested.

At the same time, Henry was hoping that whatever he had to pick up would be small or concealable. Surely, this Tom fellow, if not Patrick, had factored in he would be with Roger all day.

Henry had finished his latte and was eyeing off the torte when his phone rang.

"Sorry," he said disingenuously to Roger.

"Tom here, Henry. Is Roger with you still? I forgot all about that."

"It's not a problem. I have that covered."

"Oh, good. Well look. Where are you, sorry, don't answer that. Are you at the store?"

"No, but it's not far away."

"Superb. Can you make your way there now? It shouldn't take long."

"Yes. That should be fine." Henry was being given a task and he felt he excelled at tasks, generally. People knew, somehow instinctively, that they could rely upon him, he quietly considered to himself.

"Lovely. Call me on this number when you get there and I will run you through exactly where to go, and what to pick up, if possible, as it will be much easier that way," Tom said.

"Are we talking something that is large, given the present position?" As far as Roger was concerned, which he wasn't, they could have been talking about a share portfolio.

"No, that shouldn't be a problem, I just hope it's still there for you to pick up," Tom reassured him.

"And once I have it?"

"If it's still there, we can talk more about what to do. If not, well, we will see."

"Okay."

Henry turned to Roger after the call ended. "That was him, I'm afraid. I shan't be long. I will be back soon. Give me 20 minutes, max. I recommend the one with the raspberries on it," he said, pointing to the cakes, as he got up.

"No problem," said Roger, as he was more interested in the football highlights on the television.

Henry trotted off at a quick but comfortable pace down the road to Gerald's department store with a spring in his step. As he approached the entrance, he checked his phone for Tom's number. He dialled it as he walked in.

"Are you in the store now?" asked Tom.

"Yes. I have just arrived. Now, where am I heading? I hope it's there," replied Henry.

"So do I," said Tom. "Okay. Do you see the lifts? Make your way to the right, as it's near the 3rd floor, I believe."

"I can see the lifts. Just passing the men's section now."

"The lifts aren't super quick from memory, Henry."

"Should I take the stairs? I will take the stairs," replied Henry quickly.

"Oh, no, please don't! It's the lift you need to take. I will explain," Tom said, as quickly.

Henry got in the lift. He told Tom he had done so. He pressed the button that said level 3. He told Tom he had.

"Going up," Henry said.

And then Tom said, "Is it there? Have you picked it up?"

"I am not out of the lift yet," Henry said, with a smile. There was no one else in the lift. The lift seemed efficient and he got out on the 3rd floor. "Okay, I'm on the 3rd floor," he said. "Where to now?"

"I would have thought if it was still there, you would have picked it up by now," Tom said.

"How could I? I have just set foot on the 3rd floor," replied Henry.

"You've gone too far, I never said get out on the 3rd floor."

"I am confused. You said it is on the 3rd floor. What the hell is it, anyway?"

"I have never said it was *on* the 3rd floor. I said it was *near* it," Tom corrected him.

"Whatever. What do you want me to do?" Henry realised he was now feeling a little tired and just wanted to pick the thing up and go and have another cup of coffee and that raspberry slice.

"I want you to go back into the lift," Tom said.

"Okay," he said, wishing to co-operate but raising his eyes.

By now a lady had arrived and got into the lift with him. She pushed level 2.

"I am now on my way to level 2," he said with a tone of frustration.

"That's fine, have you picked it up?" asked Tom.

"For God's sake, man! I have told you I'm on my way to level 2. How could I have picked it up?"

"I am surprised you haven't by now."

The lady got out at level 2.

"I'm still in the lift, Tom. What do you want me to do?"

"Ok, I'm sorry. Go back up to level 3."

Henry pushed the button harder than need be and when the doors didn't close immediately, he jabbed it again even harder.

"Going up, again," he said, with more frustration in his tone.

"Good. Is it still there?"

"I wouldn't know, would I? I am not out of the lift, am I!"

"I think you should tell me if it's still there," Tom said, in a slightly more serious tone.

"Look!" Henry raised his voice.

And then Tom said, "That's the point, Henry. Are you still in the lift?"

"Of course!" He was slightly angry now. "What am I looking for?"

"I don't want you to look, Henry. I want you to smell, breathe in, son."

"Why would I want to do that?"

"Because what Paddo accidentally left there, in that lift you're in, was a fart. Somewhere between the 2nd and 3rd floor, I believe around 10 am this morning. Now he can't go back, like I told you. It was several hours ago, but we were all curious if it was still lingering there, son. Apparently, it was something to behold. And if it was, well, I'm sorry, we wanted you to pick it up. Can you? Tell me." Tom waited.

A moment passed and he thought the line had failed.

And then, Henry got out on the 3rd floor. The thought of being in there was repulsive, on every level.

"You fucking prick," Henry said in a kind of slow, hateful way. For a moment, a split second, he hated Tom more than anything. More than a four per cent plunge in the market, even.

"Oh, don't be like that, Henry. We had hoped it might still be there, that's all, but let's not get too upset, if you can't pick it up. Thankfully, it doesn't last forever." Tom could not help himself. "Just be sure you treat Mrs P-S and others with just a little bit of respect, in future, just as something to take away, anyway," he added.

The phone went dead.

"Henry, Henry, are you still there?"

CHAPTER FOUR

Three days before Tom was due to fly to Sydney, Paddo quit his job at the café. He gave the owner a week's notice. To his pleasant surprise, the owner suggested he leave immediately and paid him for an extra week. The departure was on good terms that recognised what amounted to bonus years of service by Paddo to the small business.

"I'm off to Australia," Paddo told everyone at the café and they were all very happy for him. When a few of the staff suggested they take him out for drinks after work to celebrate, he politely declined. That day he left the café for the last time, it was mid-afternoon and there was enough time to walk to the travel agent down the way and book a flight. He had no accommodation booked or other plans, but was overjoyed with the sheer spontaneity of his decision and he rang Tom to tell him about it.

"Why don't you stay with me, at least for the first week or so?" offered Tom. Paddo had no hesitation in accepting, although he had no idea where Tom was staying. They caught up for an ale the next day and discussed where they would meet.

Less than a week passed and within that time, Tom had left Norwich, and Paddo had only a matter of forty-eight hours until his own departure.

Miriam was a little upset at first, but she quickly came around. Lachlan was quite supportive and insisted he help in the only real way he knew how, which was to suggest he transfer some money to Paddo's account. When it was refused, he equally accepted the position and added it was always there if he needed it.

"Thank you, Dad. That's reassuring," Paddo said, sincerely.

"Tell me again why you are going to Australia?" his father asked, both knowing full well Paddo had never offered any reason to date.

"Because I can, Dad, and because I want to. I figure this is one more journey I need to take before I get serious about a job."

"Well, I think that's smart. Listen, Patrick, I do wish you all the best. I'm very happy for you and proud that you have a good head on your shoulders. I'd like you to know that. When you are young and footloose, it's a good time to travel. I'm envious, to tell you the truth."

"You travel all the time, Lachlan," observed Miriam.

"Ah yes, but I am not footloose and fancy-free, my dear, and that explains the envy."

He shook his son's hand. For a moment, just a moment, Paddo felt a real sense of closeness to his father he had not quite felt before. It occurred to him that it was coming at a time when he was preparing to leave and perhaps it took a sense of impending distance to bring such a feeling to the surface. It also made him think that his father was getting older and mellowing.

Paddo smiled. His father stepped away, then looked at Miriam before turning back to Paddo. "Your mother and I have discussed something and I wanted to mention it to you before you left so you can think about it when you're over there. I've wanted to discuss this with you for a while and I'd like to know what you think."

"Yes?" Paddo said, noticing the change of tone in his father's voice and how he now stood with arms folded.

"When you come back, I want you to join me ... well help me, really ... with the businesses I currently run and a few I will be looking to start. Roger is too committed in London and I want to have a financial succession plan within the family. I could use your help."

Paddo looked at his mother who smiled and nodded.

"Dad, I don't think that—"

"Just hear me out. I know you're not thinking about that sort of thing as a career. I'm still very busy but I'm getting a bit tired and I'm not getting any younger. I'd like to show you the ropes while I'm still reasonably fresh. While you're away you'll have some time to mull it over."

Paddo turned his head slightly as if he was about to say no but at that moment he caught another glance from his mother. He looked at the floor, paused, and considered what was being asked of him. He realised he was annoyed. Annoyed that despite everything he had done to show his parents how he felt, they were still applying pressure.

"He's only asking you to think about it," Miriam said, filling the void.

Paddo ran his hands through his hair. "Of course." A shrug of resignation. "I'll try."

* * * *

He rang his brother and told him he would be gone for three to six months. *It was only right*, he thought. He added he was sorry for being so unkind to Henry.

"What do you mean?" asked Roger. It quickly occurred to Paddo then that Henry had no reason to and probably did not mention to Roger anything about his embarrassment at the hands of Tom.

"I just meant, I probably could have been nicer to him," Paddo said, thinking quickly.

"That's fine, he is a big boy. Look, don't get eaten by any sharks down there. Stay alive and well away from the snakes as well," Roger said.

"And the spiders and the octopi," quipped Paddo.

"Those too."

It seemed that in no time at all Paddo was sitting, thinking to himself, on the train at Paddington station waiting for it to leave the platform on its express journey to Heathrow. All he had was an address for Tom, scribbled on the back of a beer coaster. He had no telephone number for him. This would be a rendezvous in the old fashion way. He wondered if he could join a theatre group in Australia and what city he should consider spending the most time in. He thought about writing a travel journal, of sorts, but the idea did not really appeal to him. It did occur to him that he was about to embark on a very long flight. At twenty-two hours, did he really make the right decision to refuse his father's offer to upgrade him to business class, he pondered, as the train pulled away from the platform. By the time he got to Singapore, he realised to have refused business class was one step too far in his zeal to shun the financial offering of his parents.

It had been made known to him that the long-haul flight extracted its toll on some people, not so much on the journey from the southern to northern hemisphere, but on the reverse leg. But Paddo was young and agile and despite economy class, he arrived bright eyed. He managed to pass out somewhere over the desolate outback.

He climbed into a taxi waiting in a line outside Sydney airport.

"Where to?" asked the cab driver.

"Good question," he replied, as he reached into his pocket hoping he hadn't lost the beer coaster. "Hang on, I have to read someone else's handwriting," he added. "I believe I have to go to Woolloomooloo, um, that's with four o's."

"Four o, you mean 40, what street?" asked the driver.

"I meant it's got four o's, the name. No, it's not 40, let's see. It says here, 'Bourke Street' and 'backpackers'. Is that going to get us there? I don't have a street number."

"Sure," said the driver. "Eight o's actually, mate."

From his trips outside of Norwich, he had noticed that the first ten minutes in a foreign place, outside of the airport or a railway station, perhaps in a cab or a bus, could be some of the most vividly meaning-ful, yet at the same time superficial imagery to be experienced. It was all fresh and unseen and the beginning of something new. The sun was so bright and the sky so blue. He was looking around everywhere, includ-ing for his sunglasses, as the cab driver got onto his usual route heading in the direction of the city.

It was 10 am on a Monday. He felt excited. He felt, in fact, he had achieved a dream and that always felt good. And he was looking forward to seeing Tom.

Spring was on its way in Australia. The air felt warm and the mild winter was fading.

"Are you going to go to The Cross?" asked the cab driver, as he stopped at a traffic light.

"The Cross? Is that a religious area?"

"I wouldn't describe it as a religious area. Probably just the opposite. It's right near where I will drop you off. All the Pommies go there, at some stage."

"Why, what's at The Cross?"

"Lots of lads looking for a good time, if you know what I mean, late at night," he replied, with a smile.

"It has a red-light district, is that what you mean?"

"You might say that but, to be fair, it's more than that. It has plenty of bars and nightlife and that sort of stuff. Colour, plenty of colour. Maybe a bit like Amsterdam but without the canals, the pot and the Dutch," he said, as he chuckled to himself. "But, it does have the Poms. I have been a cabby for a long time, too long, and I wish had a dollar for each time I dropped someone to The Cross."

Paddo decided that maybe it was not the best idea to engage the cabby as a tour guide. It also occurred to him that he probably did get paid more than a dollar each time he dropped someone to 'The Cross.'

"Sounds interesting," said Paddo, insincerely.

As they pulled up at the backpackers the cabby said, "That'll be $42.00."

Paddo gave him a $50 note. He had withdrawn cash at the airport and was intrigued by its colours and its feel of plasticity.

"Have a nice time in Australia, mate."

"Thanks," said Paddo.

He stood on the footpath with his backpack at his feet and a small bag around his shoulder. With the lack of detail given by Tom, he could only assume he had arranged for him to stay in the backpackers with him, and it was now time to find out. He pushed through some glass doors and entered the reception area. "Good morning," said a young lady sitting behind a counter, with a smile bigger than he was expecting.

"Good morning. I don't have a booking but I have a friend staying here, at least I think he is," he said.

"Let me see," she said, as she looked at the computer in front of her. Paddo looked at a wall covered in information pamphlets and tour brochures.

"Name?"

"Mine? Oh sorry, you mean my friend."

She smiled. He wanted to ask her name and noticed she had no name tag.

"Tom …" He then had a mental blank trying to think of Tom's surname. "Sorry, Tom … oh, that's ridiculous," he said, adding, "I just got off a flight, sorry, Tom …" He pulled away from the counter for a moment and grabbed his brow.

"You're right," she said, smiling again, meaning to reassure him.

"Oh, bugger, sorry," he said in frustration, even more embarrassed now. So much for thinking he was all fine after his long flight.

"We have two Tom's staying with us." She thought that might help.

Paddo returned to the counter, this time more relaxed and lent his elbows on the top ledge. He tried to look cooler, just a little less flustered. Usually good at details, this momentary absence of information at the beginning of the trip may just turn out to be quite disappointing, something now painfully obvious to him. Trying to think was making it harder. It was all too casual and rushed, what they had planned, it dawned on him now.

"We have a Tom Morelli, from Italy and a Tom Aston, from England. Actually, it says here 'UK'," she said, studying the screen closely. Paddo had a mild moment of not panic but a 'that can't be right' feeling.

"Are you sure?" he said. "Sorry, I mean … no. That's not his name." She could see he was feeling anxious and probably more tired than he realised.

"I think so," she said slowly, almost to herself, still looking at the screen.

"Right," Paddo said, a little bewildered, scratching his head and looking out the window, thinking he will be returning to the pavement that he had just stepped in from very shortly. "It's neither of them."

She could see his disappointment and wanted to help in some way. "When was he supposed to have checked in? Maybe he has but since gone. I can go back a few days," she said.

"Actually, I don't know. Ah, it's my fault, I think." He shook his head.

"Maybe he is due to check in," she was now looking at him.

"Yeah, maybe, I don't know."

Two people came through the door with bags and it was obvious to him that he should vacate his space at the counter.

"Well, thanks for your help," he said. "I am sorry to have taken your time."

She smiled again and said that it was no trouble at all. He excused himself past the others and they made their way to the counter.

Outside, he stood for a moment in exactly the same spot the cab had dropped him off. Should he turn right or left? Then it came to him: Greer, yes, how could he have forgotten Tom's name? He punished himself with an unflattering description under his breath. But it didn't matter anyway because there was no Greer there.

Before he was about to step off the curb, he heard a voice call out, "Paddo!"

Tom came bounding down the street, almost at jogging pace and then wrapped his arms around him in a warm embrace.

"Wow, looks like I nearly missed you! How are you, son?" Tom asked, smiling and catching his breath.

"Good, I guess. Well, I'm good now!"

Tom was dressed in a tee-shirt, shorts and thongs and looked very relaxed and almost already 'Australianised'.

"I've just been in there and they had no record of you. What's the go?" asked Paddo. A small sense of annoyance was still with him, despite the fact he was happy to see Tom.

"Oh, yes, well I couldn't get in. I got here a few days ago and they were all booked out. I've got a new phone and I didn't save your number. I knew your flight number and time so I figured there was a good chance of seeing you if I got down here about now. Looks like I just made it."

"You sure did. I was about to wander off into the wild blue yonder."

"Here, let me grab one of your bags," said Tom, as he lifted the small bag. "I'm booked in just down the way, in Kings Cross. We can walk there from here. I've got a double room. It's nothing fancy but I think you'll like it."

Paddo would like to have stayed at the backpackers, if for no other reason than he could see the lovely girl at the reception again and perhaps let her know he wasn't quite the fool he felt.

"Maybe I should check in here. I never asked if they had room."

"For tonight, stay with me. I've got two more nights booked. We can come back here tomorrow if we like and see if they can take us. Let's go and get a beer. Are you thirsty?"

"Can we drop these bags off first?"

"Sure we can."

It took about half an hour for them to reach the apartment which was on Bayswater Road and technically Potts Point, not The Cross.

They wasted no time and off-loaded the bags before walking to Darlinghurst Road, which seemed to them to be the main street of The Cross. Paddo had never been in the type of area he now found himself in and was taking in a display of strip clubs, bars, restaurants and cafés, whilst trying to stay out of the way of the pedestrian crowd. It seemed evident that the taxi driver's description as 'colourful' was apt. The only Kings Cross he ever expected to find himself in was in London. The Sydney namesake was originally called 'Queens Cross' but for some reason the name got changed, Tom mentioned, as they walked.

"Why did you choose to stay here?" asked Paddo, as they slowed to a stroll, peering at the displays and signs advertising cocktails and lap dances.

"No real reason. I have a friend in Norwich who told me about it and said put it on your list to visit at some stage." They crossed the street. "So, I figured it seemed pretty central and convenient first up," he said, as he entered a pub like it was his local already, with Paddo hardly noticing but following. "Mind you, he is a party animal and I think his idea of a good time is a little different from mine. He would have hit the strip joints a lot and probably paid for some entertainment."

Keen to try something they hadn't consumed before, they both ordered an Australian pale ale. "This beer," explained the fellow behind the bar, "is definitely a session ale. If you want an upgrade, have its big daddy, mate, this red ale here, which packs a lot more punch."

Both Tom and Paddo were used to cask ales that mainly ranged from 3.8% to 4.5% alcohol per volume. After the second pale ale, Tom ordered the stronger red ale but Paddo stuck to the pale ale. They got to talking so much that it soon got to 3 pm and, as the beers were going down like water in a trek through the Sahara, they either overlooked lunch or relegated it to simply unnecessary.

"I think we should hire a car, no actually, let's buy one, and drive to Melbourne later in the week," said Tom.

"It's a very big country," said Paddo. "You think driving is the best option?"

Paddo had done a little bit of research and noted with Tom that Australia is the sixth largest country in the world and the distances were absolutely vast.

"I know, but we get so much freedom with a car," replied Tom. "We can go wherever we want, whenever we want." He added that the trick would be to get a good one, without paying more than say four or five thousand dollars. The conversation then revolved around whether "they" should spend more and get a four-wheel utility vehicle, so they could take it on beaches and other places.

Suddenly and out of context Tom said, "God, I haven't eaten," looking at his watch, which said 3:45 pm. By then, he'd consumed three more strong ales. His statement was made as if it was some major unexpected revelation, almost like he was imparting some dreadful news. He went to the bar to order a steak sandwich but got told the kitchen had closed and would not re-open until 6 pm. This came as a complete surprise and he resisted saying that's not how it's done in many of the English pubs that serve all afternoon.

Paddo felt he was travelling well, having stuck to the pale ales, although he felt he was at times still on the plane, travelling.

"Yes, I could eat," he said to Tom, after Tom had suggested they get a bite at the supermarket not far from them.

Unfortunately, the supermarket was not exactly what Tom expected either. They had some takeaway food but not as much as what he was used to in the UK. The hot chickens appeared to have been sold out and he really felt like a hot chicken, for some reason only clear to him, but he was not thinking very clearly at all. He needed to eat regularly, otherwise he was susceptible to what his mother would call an 'episode'.

"Why don't we just get some takeaway at one of the places on the main street," suggested Paddo, sensibly. "There are some good places there. We walked right by them."

"I just can't believe they don't have hot food," Tom said.

"Let's go," Paddo said.

Tom went up to one of the girls in a shop uniform. "Excuse me, miss. Do you have any hot chickens left?"

She looked at him with a raised set of eyebrows and could perhaps detect that he had been drinking and said, "Do you see any there?" pointing, looking in the direction of a stand, a mere few metres away that said, 'Hot Chickens' but which was noticeably completely empty.

"No," he said, feeling foolish.

"Well then, clearly we don't have any left." She gave him a fake smile and walked away, looking disinterested and busy.

Before she was out of ear shot, he said to her, "Are you sure? You're not about to restock the shelf soon?"

She turned and looked at him as if it was a burdensome enquiry and gave a sort of a twitch and said, "As I told you, and as you can plainly see, we don't have any. None!" And she wandered off at a quicker pace this time. Her slightly rude demeanour was providing an incentive for Tom not to be at his most charming.

He turned to Paddo and said, "Do I see any there! Did you hear what she said?" He shook his head, still staring at the empty space where the hot chickens once were.

"Yep, let's go. I'm hungry. We can do better. There's a place down the road."

"My word we can," Tom said, but he was not ready to go. He added again, "Did you hear what she said?" smiling, in an evil sort of a way now, with the button stuck, and still shaking his head. "I'll fix them," he said, and slowly wandered away down the aisle.

Paddo knew Tom well enough already to know what he might be capable of and grew a tad concerned. He could see purpose in his steps and followed him. "I don't think it would be a good idea, Tom. You have been drinking all afternoon and you need to eat. Leave it alone. She's having a bad day or overworked. Let's just walk out. Don't be an intoxicated tourist!"

"No, no, leave it to me," he said.

Paddo could see Tom's mind ticking over, like a time bomb.

Tom wandered over to the deli section and stood and browsed for a moment, staring at the display in contemplation, with his fingers slowly tapping on his chin. Plenty of fresh food was on offer, including fresh, whole chickens. Paddo followed but at a distance, so that he could observe from afar but not so distant that he could not see or hear.

"Can I help you, Sir?" came the obligatory enquiry from the young lady behind the counter.

"Ah, yes, just a moment," he said. He then added, "I would like three spatchcocks, please."

The lady looked at him and said, "Sorry, I beg your pardon?"

"Spatchcocks. Three, please."

"I don't think we have any of those, Sir," she said, with a slightly concerned expression on her face. She looked about sixteen or seventeen years old.

"Sorry, you *are* a delicatessen, aren't you?" he said, slowly.

"Yes, well, we have a deli department," she replied.

"But you have no spatchcocks?" he said, more as a statement than a question and with a pained smile of fake incredulity.

"I'm not certain I have heard of them, Sir," she replied, now feeling a little awkward.

"I can't believe it," Tom said, now giving out a little frustrated laugh and turning around, as if someone might join in with his astonishment.

"It's a small, immature chicken, split open, with its backbone removed," he said, in a more serious tone and louder, much louder. Paddo was pretending to look at jam spread in the nearby aisle and cringing. The words 'small, immature Englishman' entered his head involuntarily.

"I find this all quite unacceptable, frankly. With all due respect to you miss, what sort of supermarket, what sort of a delicatessen, doesn't stock spatchcocks! I just don't understand." He said this loud enough that a few of the other customers, not even at the counter, could hear him. He seemed intent on making a scene.

"Sir, I can get the manager if you would like," she said, hoping he would take up that offer and she could run away from him. She felt like she was walking on egg shells now. Chicken egg shells.

"Yes, please," he said loudly. "I am happy to wait, to get this whole thing sorted out."

Paddo picked up a jar of strawberry jam and looked at the label so as to disconnect himself from the whole scene. People were turning and staring.

The young shop assistant vanished and returned with the same lady who told him where to look for the missing hot chickens. She was now in the mood to tell him where to go.

"You again, Sir," she said, from behind the counter. "We have failed to meet your needs, again?"

"Do you know what a spatchcock is?"

"Yes, I have heard of them," she said, calmly. "It's more a way of preparing a small chicken, I believe."

"Then I would like three, please," he said.

"We are all out of spatchcocks at the moment, and small chickens, as my staff member has told you."

"No, she didn't tell me you are all out of them," Tom corrected her. "She told me she hadn't heard of them."

"Whatever," she replied.

"Whatever! Now that's customer service with a gold stamp, isn't it! Do you have a spatchcock section that you can point me to, that's empty?"

"Sir, I am sorry we don't have any spatchcocks and that we have run out of chickens. I am sure you may be able to find what you want elsewhere," she said in a very professional tone. The young girl was looking on, hoping she would not be in trouble. "A specialist, stand-alone delicatessen, perhaps. Not a small supermarket."

"Well," he paused and looked at her name plate, "Jane, is it? Let me just say this, Jane. I'm very disappointed. I would hope that if I ever return, you will have sorted out your dreadful lack of spatchcocks! And chickens," he said.

"We will be sure to look into that, just for you," she replied.

"Thank you," he said. "And good day to you, miss," he added, looking in the direction of the girl.

He turned to leave and stopped and turned back.

"I would like to add, your young assistant behind the counter here is very polite and is to be commended," Tom said. There was tad of red ale induced slurring of words that gave him away.

"Thanks, I'll pass it on," Jane replied in a patronising tone, confident she had come out on top with someone she had already made her mind up about.

"I can't say the same for you, I'm afraid," Tom added. "Just remember, Jane, patronising your customer is never called for under any circumstances and one day, if you happen to do it again, it might just cost you your job. Good day to you, Jane."

They went and got Turkish food, Tom passed out on the couch soon after and Paddo got a good twelve-hour sleep. He made a mental note before he dozed off never to drink too much with Tom again when Tom had an empty stomach.

CHAPTER FIVE

Jeparit, Victoria, Australia, 12 years earlier

"Winny, get the hell in here, your Aunt Molly needs help and Bessy can't do it!"

The order to Winny was to Winifred O'Halloran, aged twenty-eight, and came from her mother, Myrtle.

No one knew Myrtle's age, not even her husband, Frank. More correctly, no one was allowed to know Myrtle's age. She had five children, all now adults, except Bessy, who was ten.

There was no reason for Myrtle to tell anyone her age. She did not have any need for a driver's licence and never visited a doctor. It was estimated by the ladies in town, especially those who lived along Roy Street and observed her walk to the shops about once a week, that she was at least fifty-five. Frank knew at one time, but he had long since stopped keeping count. No one in the family celebrated birthdays, but that was not to say the O'Hallorans were not a close-knit family, at least in those days. In a matter of two years though, the only ones left living in the house would be Myrtle and Bessy.

Bessy was short for Beatrice. Her three sisters were Winny, the eldest; Margaret, two years younger; and Daphne, two years younger again. Bob was the eldest of all and he had long since moved to Mt Isa for work, and from where he occasionally sent money to his parents.

Frank once worked in Ballarat as a labourer and then later got a job with the railways. He was not in good health and no longer worked. He smoked heavily, probably two packs a day but didn't drink, mainly because it was too expensive. It was also because he wanted to stick to one vice.

On this day, Winny was summoned by her mother's bellow down the narrow hallway of the house. The house was very small and in the centre of Jeparit and it was usually unnecessary to speak other than at conversational level to be heard by anyone from any room.

Aunt Molly at that stage had just a matter of days to live. She was Frank's sister. Myrtle had been very fond of her for forty-odd years. Molly was in bed in Bessy's bedroom and had been there for thirty-seven days. Ninety-two years old and ready to die, just not in a hospital. Her large frame covered the width and her feet dangled over the end of the bed.

The bed was wet. It needed to be changed. This required Molly to be manoeuvred somewhat and the sheets taken off, the plastic and bed wiped down and fresh linen to be put on. They had done it many times before.

Frank was never required to do a thing.

When Molly died one morning, Bessy watched men in white take her body out. After a few days, she asked her mother would it be alright if she could return to her room. She had been sleeping on the floor in the lounge room.

"Of course, love," her mother said.

That year Frank had a heart attack and also died. Whilst Bessy too was fond of Molly, it was her father's death that was her first introduction to grief. Frank had always been a good father in Bessy's eyes and she loved him dearly. His death was sudden and Bessy was deeply shocked. Myrtle had suspected something like that might happen, but she was never one to discuss such things. Myrtle herself also was a large lady, overweight at a concerning level and tough as they come. Her sufferings were usually done in silence.

Within the next year, Winny got married to a fellow she had met in Geelong. Bessy never met her husband. Margaret left Jeparit one morning and went to Darwin, for work. Her mother told Bessy that after she had gone. Daphne was the last to leave. "Where are you going?" asked Bessy, one Saturday afternoon, as she saw her standing in the hallway with a suitcase.

"I'm going to Melbourne for a while," Daphne said and left.

No one, it seemed to Bessy, actually ever said goodbye.

Between the age of ten and twelve, Bessy felt almost everything had changed for her. Except the little village of 500 or so people that she felt a small part of. Riding to the shop for a bag of lollies was the highlight of her week. She was not unhappy, although she missed her father terribly.

There was a swing in the backyard and in those years, Bessy would spend a lot of time on it, almost as a ritual. Pondering her world and watching her dog, she would swing and swing, sometimes from just after school until dinner. Myrtle never called anyone for dinner, except Frank, and whilst it was never served at the same time, everyone knew just when to sit down at the table.

But eventually the table was set for only two and it was in those moments that Bessy got to know her mother really for the first time.

At some stage when Bessy was around thirteen years old, she asked her mother that if she was her, what would she be when she grew up? Myrtle thought for a while about that question and said, "Well, there is not much choice, really."

"But Mum, Mrs Prentice at school says we all should think really hard about it, really hard, because we have a 'world of choice.' That's what she said," she replied, as she shovelled some minted peas into her mouth with a spoon. She was pretty confident that her mum was going to be not quite right and Mrs Prentice had it right.

"Hmmm," said Myrtle, leaving Bessy hanging.

"So, what would you be Mum, I mean, if you were me?"

"She is a wise woman, that Mrs Prentice," said Myrtle.

"Yes, she is Mum, but what would you be?"

"The only choice you really have, my dear, is to be yourself," her mother said, and gave her a soft pinch on the cheek. And then grabbed the ice-cream tub out of the freezer.

Bessy was thoroughly dissatisfied with that answer.

"But Mum, I am myself."

"I know you are, child, and never stop. Now, let's have some ice-cream."

* * * *

By the time she was sixteen, Bessy had been to Geelong with a girlfriend to see a game of Aussie Rules, to Ballarat for a weekend with another girlfriend's family and to Melbourne for three nights on a school excursion. She had also been to Rainbow, the next town, where she attended high school and all over Jeparit, which she knew like no one else.

Her birthdays had begun to be marked now and had been since it was only the two of them in the house. Myrtle still never let on about her own birthday and would make a sponge cake on Bessy's.

On her sixteenth birthday, Bessy received her first birthday present. It was a ring that Myrtle gave her.

"I want you to have this. It was my mother's ring. It's very old. I think your fingers might be the right size now."

When she brought it out and placed it for the first time on the dining room table, it was wrapped in an old, soft, grey cloth. It looked very thin to Bessy, although as her mother never wore any rings, she had not paid much attention to rings at all. She looked at her mother's fingers and noticed how large they were compared to the ring.

"Your grandfather gave this to my mother when they were courting."

Bessy was in awe and didn't know what to say. "You mean when they were going out?"

"Yes." Myrtle held it up and started to rub and polish it with the old grey cloth. She then put it in Bessy's palm.

"Oh, Mum, it's beautiful. I shall wear it forever."

* * * *

One rainy afternoon in winter, when Bessy was seventeen and in her last year of school, she arrived home with some good news. Her grades were improving and the date had been set for the parent-teacher night, to discuss everyone's progress. She was excited to tell her mother.

She walked through the backyard and into the house and threw her bag against the usual spot.

"Mum ..." she said, expecting her to be in the kitchen.

But she wasn't.

Bessy walked into her bedroom and took off her tie.

She went into her mother's room and found her on the floor. The doctor said she had most likely been there since morning and it was sudden and she had felt no pain.

CHAPTER SIX

After three weeks, Winny came to stay with Bessy for two nights. Bessy was told that she could finish school and stay in the house until the end of the year but then it was to be sold.

With her share of the proceeds, she said, there would be enough money to rent, even in Melbourne, if that was what she wanted to do. Bessy was still in a fog of grief and it would take all her courage to try and focus on the remainder of the school year.

Occasionally, some of her girlfriends stayed overnight. The mothers of each friend cooked and brought food to the house every week. Everyone in town knew of her plight but most stayed away. Not because they were not worried but because word eventually spread that the girl was doing alright, that she was very strong and had become increasingly independent. Word in Jeparit was that Bessy was the best of the O'Hallorans and soon they would all lose her to the city.

And that is what happened, as soon as the house was sold.

Apart from the day of the funeral itself, Bessy did not see her brother or Margaret or Daphne before she left. Winny returned again to organise a removal truck for some things in the house and left shortly after the truck left.

It seemed like half the town stood in Roy Street to say goodbye on the day that she left on the bus. All of her girlfriends were there, hugging her. As the bus left the main street and headed to Melbourne, Bessy let her head rest against the glass window and closed her eyes. She let herself be transported, to be taken away, letting the hum of the bus distract her from thoughts of Jeparit and all that she was leaving behind. Most of her tears had been shed except a few that she let fall against the glass.

* * * *

Whilst Winny had arranged for Bessy to open a bank account and money got deposited into it after the house was sold, Bessy was not informed exactly how the proceeds of the sale were divided or, for that matter, what the sale price was. After paying two months bond for her flat in Melbourne, buying a bed, a small dining room table, washing machine, fridge and some kitchen utensils, her account totalled $7986.15.

Bessy did take some things from the house, including some linen. Lots of things that she could have used, such as pots and pans, cleaning and other household items all went in the removal truck. She sat at the kitchen table, in her tiny one-bedroom, first-floor flat in Flinders Street. The only window looked out over the street and could not be opened. On that first day, she sat and thought what use was it to think hard, like Mrs Prentice had told everyone to do, about what you wanted to be. It seemed that for her, things had been decided, anyway.

But this girl from Jeparit was not one to feel sorry for herself too long. It was time to get a job and start her new life. A life that would never, ever, lose sight of where she was raised and the good people there. The word in Jeparit was the girl had spirit and that she would do Myrtle and the town proud, one day.

Not far from the flat in Flinders Street, a new shop had recently opened and there was a sign in the window that said 'Counter Staff Wanted'. It was a gourmet delicatessen that also served small meals and even had a liquor licence. Bessy walked in one morning, not long after opening time. She marvelled at the selection of foods and beautiful, exquisite displays, both behind the glass display and in jars and packages on shelves that lined the walls. There was an eating space for maybe ten or so people inside and half a dozen outside. Flowers hung from the ceiling inside in cane baskets and also outside, near the sign that said, 'The Posh Prince'. As she slowly wandered and browsed inside, she could not help but feel uncultured, as there were so many things she had never heard of before. What is a truffle, she wondered and why is it in butter? She stared at a small jar that had foreign writing on it and said to herself, almost audibly, 'Escargot', pronouncing the last letter. She turned the jar around and saw the price and raised her eyebrows, being careful to return it securely to the spot in which it had been placed. *Must be good whatever it is,* she thought.

"Can I help you, miss?" came a voice from behind her.

"Oh, um, no. I mean, not really, I was just looking at your ..." She didn't know what to say.

"The escargot?"

"I think so," Bessy said.

The lady smiled. She was about forty years old and the owner. There was only one other customer and he was sitting down with a cup of coffee and newspaper. The lady could tell Bessy was very young and feeling a little nervous.

Bessy felt a sudden urge to make her way casually to the exit.

"Would you like to try some?"

Bessy was a little surprised by the offer.

"You mean the escargot?" again pronouncing it as it was spelt.

"Yes, why don't you take a seat and I'll bring some over."

Bessy looked around.

"Just over there is fine. We're not busy at the moment."

Bessy looked behind the counter and saw one other girl, who was probably about twenty-one years old. She sat down and the lady brought over an opened jar on a small white plate, with the littlest fork she had ever seen and another small white plate with a serviette on it.

"Some of the writing on the back is French, and there is only a morsel or two left in the jar," the lady said.

Bessy looked at her with a slightly worried look.

"Don't worry. It's free, complimentary." She said it with a small laugh to put Bessy at ease and disappeared behind the counter and then into the kitchen. Bessy picked up the fork and jabbed it into the pickled product. Taking a look at it for a moment she then put it into her mouth.

She thought it probably polite to eat a second piece but leave the last in the jar.

The lady returned after a little while and pulled up a seat next to Bessy.

"What did you think?" she asked, again with a smile, this time gazing into Bessy's eyes.

Bessy really didn't have too much of an opinion on it, one way or the other. "Nice," she said. "Do you mind if I ask, what it is?"

The lady smiled and said, "Snails."

That was not at all what Bessy was expecting. "Oh," she said, not knowing what to say next. Bessy thought not saying anything at this point might be best.

"Did you come in because you saw the sign in the window?"

"The sign?" Bessy asked.

"The sign that says 'Staff Wanted'."

"Well, yes, sort of," Bessy replied.

"I thought so," said the lady. "What's your name?"

"Bessy O'Halloran."

"And how old are you, Bessy?"

"I'm eighteen. Well, I'm almost nineteen."

"Have you had a job before?"

"No, miss."

"Are you interested in applying for a job, working behind the counter here?"

Bessy again didn't know what to say, exactly, but she knew she should say something. "Well, I …."

Before she could finish, a group of people walked in.

The lady got up. "Look," she said. "If you are interested, put together a piece of paper and write all your details on it. Say something about yourself and why you might like to work here. It would be three days a week. Put it in an envelope marked 'Veronica' – that's me, and hand it to one of the girls across the counter. Make sure you include a phone number, so we can ring you."

Veronica started to serve the other customers.

Bessy went outside and took a deep breath. She raced straight back to the flat. Her immediate thought was that she wanted to tell someone, anyone, what had just happened. But there was no one to tell. She knew absolutely no one in Melbourne. Her sister, Daphne, had left Melbourne without telling her where she was going. And how would she tell anyone in Jeparit? She had no phone. A phone! She needed a phone. *That's right,* she thought, her heart pounding a little with excitement.

She left the flat and went to the nearest shopping mall and bought a cheap pre-paid mobile phone. She could remember three phone numbers. Two were the home numbers of her two best girlfriends in Jeparit and the other was the home number for the house in Jeparit. No use for that now, so her contacts comprised Jenny and Raelene.

Disappointed when she realised that she would have to handwrite her job application, she started to feel better when she acknowledged to herself, as she wrote, that she had good handwriting, mainly due to the patience of Mrs Prentice at school. It was almost 5 pm when she had finished what amounted to two pages. Finding it hard to cover the bit about 'something about yourself', she stuck to the basics, including where she lived, where she was from, that she had done 'average' at school, had three sisters and a brother, and liked Aussie Rules football. She added she would love to learn more about food and about cooking but 'I am not developed in my knowledge' and added at the end she was 'hard working and keen to learn'.

She put it in an envelope and marked it 'Veronica' and raced down the street, hoping the place hadn't yet closed for the day. Relieved to find it open, as instructed, she handed it across the counter. A minor panic on the way home ensued as she thought about whether she had spelt 'Veronica' correctly. When she got home, she convinced herself that many people of far more talent and experience would apply for the position and she had no real chance. She tried not to think about it anymore and fell asleep early. It had been a big day.

There was no phone call the next day and with none the following day as well, her doubts had converted to certainty in her mind. But then the next morning, a call came. In her anxiousness to answer, she pressed the wrong part of the phone and killed the call after two rings. Still cursing herself, the phone rang almost immediately again. As no one else had her number, she knew who it was. However, when she answered, a male spoke, which she did not expect.

"Hello, Bessy, my name is John. I'm Veronica's husband. Are you able to come down today for an interview?"

When she got to the interview, it was with John only. Bessy was not to know it, but Veronica had already made her mind up to give her a go. Veronica made decisions on instinct but John was more the deliberating type. He was concerned that she had never had a part-time job at school and there was no one who could vouch for her. But he was impressed by her honesty and innocence and that swayed his judgement, even though they had only just made the position available the morning the sign went in the front window and no one else had yet applied. He asked her could she start the next morning. She of course said yes.

As soon as she got home she called Raelene and then Jenny. Both were overjoyed to hear her news. She told them she was very nervous and hoped not to make too many mistakes. It was not really clear to her what she was going to be doing. John had explained training would be given both in the kitchen and in the front of the shop.

Both of her friends promised to come and visit soon. Raelene was hoping to move to Geelong soon and Jenny was working at a general store in Rainbow, down the road from Jeparit.

On her first day, Bessy thought she had made it through without a mistake until just before closing, she dropped a plate on the tiled floor in the kitchen and it smashed.

"Don't worry about it," reassured Veronica. "I've broken dozens in my time and it's all part of the job in a busy kitchen. It will not be your last, be assured of that, Bessy."

Veronica was very hands on, although she wasn't there every day.

Soon, Bessy was asked to work four days and then on Friday and Saturday nights, when extended trading hours applied. She grew in confidence and at a good pace. At first, she was in the kitchen for most of the time, learning how to present the plate and cleaning and stacking.

Two of the other girls did most of the food preparation. They would also attend at the counter and Bessy was kept in the kitchen only for two weeks.

One day, Veronica suggested it was time for her to have a stint behind the counter. She asked her whether she had noticed how the girls did their job in that section.

"I think so," she said.

"Well, always look the customer in the eye. Don't ask if you can help them too quickly. Let them browse, if that's what you think they are doing and remember, no matter what, they are always right," Veronica advised.

Bessy was a good listener at the best of times but listened especially carefully to Veronica. At this age, Bessy had stopped growing. She was not tall but not short, neither overweight for her height nor underweight and usually wore her brown, shoulder-length hair down. By now, she was used to wearing her hair up and mostly in a thin cap at work, to meet the hygiene standards for food preparation.

Her confidence and skills grew each day and Veronica was very happy she had given the girl from Jeparit a chance. She told John she had yet again demonstrated her good instincts, which he dutifully acknowledged.

Not everything went perfectly, and one day Veronica quietly pulled her aside not to chastise, but to explain the finer points of customer service. An elderly lady had wandered in and was browsing around the shelves that displayed the various and sometimes quite expensive delicacies. She wandered from section to section, occasionally picking up a jar and reading the label carefully, just like Bessy had done on her first visit.

Bessy decided to venture out from behind the counter where she and Veronica were working that morning. She thought she had allowed sufficient time before asking the lady whether she could assist with anything. The lady was looking at the jar of pickled escargots.

"I'm fine, thank you," the lady replied in a soft, almost frail voice.

Bessy was most eager to help. "Do you know what they are?" Bessy asked the lady.

"Yes," the lady said, nodding her head as she did so. She had a lovely faint-pink hat on, with some yellow stitching that matched the embroidery on her blouse.

"They're escargots," said Bessy, this time making a point to clearly and in a slightly elevated tone leave the letter 't' silent. "Snails," she added, confidently.

"Yes, I know," said the lady politely, glancing towards Veronica, who was now watching from behind the counter.

The lady returned the jar to the shelf and sat at a table. Veronica attended upon her and she ordered some blueberry cheesecake and a small pot of tea.

At the end of the day, Veronica sat with Bessy for a while in the kitchen. "How are you feeling? Are you enjoying the job?" Veronica asked.

"Oh, yes, Veronica, and I'm so glad I have been given the opportunity. Am I doing okay? I mean, sometimes I feel I could be doing better, like the other girls seem to be."

"I think you're doing fine. Each day I am seeing you grow in confidence," said Veronica.

"Thank you."

"Just one thing, Bessy. Today, do you remember the older lady who came in?"

"Yes."

"You remember when I said the customer is always right?"

"Yes."

"Well sometimes, we all know they are not right all the time. She was a sweet old thing," said Veronica.

"Yes, she was lovely. And she knew what snails were called, too!"

"That's it. She did know. But, how can I put this? It's like a sub-set or a part of the 'customer is always right' thing," said Veronica, raising her hands and two fingers making an inverted commas sign as a quote.

"How do mean?" she replied, not familiar with the gesture made in an endeavour to make her point.

"Well," Veronica slowed her speech down a fraction, ever so careful not to put a dent in Bessy's emerging confidence, in case there was fragility there. "What I mean to say is that, probably best not to test the customer. To make the customer feel like you are quizzing them. They may not know the answer and feel a little silly. You remember when you didn't know what they were?"

"Yes, I do."

"I waited for you to ask. That way, you let the customer set the pace of any conversation that may then occur. They usually don't come in for a lesson, so just offering information they might ask for, just enough, is probably better than telling them things before they ask."

"Kind of like, so you don't make them feel silly?"

"Exactly."

"I get it."

"They may very well be the silliest person in town, but we can never make them feel that way."

Bessy had worked fifteen out of the last eighteen days. They sat and chatted some more.

"I want you to take a couple of days off, Bessy."

"You do?" she said quickly, quite surprised. "Is it because of what I said to the lady?"

Veronica laughed. "No, it's because I want you to have a break. I can't pay you for the times you are not here, of course. But, a young girl like you needs to make some friends and have a life outside this place. I want you to have five days off, relax a little and try and see some of this city. I know this job has consumed your every move for a while. And you will be no good to me if you burn out, girl."

On the way out, Bessy was told to come back for the morning shift on the following Monday. She would have a long weekend to do what she pleased. As she walked home, she wondered what that could possibly entail. Her mind drew a blank.

CHAPTER SEVEN

By the next morning, two things had come into Bessy's mind. One was to buy a clock radio that she could put by her bed and use as an alarm as well. The other was to go to a butcher and buy a T-bone steak, to treat herself.

She hadn't eaten a steak since Jeparit, in fact since her mother had died. Then, it was three times a week, usually with mashed potatoes or peas, sometimes both. Her mother could not afford the quality cuts, so it was more often than not blade steak. Myrtle had a variety of ways she used to tenderise the steak, including half a kiwi fruit or any citrus and plain old bashing with a large spoon. T-bone or rump was a rarity and eye fillet, that was beyond consideration. Myrtle could cook reasonably well, although she only had about eight or so dishes, rotated.

Bessy had not been spending money, except on the basics and she noticed her account had made a jump. She reminded herself that she needed to keep saving and not frivolously spend. It was not something that she had drawn from her mother or father, to be careful with her spending. In the O'Halloran house, there simply wasn't a lot of spending anyway. It was more something to do with her common sense.

Bessy had watched her mother cook and, if it came down to it, she could cook all her mother's dishes.

She unwrapped the clock radio and placed it beside her bed. She set the time but not the alarm, as that wouldn't be needed for a few days.

She placed the large T-bone steak in the fridge and placed two peeled potatoes in a bowl of water. *Just the peas now*, she thought, but she would leave them for later.

She rested on the bed and turned on the radio. After flicking through the stations, she fell asleep, waking about an hour later to her phone ringing.

"What are you doing Saturday night, Bessy?" It was Sophie, one of the girls she worked with.

"Nothing," she answered.

"Would you like to go to a party? It's not my party, it's a friend of mine's."

"Well, yes, but ..."

"Phil is a bit of a party animal. He loves it when I bring new people to his parties, particularly girls. He is a bit out there but he's nice," Sophie said.

"What's the party for?"

"No reason. Just because Phil likes to throw them. He goes to Monash and has a party almost every couple of months with his uni crowd. I went to school with him."

"Oh, okay, sounds good. How will I get there?"

"I will pick you up. You live in those apartments up the other end of Flinders Street, don't you?"

"Yes."

"I'll be there around 8."

"Okay."

When Sophie hung up, Bessy regretted not asking what she should wear. She went to the closet and looked at all her clothes. Nothing seemed suitable but then again, she considered, what was suitable to wear to a party that was just a party, with people who did not know her? Tomorrow's agenda had now been set, which was to find something to wear.

Bessy had heard that the department stores in Melbourne were very good but the smaller fashion stores were exceptional for women, particularly some independent ones. It would greatly help if she had an idea what she was looking for. Deciding that she needed help, she rang Jenny. Jenny advised to look for something casual but smart and not too expensive.

"If they're uni students, Bess, even if they're rich, they like to dress like they are poor but not too poor," Jenny advised.

"I don't want it to look brand new," said Bessy. They discussed the ins and outs of appropriate attire for a bit and settled on a pair of jeans, probably faded, with some holes or slight tears, a black shirt, perhaps with a slight pattern, some funky bangles and maybe a necklace of sorts.

"I wish you were here to help me," Bessy said.

"I'd jump on a bus but I can't get off work. You'll be fine."

Bessy set out with a budget of $120.00. In the first shop she went into, she went up to one of the staff and said, "Do you have any jeans with tears in them?"

"Yes, this way," came the reply, and she led Bessy to three large racks, full of all sorts of jeans with holes and tears. After spending about 20 minutes and trying on three pairs, she decided to shop around. This is just the first store, she told herself, and she did not want to make a mistake. After half a dozen other stores and a large department store, she returned to the first store and bought the very first pair of jeans she had tried on almost two hours prior.

"Nice choice, they fit you very well," said the store assistant. She returned to the department store and bought a black shirt where she also found a necklace. She decided to give the bangles a miss, as she had already spent $20.00 more than her budget. When she got home, she tried them all on and looked at herself in the mirror. She called both Jenny and Raelene.

Raelene told her to wash the jeans and shirt and she did that immediately. And, not to over iron them. She hoped they would be dry by the party tomorrow night. One of the things she did not like about the flat was it had nowhere to privately dry clothes, except in the flat. So, she went up to the top floor which had an outside roof space with a clothes line, for a quicker result. She had never used it before and felt a little bit nervous about leaving her new gear out of sight.

As she was hanging up the jeans, a voice behind her said, "Hello, there."

She turned around, thinking there was no one up here when she had come up, barely a moment ago. The man was probably sixty, unshaven and he smiled at her, revealing numerous missing teeth. He reeked of something that either emanated from his breath or his clothes or some combination. It was not a pleasant odour. It hit Bessy like a force field and she had to take a step back.

"I'm Bill. You live in 2C, I've noticed," he said.

Bessy thought that best not confirmed, just for the moment. He extended his hand out. She put the pegs down and shook his hand. It felt limp and sweaty. She resisted the urge to wipe her hand on her pants.

"I live on the top floor. You're new to the building, aren't you?"

"I suppose. I've been here a little while, now." She was trying to work out quickly if Bill was harmless or not.

"I do a bit of janitor work around here, so if you ever need anything done, just come and see me. I'm usually home." Bill was nodding his head continuously she noticed, like he had no control over it. His hands were slightly shaking as well.

"Thanks, I will keep that in mind, Bill," she said.

"Can I give you a hand there?"

"Oh, no, I ... as you can see, I only have a couple of items. I'm done really."

About a week later, Bessy met a lady who lived on the second floor. She invited Bessy in for a cup of tea and they got to talking about the building and its age and its various faults. There was a big list of things wrong with her flat, all fairly minor, and she wanted to tell Bessy all about it at some length.

"My taps and shower are always playing up. And the stove! It seems like every six months something is broken."

Her name was Deidre. "Have you met Bill, yet?" she asked, after relaying several other problems with the oven and cupboards that wouldn't close properly.

"Once," she said.

"Well, whatever you do, if you do get something wrong, don't get Bill to fix it. He's quite competent, apparently, but a bit of a weirdo."

"I've noticed," said Bessy.

"He's been here for years. Much longer than me. There was a rumour I heard when I first moved in; I don't know whether it's true or not. The lady who told me is gone now. I think she's dead. Anyway, she said there was a lady who lived in … I think it was your apartment, I can't remember. But, she used to hang all her clothes on the roof. And I mean *all* her clothes, apparently. You name it, underwear and bras and even skimpy skirts. She spent a fortune on clothes. Well, some of it used to go missing from the line and then mysteriously return. It turns out that old Bill used to take the clothes off the line and into his flat where he would try them on. He was particularly fond of the panties apparently. He might keep them for an hour or so and got clever about hanging them back exactly where they had been and timing his secret delights. She never found out until he had been doing it for months, then flipped out." She sipped on her tea, before adding, "As you would expect."

Bessy's stomach turned a fraction and the blood drained from her face.

"I don't know how he got caught. The cops were apparently called but as far as I know, they either didn't follow it up, or they gave him some stern warning or lecture or something," Deidre said. "If you get a problem, ring the agent, would be my advice."

"Thanks Deidre, taken," she said, thinking she had never spoken a truer word.

She was very glad that there was no way old Bill could have fitted into her jeans, certainly not without stretching them so badly that the holes and tears would have been even bigger.

"It's a strange old world, my dear," Deidre said, placing her hand on Bessy's.

By the time 8 pm arrived on the night of the party, Bessy had been ready to go for roughly an hour. Once dressed in the new clothes, the necklace went on and off several times, before it finally made the cut. When Sophie arrived to pick her up, the very first thing she said was, "Nice necklace."

On the way, they stopped at a bottle shop not far from Phil's house. Phil shared a house with four other guys, all roughly his age – twenty-three, except for Josh, who was in his first year at university and was twenty. "What's going to be your poison?" asked Sophie, as they pulled into the drive-through liquor store. "Let's get out and have a look," she said, without waiting for an answer.

Bessy noticed the drive-through had two lanes and one said 'browsing lane', which was not the lane Sophie had stopped in.

"What do you drink?" asked Sophie.

"I don't know," Bessy said.

"You don't know? I thought all the country girls knew what they liked to drink. Let's see what's on special," she said, as she trawled up and back along the cold section.

Bessy could not recall ever being in a bottle shop before. She would have had no idea what to get, or what she liked. Up until that moment in her life, she'd had one shandy with her brother when she was about eight years old and it was a Christmas Day. She remembered him saying, "Drink it quickly, before Mum finds out I gave it to you." Her memory was that it was in the backyard and it was stinking hot and the beer gave her a light head and made her burp the biggest burps. At a school disco when she was fourteen, Raelene had smuggled in a silver bladder of white cask wine and made her have a big gulp out of the nozzle, before Raelene later spilt half the wine down her shirt and then later vomited the rest of it in the paddock behind the hall. Bessy was more amazed that Raelene was still able to pash Rodney Highland shortly after.

"I think we should get these," Sophie said, pulling a six-pack of vodka pre-mixes off the shelf. "Here, hold these," she said, handing Bessy the pack, "and maybe these, in case it's a long night," grabbing what looked like a cheaper, budget brand version of the same thing.

Sophie paid for the lot and they got back into the car. Before they arrived at the party, Sophie said, "They've offered me one of the bedrooms. Josh's, I think. You can sleep at the other end of the bed, if you like. Josh was told to put clean sheets on and crash on the couch. Have you got some money on you?"

"Yes, do you want some money for the drinks?" asked Bessy.

"You can shout next time. I just thought if the party's not your scene, you can, or I can, call a cab for you. It'll probably cost you $25.00 or so." Bessy had given virtually no thought to what the party might be like, or whether it would be her scene.

On arrival, Sophie led Bessy by the hand through a narrow side yard, then a crowded lounge room and kitchen to a back veranda, which was less crowded but very loud. "Phil, this is my new friend Bessy," she said. Phil was holding a massive German stein glass that was filled with something that didn't look like beer. He greeted her with a smile and said it was really good she had come along.

Phil looked like he'd already finished a stein or three and not every word was being pronounced as intended. "Get a drink, girls. Actually, you can put your cans in the bath," he said.

The house was very big. The biggest Bessy had ever been in. One of the bedrooms had an ensuite with a bath, and that was Phil's room. It had various signs on the door, all that looked like they had been stolen from a construction site, including 'Hazardous Material' and 'Enter At Own Risk.' Sophie knew from experience that the bath full of ice in Phil's room was the place to stash the alcohol and was already on her way there.

"What do you do?" asked Phil, looking at Bessy with one eye pointing in a different direction to the other.

"I work with Sophie, at the deli café in Flinders Street."

"Oh, that place, the Posh Ponce, sorry what is it called again, Posh Pimp?" Phil said, not really trying.

"Prince," Bessy said. "Posh Prince."

"Oh yes, same thing. Is it good there?" he asked, saying the first thing that he could think of to ask.

"I guess so, we have some really yummy stuff."

"That's great. I love yummy things," he said as he checked out Sophie's 'new' friend and what she was wearing.

Sophie returned with a can each. They left Phil and wandered. Bessy could smell something sweet and smoky in the air, to which she was unfamiliar and wondered what it could be. She looked at what the other girls were wearing and then looked at her shoes. She was wearing brown boots and thought they didn't really go with her black shirt. A slight pang of embarrassment ensued.

Sophie got to talking with a group of people she knew. Bessy asked her if she knew everyone at the party. "I don't know half the people here," she said, adding "and I don't think I want to. Though, I reckon there are a few cute guys we should hover around."

Bessy looked around to see whom she might be referring to but failed to see anyone in particular that she thought fitted the description.

Before long, Sophie had knocked back two cans to Bessy's one and she was, at that stage, wise enough to suggest that Bessy not try and keep pace with her. When she wanted a drink, she told her to just turn left down the hall and go into the bedroom that said 'Industrial Zone.'

It would be an hour after Bessy had finished her can when she took herself off to the industrial zone. When she got to the bathtub, she could not believe how much ice and beer and other drinks were in it. It seemed like a lifetime supply.

"Come on. I want to introduce you to Josh; you'll like him," said Sophie, leading her by the hand again.

Josh was sitting on a couch in the lounge room talking to one of his mates.

"He's a gentleman, Bessy. I am gonna leave you with him," she said.

Bessy was used to doing what she was told. "Sit there," she said, swinging Bessy around so that she landed right next to the vacant space on the couch.

"Josh-Bessy, Bessy-Josh," and she left, vanishing into the crowded room.

At that moment, the friend Josh was talking with got up and went off in Sophie's direction, as if he was going to look for her.

"Hello," said Josh, turning slightly in her direction on the couch. He held out his hand to shake hers. She put her hand in his and he kept it there for a moment longer than she expected. She could tell he hadn't been drinking or, if he had, certainly not to Phil's level.

"Are you studying?" he asked her.

"No, I work in a café. Well, it's more like a delicatessen."

"Oh, that's interesting," he said. There was something about the way he said it, that made it sound interesting.

"Are you studying?" she asked him.

"Yes. I'm studying architecture. I'm not certain it's what I want to do though," he said.

"That must be so interesting," she said.

"Well, a lot of people say that and they're right, I guess. My father is an architect and he said it's interesting to a point, I figure, like a lot of things," he replied.

And so, the conversation went on like that for some time about things that seemed interesting on some level and Josh told her where he went to school and how he came to be house sharing with the others. It became very loud and Bessy could hear music coming from somewhere.

"Do you like living in Melbourne?" he asked her.

She said that on the whole, yes, but she missed some parts of her life in Jeparit.

"Will you ever go back there, you think, I mean to live?"

"I don't think so. I don't think I can."

"Why is that?"

"I think even if I wanted to, and even though I miss it, terribly at times, I couldn't have the life I used to have. My parents are gone and so is the house. I mean, it's still there, but someone else owns it now."

He nodded and listened.

"I still have friends there. Girls I went to school with. But they too will move soon, I think. I hope they come to Melbourne, but I don't think they will."

"What are you drinking there?" He had noticed that she had sat down with a drink and placed it by the side of the couch on the floor. "Is it almost empty? I'll get myself a beer and be back with another one, for you?" he said it in such a way that it was a question, rather than Sophie's more forceful yet still friendly style.

"Okay," she said with a smile. He did not leave her sitting by herself long and returned with one of the cans out of the bath. It was icy cold which was in contrast to the stuffy, hot, overcrowded lounge room.

"How did you know where the cans were?"

"Well, let's just say Phil throws a few parties and I know who his favourites are."

They talked more and more and Josh told her about his family. Bessy said she was not close to her sisters and hardly knew her brother at all, as he moved away when she was quite young. She told him about Jeparit and collecting golf balls at the course for pocket money. When she told him about finding her mother on the floor, it occurred to her it was something she had never really talked about before, not even to Jenny and Raelene, probably because the girls knew the details already and didn't want to raise it with her. The conversation with Josh was something she was enjoying a lot. He seemed such a wonderful listener. She loved looking into his eyes.

The party started to thin out and midnight had long passed. They were still sitting on the couch. By this stage, Josh had his arm around the back of the couch. Bessy didn't know that she was, by this point, resting her hand on his knee. He leant over to kiss her and she let him give her a small, brief kiss on the lips. She looked at him and for that moment, no one else was in the room and if someone was watching, it didn't matter. She leant in and this time she kissed him and held her lips to his longer. They kissed for a long time and he held her firmly.

Sophie returned and said, "Well, take a look at you two, would you! I mean, I leave you alone for five minutes and look what happens. I'm gonna crash Bess. What are you doing? Are you hanging around?"

Bessy had no idea what her next move was. She was in the moment.

"I'm happy to give you a lift home," Josh said.

"I'm sure you are," Sophie said, forgetting her manners.

"I couldn't ask you to do that," Bessy said. "I am going to catch a taxi."

"I insist, it's no trouble. I've had three beers all night, so I'm fine to drive," Josh said.

On the drive home it occurred to her that she had basically spent the entire party with Josh. "What a great party," she said, as he pulled up outside the apartments. She kissed him on the lips and she thanked him for dropping her home. He said he would call her. He offered to park and see her in, but she smiled and said he should keep going. With a spring in her step up the stairs, she felt she could keep going all night.

CHAPTER EIGHT

Josh did not call Bessy the next day and when he didn't call the day after that, she didn't sleep too well. Lying on the bed and listening to the radio, she switched from music to late-night talk-back until the early hours of the morning. At around 1 am, she felt a fool for not having called him. After all, he may very well have expected her to follow up, rather than him. But then she doubted herself again, questioning whether it was still the case in this world that the man should make the first move. She rolled over and fell asleep, resolving she would call him tomorrow after work.

At lunch the next day, when she stepped out of the café for a walk, Josh called. "I'm sorry I have not called you earlier," he said straight away.

"Oh, that's fine. I was about to call you this afternoon anyway," she replied, trying to sound as casual as she possibly could.

"My parents paid an unexpected visit and they didn't leave until this morning," Josh explained.

He could not recall whether he mentioned to Bessy that it was in fact his parents who owned the house that he shared with Phil and the other boys. They arrived at 9 am without warning on the morning after the party. He explained that they were not at all impressed with how the house had been left after the party.

"I think Phil may have to move out," Josh said.

"Really, why?" asked Bessy.

"There are a few reasons. I thought my parents had gone to their holiday house in Lakes Entrance for the week, but they decided to return early. That gave us no time to clean up the place, unfortunately. Phil's bedroom is a disaster zone, rather than an industrial zone and someone spilt red wine in one of the other bedrooms. My mother was not impressed and Phil's going to have to take the fall I think. My parents really don't know the other guys. It didn't help that he spent their visit in the bathroom vomiting."

"That's a shame," Bessy said.

"It's okay, really. It's time for Phil to move on and grow up a little anyway."

"I would have come over and helped clean up," she said.

"Believe me, it wouldn't have made any difference to Phil's fate. My parents were tipped off, I think. Word of the last party made it to them when they were overseas and couldn't visit then. Anyway, I was wondering if you would like to get together this Saturday?"

"Yes, that would be lovely. I have to work on Sunday but Saturday day and night is free."

"That's great. I was thinking we could go for a drive in the day and have dinner in the evening," he said.

"Sounds wonderful."

'Wonderful' was Bessy's new favourite word, since her move to Melbourne.

"Okay, well maybe an early start. I'll pick you up at 10 am, if that's alright?"

"That would be great."

Bessy had never been on a date before. Here she was nearing twenty and her time had arrived. She was very excited about this charming man named Josh.

Josh arrived precisely on time that day and came to the front door of the apartment. He gave her flowers and Bessy tried hard not to blush. She felt her face turning a warm shade of pink. Her fair skin had been inherited from her father and she had some freckles like her mother.

Josh's car seemed very fancy to her. It was an old silver Audi station wagon, which was formerly the family car when he was a young child. They were soon on the road.

"I thought we could take a drive to Ballarat. We could be there just before lunch, if you are keen?" Anywhere was going to be just fine. "I thought we could stop in at the art gallery. The Archibald Prize exhibition is on there. And maybe the site of the Eureka Stockade memorial. I haven't been to Ballarat for a few years. Bit of culture and history, with some local tucker, maybe. What do you think?"

"Sounds great," said Bessy. She had been to Ballarat once before but she could not really recall much.

Josh did most of the talking along the 100 kilometre or so journey. It was a beautiful warm day and there wasn't much traffic. He explained that he had been to Ballarat many times and really liked the small city. His father had first taken him there as a child and explained to him it was probably the best example of early architecture in Australia.

"I really like the old buildings. When my father took me there the first time, I must have been only about ten. He explained in intricate detail the differences between much of the colonial architecture, the Victorian and the Edwardian styles and some styles that were typical of the days of the gold rush. It's a shame they don't have the patience to build them that way now and knocked down so many in Melbourne. Sydney has had a lot of its gems knocked down. More than Melbourne, I believe."

Bessy was impressed with what seemed like a worldliness about Josh, despite his young age. Besides, he spoke with an educated sort of tone to his voice. They arrived at noon and Josh suggested that they drive out to the memorial of the Eureka Stockade. After parking the car, they walked up to the circle sculpture, which marked the 150th anniversary of the miners' rebellion to the government's licensing laws. They chatted and read the plaques and information and stood under the Eureka flag that was flapping gently in the breeze.

"I had no idea more than thirty were killed," Bessy said, as they strolled back to the car.

"Either did I, actually," Josh said.

He mentioned that the strong sense of protest to government folly had somewhat dissipated over time in Australia and some of the men who lost their lives in the rebellion of 1854 may well have been disappointed with how conservative the nation had since become. Bessy did not feel confident enough to express an opinion, one way or the other. Josh seemed to hold many opinions, it seemed to her.

"Did you study a lot of history at school?" she asked, at lunch.

"A little. I did take a particular interest in Australian history. I'd like to study it more. I am probably more interested in the history of architecture than architecture itself, to tell you the truth," he replied.

They arrived at the art gallery to a small crowd. It would be a day of firsts for Bessy.

"I've never been to an art gallery," she said.

"It's a good place to visit as it almost guarantees opinions and conversations, maybe even arguments," he said, smiling at her. Bessy had never seen so many well-dressed people and men wearing scarves and thick, heavy-rimmed, dark-framed glasses. At first, they strolled through the general art area, before going to the Archibald section. She could not help but hear some of the conversations between couples slowly wandering, stopping and commenting.

"I find his use of the transient abstract exquisite, Simon, but his sense of the contemporary esoteric leaves me perplexed," she heard a lady say to someone whom she guessed was probably her husband. Bessy had no idea what the lady meant and stood and viewed what they were looking at. She thought it looked like something that a pre-school student had painted on their first day. The portraits she found far more accessible.

"I can't believe some of these are paintings. They look so real, like photographs," she observed.

They had fun nominating their favourite and were surprised they both chose the same portrait. After coffee in the cafeteria, they decided to head back to Melbourne.

"I'd like to visit again," she said, as they started the drive.

"You mean the art gallery?"

"I mean Ballarat."

"I'm glad you liked it."

When they pulled into Flinders Street, they got out of the car and it seemed a natural progression to go up to the apartment. Bessy had a bottle of red wine that was in the cupboard that her neighbour Deidre had given her, and they opened it and sat on the couch. Soon they were kissing and soon, it fell dark outside.

They chatted some more in between and she thanked him so much for the day. They kissed some more.

Then Josh said something she did not expect.

"Do you think it is too early?" He said it slowly and looked into her eyes.

At first, she did not know what he meant.

"You mean dinner?" She looked at her watch.

He smiled.

"I meant something else."

There was a moment of silence but she did not avert her gaze. It was like a butterfly had dropped into her stomach causing a nervousness and her heart to pick up a notch so that she could suddenly feel it beating. It was not something she had been thinking about. But she felt something she had not felt before. It was a sense of wellbeing and safety and passion, all rolled into one.

She took a slow swallow and Josh held her.

"I am not certain we should, so soon. I certainly don't want to move too quickly. I really don't know," he said after a little while and in a very soft voice. She could feel his breath on her cheek.

She grabbed his hand and stood up and led him to the bedroom.

* * * *

The romance of Beatrice O'Halloran and Joshua McAllister would have made the front page of the Jeparit newspaper, had the town had one at the time. But news soon spread anyway that the girl had landed on her feet and met a fine young gentleman.

Some of the older ladies in town would ask Raelene's mother what the latest news was of Bessy, as if they were following the tabloids that were reporting on the trivial activities of a duchess. "I always knew that girl was destined for great things," said Virginia Partridge, who had lived in Jeparit for all of her eighty years. "And she was the best of those O'Hallorans," added Emily Thompson, who had moved to Jeparit when she was twelve and at eighty-two, some say had never left.

For the next two years, Josh became a very important part of Bessy's life. Not once did she hear from any of her sisters or her brother. She managed to track them down and called all of them and left messages at their home numbers, several times in the case of Winnie, but she never received any reply. Her sadness was lessened by her bond with Josh. Slowly, she adapted to the serious possibility she would never see them again.

The job at The Posh Prince continued, despite Veronica and her husband selling the business. The new owners kept everything the same except the name, which they changed to 'The Gourmet Pheasant.' In truth, Bessy was not fond of either name. She thought the new name had lovely colourful signage but as they stocked a variety of game, including venison and rabbit meat, which only made up a tiny proportion of their food, she thought the choice was odd. The new owners were a young Italian couple and they were far less experienced than Veronica and John, but their confidence, which was a little misplaced, was sky high. Sick of people asking him about the change of name, Lino, the husband, explained to the staff that it was intended as "a play on words." He said this in his thick, almost musical accent. "I wish to say, 'peasant,' as much as 'pheasant'," he added very seriously, holding his left hand out in front.

Sophie had left and Bessy largely took over her position, which involved a lot of the ordering of the stock. Lino and his wife, Abriana, were far less involved in the day-to-day running of the place and Bessy sometimes wondered whether they thought it could be managed by remote control from their house in Carlton.

Lino was a passionate man, as he told the staff constantly. "I am passionate. I want everyone to be passionate," he would say every week at least once. Occasionally, he would explode 'with passion' as he would later explain, usually at the same time as he was apologising for blowing up about something minor.

Abriana would usually make an appearance shortly after one of Lino's meltdowns, to ensure the staff hadn't walked out.

Raelene and Jenny separately visited not long after Bessy started to see Josh but, as time passed, she heard less and less from them. Both moved from Jeparit and left Victoria altogether.

After the new owners had settled in more and Bessy got used to their style, she thought for the first time about leaving the job or at least taking a holiday. She was now full-time and had four weeks leave due. It seemed the holiday option was the better and she decided to talk to Josh about it.

"I was thinking I might take some time off," she said, one day over dinner.

"Where would you go?" he asked.

"I have no idea. I don't know, maybe Sydney. I've never been there. Or Queensland."

She was hoping he would also be able to take some time off, too.

But the discussion veered off that topic and was not raised again for weeks. Josh had continued his architectural studies. His interest in architecture seemed to have strengthened and he mentioned a few times some business options he was considering. They met after Bessy had finished work one afternoon for coffee in Lygon Street.

"I have a six-week break coming up in a couple of weeks. Mum and Dad are going to the UK and want me to come. I'm considering going," he said.

Bessy was immediately disappointed but quickly ensured she did not show it. "Oh, that's great," she said.

"Yeah, well, I haven't made up my mind exactly but I think I will, probably."

She was getting the impression he had in fact made his mind up.

* * * *

Josh had been away for four weeks. This seemed an eternity to Bessy. She was a little unhappy that he had seemed unusually distant with her in some way before he left. It was not something she could put her finger on. The physical distance then compounded her unease. All sorts of thoughts entered her mind in his absence, including that she somehow felt that his parents did not approve of her. Sure, she had been invited to dinner, even to Josh's father's fifty-fifth birthday at their acreage in Gippsland for the entire weekend. But she trawled the self-assessment net across her mind, back and forth, to see if she could catch whatever faults and insecurities that might lurk in the depths of her emerging despair. She could see and hear Mrs McAllister say to her on that weekend, as she stood on the porch, "Where did you say you are from again, dear?" She could recall no other conversation with her since.

Two days before Josh was about to return, Lino had the biggest of his fits and Bessy was about ready to chuck it all in on the spot. All over a broken plate. She recalled what Veronica had said to her on her first day.

"I think you need to calm down your approach to things, Lino," Bessy said, now the one handing out advice.

"Calm down, calm down, fungula … this place, she's a pezzo di merda!"

Admittedly, the plate that got dropped was a large, expensive plate, imported from Italy.

"Shall I call Abriana?" asked Bessy, calmly.

"Fungula, non me ne frega un cazzo!"

When Lino went into a spasm of temporary plot loss, he reverted to his native language, sparing the vulgarity on those who did not understand, but nevertheless might guess what he was saying.

But she held it together with the knowledge that Josh would be with her in a matter of days and after throwing the self-doubts overboard and letting any other insecurity fall through the net, woven now with a larger mesh, she allowed herself to look more positively as to what might be in store.

CHAPTER NINE

It was about this time, if not exactly, that Paddo and Tom were dealing, then wheeling, in relation to a car in the western suburbs of Sydney. "I am not paying that. I can tell you that now," said Tom to Paddo, after calling him to the side for a private discussion on the edge of a steep driveway in Rooty Hill.

They had taken a train from the city and arranged to meet a fellow by the name of Albert at the Rooty Hill RSL club, so that he could collect them in another car and take them to his brother's place to show them the car they were interested in buying. It was a 1996 Toyota Troopcarrier, a six cylinder 4.2 litre diesel, white, with not much rust and 451,000 km on the odometer.

When they called the number in the advertisement, Albert explained he did not own the car but that his brother, who did own the car, had given him permission to sell it.

"Is your brother going to be there?" asked Tom.

"Yes, the car is at his place but you will be dealing with me."

Albert stood about 6 feet 8 inches. His brother was not as tall, nevertheless was a large man as well and did not speak very much English, it seemed. When Albert stood next to Tom, it looked as if Tom was a dwarf.

"Are you going to be able to reach the pedals?" Albert asked Tom, as they stood at the top of the driveway.

Tom left Paddo's side and got into the Troopy, ignoring Albert's question. He started it up and then turned it off. Paddo looked under the bonnet. They gave it a thorough examination inside and out and Tom climbed underneath and checked for signs of rust.

"Your brother has some paperwork?" asked Tom. He had told Paddo on the way out in the train to let him 'do the talking.'

"What sort of paperwork?" said Albert, with a look on his face as if Tom had suggested something outrageous.

"Registration," Tom said.

Albert turned without saying anything and strolled further up the driveway and went into the house.

"Listen," Tom said to Paddo, lowering his voice. "He's asking too much. It was well past its prime a decade ago. I'm not paying $11,000. That's more than we want to pay, you know that."

"I agree it's more than we want to pay," said Paddo. "But I think it might be tough to get him to budge. It also seems to be on the money, the market price for this thing, even with that many miles on it."

"It's not going to be easy to get the big bloke down. I just hope his brother – where is his bloody brother anyway – has some sense. Anyway, leave it to me," said Tom.

"Righto."

"The tyres are in good nick; they look almost new," Tom said, and kicked one. Just as he did, Albert returned with his brother. He handed Tom the registration paper and Tom handed it to Paddo to look at.

"Is the tyre okay?" asked Albert, smiling and turning to his brother, then looking at Paddo.

"How do you mean?" asked Tom.

"I see you kicked it. There is a boot mark on it now."

"It's fine, we were just saying how good they are," Tom said.

"Is that right," Albert said. He sniffed and glared at Tom from his lofty height, a look of insolence in his eyes, his large hand slowly rubbing the stubble at the bottom of his chin. They all knew it was now coming to the money part of the deal with exception of a test drive.

"Can we go for a spin?" Tom asked.

Albert nodded, and all four of them went for a drive to Rooty Hill and back. Tom drove into town, then Paddo drove back to the house. No one spoke. Tom kept his observations in his own head and thought about his approach when it came to offering the money. They got to the top of the driveway and everyone got out.

Tom decided to break the ice. "Are you open to offers?"

"It depends what you're offering," came the reply. Albert's brother still had not said a word.

"Well, we were thinking we didn't want to pay exactly what you are asking," Tom said.

"If you are talking about money only, which I am taking that's what you mean, then it's $11,000 or you can forget it," said Albert. His brother stayed perfectly still, a blank, disinterested look on his face.

"We don't have anything else to offer," Tom said, a little bemused.

"No problem. Then it's eleven grand."

"We were thinking ten," said Tom, confidently, looking first at Albert then at Paddo.

Paddo looked at the brother to see if it registered. The brother looked at Albert and said something in a different language. Albert scratched his nose and turned up the side of his mouth a little. His brother lit a cigarette. There was an unnerving pause.

"Do you want me to call you a cab back to the station?" asked Albert.

"A taxi?" asked Tom, confused.

"That's right. I don't want to waste any more time." He pulled out his phone.

"What about ten and a half thousand?" Tom asked.

Albert pressed some buttons on his phone and said, "Cab for two to 336A Kahalan Place, Rooty Hill. Yes, they are ready now." He started to walk back to the house.

As Paddo carefully and slowly drove down the driveway in the Troopy not long after that, he could not help himself. "Remind me, please, to leave you to do the talking when we sell this thing. That's if we can ever sell it. Your negotiation skills are so damn good!"

* * * *

Bessy felt nervous about calling Josh. She knew that he had arrived back in Australia yesterday and her concerns about their future hardened when he didn't call. Although, the flight had not been due in until 9 pm, so again she checked herself and let the voice of reason in her head dictate that she was just being a little paranoid and that it was all a natural consequence of absence.

She picked up the phone at 10 am, enough time for at least a bit of a sleep in after the long flight. When it went through to his message bank, the voice of concern in her head made a brief return, only to be interrupted by her phone ringing five minutes later.

"Sorry, I missed your call. I haven't been long up and had just gotten out of the shower," he said. The words soothed her and she tried to hide her relief.

"Hey, I am so glad you're back, safe and sound. I missed you. I can't wait to hear all about your trip."

"Yeah, thanks. It was great. I am a bit flight from the flight, sorry, tired from the flight. It's a monster. My parents are suffering more than me."

"And they had a good time?"

"Yes. Mum got a little ill in the first week. But she recovered, and I think they enjoyed themselves."

"That's great. Is she okay now?"

"I think so. She seemed to think it was some sort of bug she might have picked up on the plane. She was laid up in the hotel for a couple of days but she's fine."

"So, what are your plans? Are you up for a visit today?" she asked.

"I was thinking tomorrow, if that's alright?"

"Yeah, sure. I'm working until 3."

"Okay, well, what if I meet you at that place in Lygon Street that I like, Jensen's Café, shortly after?"

"Sounds great. See you then. Love you."

"See you then," he replied.

In the little over two years they had been seeing each other, Josh had never been one for showing much social contact with her other than in person. It was not entirely surprising to her that she had not received contact whilst he was in the UK. On average, they had seen each other three and sometimes four times a week. On some weekend nights, he would stay over. She was very much looking forward to the weekend.

Work seemed to drag the next day and Bessy could not focus. It wasn't busy, which made it worse. She fixed her hair up in the bathroom and darted out the door at exactly 3 pm. When she got to the coffee shop, Josh was already waiting. He was sitting in their usual spot and looking at his phone. She could see it was a new phone with a much bigger screen.

"Hello," she said. He got up and she gave him a hug and a kiss.

"New phone?" she asked, as they sat down.

"Yeah, I got it just before I left." They ordered some coffee and Bessy ordered her usual slice of carrot cake.

"How are you feeling today?" she asked.

"Good. Better, anyway. It's twenty-two hours, that flight. A bloody long thing, I can tell you. We were in business class, though. I am thankful at least for that."

"You know, I have never been on a plane yet," Bessy said.

"How have you been?" he asked.

"I've been good! Work is a bit crazy, in a crappy sort of way. The new owners are driving everyone bonkers. I like them, though. Especially, the lady. She is funny and so is he, in a way. Same old routine, though. Old Bill from upstairs got dragged off to a nursing home last week. The whole place is relieved we will be getting a new tenant."

"He was one weird dude, that guy," Josh said.

"What was the highlight of your trip?"

"It's hard to say, really. I hung out with the olds for most of the time. They paid all the expenses, which I felt a bit bad about. But maybe London, I suppose. It's pretty cool. Working there would be good one day. I'd like to do that."

"Yeah, I'd love to go to London. Anywhere, really," she laughed. "It's so good to see you," she smiled and placed her hand on his.

His phone rang and he removed his hand from hers.

"Sorry," he said to Bessy. "Yep, thanks. I know that. Can I call you back?"

Bessy noticed that the caller must not have immediately answered yes to his question and watched him listen a little longer. "Yes, okay," he said a little impatiently, before ending the call. He apologised to Bessy again.

"Who was that?" Bessy asked.

"It doesn't matter. I will call them back."

They chatted some more and Bessy had a bite of her cake. They discussed the weather and the football news. Bessy wanted to turn the conversation to more meaningful things but it wasn't working.

"Do you have plans for the rest of the week? When are you back at university?"

Josh seemed to take a long while to consider his response to these things, as if he heard the questions but was already considering something else. Bessy had noticed he seemed stiff in his seat.

"Not really," he said.

"I'd like to take you to the new Argentinian restaurant around the corner on Saturday," she said.

"Don't think I can."

"Is Friday better? It's also open for lunch. You still have Fridays free?" she pressed.

The waiter came over and asked if he could collect their plates. Bessy had only eaten a couple of mouthfuls of cake. Their usual chemistry seemed missing to her but again, this would only require an adjustment owing to his absence, she felt.

"Would you like some?" she looked at Josh and he said no and the waiter removed the plate and cups. She was now resting on her elbows almost halfway across the table and leaning forward and he was leaning away, back on his seat.

He looked around for a moment and ran his hands through his hair. He scratched his hand. The new phone was there next to him on the table.

"Is something wrong?" she eventually said.

When he did not immediately reassure her, she felt a hollow pit develop in her stomach.

He paused and bit his lip. "I um …"

"What is it?" she said.

He was again silent.

"Say it, Josh."

"I have met someone," he said.

At first, she allowed herself for a moment to think he might be referring to a professor or a businessman who might have something to do with architecture. But such a thought was as fleeting as it was misguided and self-deceiving, and she knew it.

"You have met *someone*?"

"Yes," he said, nodding with reassurance as if she had made some outstanding guess that turned out to be correct. He now looked at her more closely and sat casually in his chair, waiting for her to say more, as if he was de-burdened now.

Bessy expected it was him who should be talking. "Who is she?"

"It doesn't matter."

She pulled back now and looked around, but she didn't see anything around her. She paused. A lump developed in her throat as she tried to talk. She shook her head and returned her gaze to him. Her eyes pierced his like weapons designed to wound.

"Please don't," he said.

"Please fucking don't?" she said, now holding back tears. "How dare you tell me that!"

He had never heard her say that word. Possibly, it was the first time she had used it.

She gathered herself. She turned her head away again and stared at something outside. He said they should leave.

"No!" she said, sharply and loudly. She paused again and swallowed heavily, trying to clear that lump. "When did you meet her?"

"Bessy, it's not … I don't think going through it …"

"When did you meet her?" She raised her voice even louder and he looked around.

Josh had never seen Bessy in this way.

She had never had an experience anything like this.

He could see she was more than upset. "Look, I don't know …"

"Don't lie to me, Josh," she said. "You owe me the truth!"

"Just before, I think, it was just before I left for the UK."

"Right," she said, now blowing her nose with a tissue.

The waiter came over to ask if he could get them anything more and Josh said they would be leaving soon.

"Do you love her?" she asked, clenching the tissue so hard that the whites of her knuckles showed.

"Bessy …"

"I just think that you should tell me. Do you?"

"I don't know. We have only been …"

"Don't tell me," she interrupted him, holding up her hand.

She ran her hand up and down her face and smudged the small amount of eyeliner she wore. They sat in silence and then she held a hand clenched over her mouth.

Josh looked into her eyes and could see they were red. But the imagined daggers and arrows had disappeared. Instead he could see intense pain. "I'm sorry, Bessy."

She nodded, but it was a nod to herself, not in acceptance of his apology. It was over and it had been over long before he told her.

"We had some good times," he said.

"Obviously not bloody good enough." She shook her head again and breathed out. "And that's supposed to make me feel better?"

"No."

"Good, because it doesn't!"

"Okay."

He could see she was starting to process it and cool down.

"Can we leave? I think we should," he said.

"Whatever you want. It's all about what you want," she said, as she pushed the chair out from underneath her. As she got up, she felt the first stab of bitterness in her stomach after the pain of having her heart severed from him at the table. Her legs carried her to the exit but she didn't notice a thing, including Josh hurriedly fixing up the bill. A numbness had taken over like a sedative had been injected into her legs.

"I want to walk you home," he said, when they got outside.

"No, you don't," she said.

"Please, Bessy. Let me."

She gave no response and turned and he followed a step behind, before deciding to walk next to her. She walked slowly. It wasn't far.

When they got to the foot of the stairs outside, he grabbed her hand. Her arm was limp and she felt drained and lifeless. Whatever he said and did now didn't matter. He gave her a kiss on the cheek and she had no power within her to do or say anything. He turned away and walked up the street. She put the key in the door, went upstairs, got into her bed and cried. And, after a while, she fell asleep.

* * * *

"It's noisy," Paddo said, as they rattled down the Princes Highway. They had decided to give themselves four weeks to make it to Port Augusta, travelling along the south coast of New South Wales, into south-east Victoria, onto Melbourne then South Australia.

"And don't forget it's diesel when we fill up," Tom said.

Paddo was driving. "Can you tell me how long this highway is?" Paddo felt he almost needed to shout.

"It says here 2256 kilometres," replied Tom, looking at a map he picked up at the last service station.

"What's that in miles?"

"I think it's about 1300 miles, maybe a bit more."

"Oh good, that sounds less," Paddo said.

They'd picked up some camping gear and had thrown it in the back.

"Where's the best swimming beach on this stretch of road?" asked Paddo.

"I don't know," Tom said. "My name is Greer not Google."

"Haven't you got that Lonely Planet there somewhere?"

"I think I left it in the last place we stayed."

"Great. Well try your phone and Google it."

"I don't like doing that in the car. It makes me feel sick."

Paddo shook his head and turned on the radio. Soon they were approaching the town of Ulladulla.

The sign said 'Welcome' and as they had been travelling non-stop for more than three hours, they decided to get out, stretch their legs and have something to eat.

"Lots and lots of places have Aboriginal names. I think I should make a point of noting what they mean. I reckon that would be cool," Paddo said.

"Right," Tom said.

They strolled around town before stopping at a bakery. Tom ordered a meat pie and Paddo had a salad roll.

"It says on that sign over there Ulladulla means 'safe harbour'," Paddo said.

"I don't see any harbour."

"Well not from here, you can't."

"I'd rather you didn't use that language," Tom said.

"What language?"

"Can't. I don't like being told that I *can't* do something." Paddo just shook his head and continued to eat.

They noticed some signs that said 'Mollymook' and 'Narrawallee' and Paddo made a mental note to look up their meanings. They decided it was best to keep driving and maybe find a beach further south.

* * * *

Bessy got up and made herself a cup of tea. She had decided to call in sick to work in the morning. That would not be a lie, she concluded. It would be her first sick day ever, so Lino could hardly complain, not that it would stop him anyway. Lino 'could go and f…'. She stopped herself. Enough swearing had been going on. She shook her head; it wasn't right. She flipped between anger and sadness. After the tea, she felt wide awake.

Stretched out on the bed again she switched on the radio in an effort to stop thinking and to halt the replaying in her mind of the events of the afternoon. But it was hard. People were telling their life stories on talk-back and she kept thinking what her story was so far? It added to her agony. She switched it over to music. Years ago she had felt alone but not unhappy; now she was alone *and* unhappy. But it was more than unhappiness; it was sheer raw pain. Someone had told her once –maybe it was her Aunt Molly – there were different types of pain in life. Some comes and goes briefly. Some only heals with time and you hope it doesn't leave a permanent scar. And some never leaves.

Grief was not a word she used often. It was however upon her again. With her eyes closed, she counted the people she had once loved who were now gone. Gone forever. Now one more had to be added to the list.

She decided one thing in the hours she remained awake on that bed. In the next month, she would have to make some decisions about her life. Firstly, she would almost definitely resign from work and take a break – travel somewhere, anywhere – and just get away. She figured she had enough money to keep the apartment and travel on a tight budget for up to two months. So what if she spent all her savings? What else was she going to do with it anyway? Travelling alone would be a chance for her – a chance to meet new people and expand her horizons. She liked the way that sounded, as she tossed questions and everything else around in her mind, before she switched the radio off and started crying again.

CHAPTER TEN

Narooma, NSW

By late afternoon, Paddo was very tired. He had driven what felt like all day, although the traffic out of Sydney accounted for much of his fatigue. When they arrived at Narooma, it was time to stop for good, regardless of its attractions. Before they realised, they had gone too far and crossed the bridge that spanned the azure waters of the Wagonga Inlet and found themselves heading out of town. Paddo turned the Troopy around and went back over the bridge, so low in energy that he didn't bother checking with Tom and parked in the car park on the edge of the water.

They took a slow stroll along the boardwalk on the edge of Mill Bay and gazed down to see the variety of sea creatures in the clear, shallow water. They watched schools of small fish and the occasional crab, seemingly basking in the soft sunlight. A large stingray gently flapped its way along near the surface of the deeper blue water further out from the shore. Families with toddlers passed by in both directions, with children on tiny bikes and scooters. Pelicans glided in like they owned the bay. The smell of fresh ocean air invigorated Paddo and he said they should stay the night, if not several. Tom offered no opposition and seemed to be in a world of his own as he wandered to the end of the boardwalk, occasionally pointing to something interesting in the water.

With still plenty of daylight left, they decided to go for a drive around the town. They paused to read the tourist information signs which was followed up by some research on Paddo's phone. After a small bite to eat at a corner shop, they settled on trying to find something called a 'primitive camping ground' at Mystery Bay, which lay about fifteen kilometres south of Narooma.

"It's says here, Tom, that this camp ground is one of the few natural camping areas on the entire south coast of New South Wales. And it fronts the ocean," Paddo said.

They had no trouble finding it and when they arrived, were surprised just how large it was. The camp sites were spread out throughout the bushland setting, with plenty of spaces available. Finding a spot to pitch the tent was easy and they chose one that was a comfortable walk to the beach, with just a little bit of privacy.

One night turned into two, then three. The weather seemed to them like a gift from the universe, with warm and still sunny days, and a mild afternoon breeze and cool evenings. Each day was almost a replica of the previous. There were plenty of activity options to fill their time and they took short and long walks in the Eurobodalla National Park, to the north and south. Tom drove the Troopy into Narooma on the third day to restock, buying some bread and water. For ice and gas, it was a short trip to a local farm. Each night provided close to ideal conditions for a fire and there was a ready pile of firewood that they could purchase on site. For the time being, their lives were picture-postcard perfect. For both, it finally sank in for the first time that they were in Australia enjoying themselves, just as they had imagined.

Tom took a swim in the mornings and the afternoons, although Paddo was less keen on swimming once the sun got too high in the sky. He was far more conscious than Tom about sunburn, although it was Tom that had the fairer skin and needed to be most vigilant about it. When it came to body surfing, it was Tom that was the more adventurous, but his small frame was pummelled constantly by the roll of the waves, washing him into the shallows dazed yet enthused for more.

Other backpackers and tourists in the camp ground struck up conversations and they decided to make some effort to introduce themselves and stay the best part of a week. On the third night, a group of girls from Denmark invited Paddo and Tom for dinner. Tom took the Troopy to

Narooma once again shortly after the invite had been made and picked up some white wine, beer and chocolate. He hoped his choice provided enough to please everyone.

Paddo tried his hand at fishing off the rocks the next day with Hilda, from Odense. Hilda caught a nice rock cod and Paddo took it off the hook, balancing on the rock ledge and being extra careful not to tumble into the water. In the process, the hook punctured the skin on his finger as he yanked it free from the fish's mouth. His hand bled onto the rocks like water dripping from a tap. They went back to Hilda's camp site where she gave him a bandage and they both had a glass of wine from a bottle that had been left over from the night before.

Tom spent most of that day retracing his steps on the longer of the bushwalks he had done earlier in the week, this time with Hilda's companions, Marietta and Freja. He enjoyed playing tour guide and chatted away as if he was employed by the local national park service. He told Paddo all about it and while Paddo enjoyed the fishing, he thought being tour guide would have been more to his liking.

When the girls packed up on the morning of the next day and the weather started to look like it might storm that afternoon, Paddo was the one who first suggested that it might be a good idea for them also to make tracks. His radar was on as if it had been finely tuned into the Bureau of Meteorology, for the precise moment Tom threw his backside onto the passenger seat after throwing the last item of rubbish into the back of the Troopy, a massive crack of thunder made them both jump.

The Troopy's windscreen wipers would soon get their first test from their new owners. When they reached the highway, they both fell silent, not that their voices would have remotely registered with either. They had never seen rain like it before and never in their wildest imaginings had they considered rain this heavy possible. Paddo leaned right up against the steering wheel and concentrated on the road. The wipers were at maximum speed but the windscreen was still a blur. Traffic had slowed to a crawl and they noticed many people were pulling over where they could. Tom suggested turning the lights on and Paddo told him they were on. The sound and force of the rain was so loud it drowned out the noise of the engine.

After ten minutes, the rain eased a little and then further along the highway, it backed off to a sprinkle, before they caught glimpses of afternoon sunshine filtering through the trees. Tom noticed that his foot was wet and they soon realised water had entered the passenger side. At least there was no need to wash the car of the salt spray.

"Is it too late to pay Albert a friendly visit? You can do the talking about your wet foot," Paddo said. "You might get your discount then."

* * * *

For Bessy, her days were less than enjoyable and barely tolerable. By lunchtime the day after her awful meeting with Josh, she had decided she would not cry anymore. She had made this decision as if it were a matter of deciding to switch off the air-conditioning in her apartment, which didn't work very well anyway. She determined that her emotions would be *under her control*, rather than *controlling her*. Besides, it was simply not in her nature to feel sorry for herself. In the face of overwhelming force, rationality and logic, she would banish the tears – dam them at the source.

However, a song on the radio just before dinner time reduced her to a blubbering mess. She sat on the floor of the kitchen and ate chocolate, almost hoping for a sadder song than the one before, again and again, until her dinner of vegemite on toast.

But the next day she went into work and felt a little better. She calmly reminded herself of the time her healing would take and that things could be worse. She could be married to Lino, for one. Or she could have some disability or she could be dying or she could have never experienced the good times with Josh that she had. These things ran through her mind, including the many happy times, as she prepared a plate of minted asparagus and creamed, spiced eggplant soup with parmesan flakes and garlic croutons with cracked pepper for a young couple – obviously in love – sitting inside.

She told no one of her heartache and resolved the less said the better. Since Sophie had gone, there was no one at work to talk about it with anyway. Again, she felt the reality of that was worth considering now. She had placed all her eggs in the Josh basket, which was fine, until the basket was empty. *It wasn't at all fine*, she thought, and she vowed never to make that mistake again, no matter how much she was taken by a man and his charms.

For a while, she felt there was no waking moment spent without thinking about her relationship with him and all its implications. Even when she served a customer, it was on her mind. When she walked home, she would revisit something she had contemplated earlier with microscopic analysis, now that she could devote the time to it away from the annoying distractions of work. She thought about him in the shower, and it went on and on for a good while.

This all had to stop, she resolved yet again. She considered joining a gym and went on a diet.

It was well into the second week of her solitude that she decided the timing and method of giving notice at work. It would be easy. Just a matter of having a brief, quiet chat one morning with Lino, hopefully when Abriana was also there and writing a short note to confirm, if they required it. Sophie seemed to be able to pull it off smoothly, so why couldn't she do it?

By the time she had decided on the day she would tell Lino, she had noticed Josh had occupied her mind far less. Time was working its slow healing power, she reassured herself, and she was pleased her theories were starting to materialise into reality.

Unfortunately, the day she chose – there was to be no negotiation with herself about any postponement – was an unusually and unexpectedly busy morning in the kitchen and Abriana was not coming in to work. It was just Bessy, Lesley, Janet and Lino, all working fairly frantically.

Just after lunch, there was a hiatus of sorts and Bessy thought she'd best seize the opportunity. Lino had seemed, by now, quite used to the lack of a siesta in Australia but on several occasions, he had already made his displeasure known about having to work without that civilised intermission. He didn't exactly use the most diplomatic language at the best of times and when he was complaining, there was a total absence. He was tired after lunch but so was everyone.

"Do you have a moment, Lino?" she asked, timing her approach and watching him pull his head out of the oven which he had been examining to see what was causing it to take so long to heat up. Perspiration dripped off his brow and he wiped his hands vigorously on his apron.

"What is it, dear?" he asked, giving her unexpected optimism about how he might take it.

"Well," she started and then paused, finding herself in a moment of last-minute mild panic.

"What is it?" he asked again, not looking at her, this time grabbing some cleaning fluid and spraying the stove top.

She moved a little closer to him.

"I have decided to move on," she said. Then added quickly, and nervously, "But of course I want to do the right thing, the right thing by you and Abriana."

"Move on, what is move on? What do you mean, move on?"

"I mean quit, give you notice of my leaving," she said.

"YOU WHAT?" he said at the top of his voice.

Lesley and Janet were serving. Lesley poked her head in and asked if everything was alright. Bessy waved her back and said it was fine but that was just a hope.

"Listen, I don't want you to get upset, Lino. It's just time I moved on. I have been here for years and I think it might be a good time for me to go."

Lino stood there in silence, motionless for about five seconds, staring at Bessy. His arms dangled with the cleaning fluid in one hand and the cloth in the other. The look on his face was something that Bessy had seen versions of in the past but this was the calm before the storm. His face then contorted into a wrinkled, anguished mess.

"Oh, this is ... my lord, WHAT, what I have done to deserve THIS? I can't STAND it!"

Bessy had known there was a fair chance he would not take it well.

"How can you do this to me, I can't ... oh, she's a ... is a not fair, you can't! LOOK at this place, how can you expect to walk out on me?"

"Lino, I am not leaving today. I need to give you proper notice."

"It's no use," he said, tossing the cleaning fluid in the corner and sitting on a chair.

"It'll be fine. You have good staff, Lino, and you will find someone as good as me, I am sure of it, if not better."

He had his head in one hand now staring at the floor. He wasn't listening.

"Look Lino, I think two weeks is fair."

"NO!" he said, abruptly.

Lesley came in again and Bessy said to leave it to her.

"I can give you no more than three weeks," she said, walking up a little closer to the chair.

He seemed to come to his senses a bit. He stretched his legs out, crossing one over the other, and rested one hand under his chin, seemingly in deep thought. There was silence for a good minute.

"Okay, then," he said after a while, with a blink and nod.

* * * *

After a feed of fresh oysters at picturesque Tathra, Paddo and Tom continued down the highway before stopping overnight at Eden.

"Can we find the garden?" asked Tom. Paddo just shook his head at Tom's lame attempt to make him laugh with a reference to the biblical Garden of Eden.

But they did enjoy the views out across Twofold Bay and took a stroll the next day through Ben Boyd National Park. Paddo was disappointed that the Aboriginal names were less prominent in this area and remarked on this to Tom, who was probably less interested than Paddo would have hoped. Tom had taken the wheel for the journey into Victoria.

"As far as I can see, we are not far from Coopracambra National Park, the home of the Bidawal and Nindi-Ngudjam Ngarigu Monero traditional country," Paddo said, reading the names from his phone slowly and deliberately.

"Fabulous, I'm hungry again," Tom said.

"And then further on a bit, let me see, near the Cann River, I think, there is the Croajingolong National Park. It says we can access it from multiple points along the Princes Highway," continued Paddo.

"I'm thinking of a burger, what about you?"

"It says there are a number of secluded camp grounds throughout the park, and it's a perfect base for beach walks and birdwatching."

"If I can get some Colman's mustard, I'm happy to make my own. And yours. I'm craving Norwich mustard!"

They continued on the road and crossed the border. Paddo continued on with his research, while Tom thought about various burger combinations.

"I think we should stop at Mallacoota. It's surrounded by the national park and there's heaps to do, it seems. The population is less than a thousand, outside holiday season. I can't seem to find what the Aboriginal name means in English though."

"I'm starved, let's get a burger there. I can see the turn off."

They arrived about 12:30 pm and Tom was happy that he could stretch his legs and fill his belly.

Paddo suggested that before they eat, they take a short walk around one of the camp sites. Tom reluctantly agreed, on the strict condition that it was indeed short. He also said that his first impression was that they should find somewhere a little more secluded.

"I don't have any problem with that. There's a lot of places not far from here to camp, I think," said Paddo.

They wandered around for a while and Tom did not have his sunglasses or his hat, having left both in the car. Paddo, he noticed, was dressed like he was ready to go hiking for a week. Tom eyed off the take-away-burger-cum-fish-and-chip shop across the road. He turned to Paddo to ask if he had seen enough and completely missed seeing an extended tent rope and kicked his toe on a steel peg in the ground. As usual, he was wearing thongs. He let out an almighty yelp and did a quick hop, skip and jump.

"What have you done?" asked Paddo, giggling at Tom's action.

While the pain peaked for a moment, Tom could not utter a word. He then let out a few expletives, very inappropriately right in front of two elderly ladies who were strolling into the camp ground. He hobbled over to the Troopy on one leg, opened the door and sat on the seat to take a good look at his toe. It was bleeding and was already starting to turn purple. Paddo brought out the first-aid kit for the first time and there was some heated discussion about whether it needed stitches or not. Eventually, Tom decided not and he cleaned the wound and wrapped it tightly in a bandage, which looked rather large on his small foot.

"Stands out like a sore thumb," Paddo said.

Tom had lost his appetite and his sense of humour somewhat. He let the seat back so he could rest while Paddo took another walk.

When Paddo got back, he found Tom asleep. He started the Troopy up and Tom gazed at him, almost as if he was still in a dream and went back to resting his head. Paddo made his way to the more secluded camp site he thought Tom might have wanted, stopping on the way for petrol, ice, beer, bread, sausages, onions, lettuce and Colman's mustard.

CHAPTER ELEVEN

There was one small favour Lino had asked Bessy to undertake for him prior to her leaving. A trade fair had been arranged some months before in the Docklands precinct. It was planned to run for two days and they just happened to be Bessy's last days working at The Gourmet Pheasant. It was absolutely ideal, Bessy thought, as she would be out of the kitchen and out of Lino's sight. But still two weeks had to be traversed beforehand and Lino had rostered her on almost every day and several nights. Again, her outlook was upbeat about that, as it would add to her savings and limit her spending. If she was to take that well-earned holiday, she would need to cover that, plus her rent.

"You will be the only girl there," Lino said, meaning she will be the only girl from The Gourmet Pheasant. "I can'ta affordo any others," he added, to no surprise.

"That's fine, I'm looking forward to it. I will fly the flag proudly," she said.

"She'sa good," he said.

"And don't you forget it, Lino." Smiles had returned to her face with their usual regularity.

She was very happy that Josh was retreating at a fast pace in the rear-view mirror of her subconscious. He no longer occupied a room in her head as much, but when he visited that room and was asked to leave, it seemed that he now fully co-operated.

To her surprise, Abriana dropped in one afternoon and said to her that she wanted to go for a drink.

"We must have a drink, no, a meal and a drink, before you go. Tonight, it suits me," she said, in her persuasive way. Her accent was as thick as Lino's but her words were delivered with more confidence.

Bessy had always liked Abriana. She didn't dislike Lino, for that matter. He was just hard work. And she felt sorry for what Lino must put Abriana through. Bessy had never met a person she disliked.

"You come with me?" she said. "We can go to my friend's restaurant in Carlton, yes?"

Bessy explained that she didn't finish until 7 pm.

"Don'ta you worry about that, we leave at 6."

Bessy took Abriana back to her apartment. They had a glass of wine and sat on the sofa. Bessy had long since stopped feeling embarrassed by her humble abode and had rightly figured that if it wasn't good enough for someone, then that someone was not good enough for her.

"I like your minimalist approach," Abriana observed, casting her eye around the bare walls.

"I wouldn't call it an approach, really, it's more that I can't afford to buy much," Bessy said, with a laugh.

"I like, anyway."

After one glass of red wine, Abriana took control of the bottle and settled in.

"You are going to travel, yes? Are you going to go back to your home?"

Bessy shook her head. "One day, I will, but just for a visit."

"Where is it again, the parrot place?"

Bessy laughed. "No, it's Jeparit."

"And there are parrots there?"

"Um, well some. It's not really known for them."

"Is it nice, there in Parit?"

"Jeparit. Je-parit. It can be. It can get hot at times. There is a lake out there that's pretty. At least, I used to like it. The yabbies are good."

"The yabbies. They sound like, scary. What are they?"

"Oh no, they're not scary. Maybe if you are three years old and they give you a bit of a nip that you're not expecting. They're like a crustacean, like, a mini fresh-water lobster, not gourmet, but fun to catch and eat."

"Ah," said Abriana. "I must go to this Parit place once, then."

They decided after another glass that they should catch a taxi to the restaurant.

"My friend, she shall be expecting us," Abriana said.

When they arrived at the restaurant it was crowded and no tables were free, at least none that Bessy could see. But soon a lady, roughly the same age as Abriana, appeared and led them through the maze of the restaurant, stopping at the very back. Bessy thought this may have been Abriana's friend but as they hardly acknowledged each other, she figured not. It was a cosy corner, with atmosphere consistent with the rest of the restaurant with a privacy reserved for just that space. The kitchen was nearby and there was a lovely plant just beside the table and art work on the wall. The smells of cooking were divine.

For a moment, Josh entered her head. *What is it now?* she said to herself. *What does this remind me of?* But then he left, and the conversation with the lovely Abriana resumed.

"What is your life?" asked Abriana, pulling her chair closer to the table and resting her chin against her elbowed hand.

"My life?" said Bessy, conscious of the sincerity of the question as well as the limitations of Abriana's mastery of English.

Just then a girl about Bessy's age appeared and said there was a bottle of wine of their choosing on the house, and she would be back, should they care to make a choice. Bessy remarked that was special but Abriana brushed it off, as if it was commonplace and to be expected. She had affixed her gaze on Bessy and there was some compulsion, in a way, to say something profound.

"Well, I guess, I …" she said.

"Yes," interrupted Abriana, eager to hear anything.

"I, well, I just, well *not just*, but a few weeks back, broke up with my boyfriend." She almost regretted immediately that was all she could come up with.

"Ah," said Abriana, this time with a slow, knowing way of saying it, relaxing back into her chair, with a nod of her head and a smile. She was after something juicy that wasn't on the menu and it was just delivered. "Where's that girl?" she said, looking around for the waitress.

The waitress appeared almost instantaneously.

"We want that one," Abriana said, pointing to a spot on the wine list, as if something Bessy had said had now predetermined it. Two glasses were promptly delivered to the table, with a carafe of water and the menu. Abriana made no comment then for a while, somewhat to Bessy's surprise but she sensed Abriana was tossing over in her mind what she would say about this news.

She waited.

The wine arrived and so did Abriana's friend, the owner. They talked quickly and loudly in Italian. Bessy was expecting a break to English at some point by way of Abriana introducing her but it never came. After kisses, the owner left through the door to the kitchen.

"Who was he, this man?" asked Abriana, saying 'man' as if he were some gutter snipe.

"Oh, he was just some guy I met, it doesn't matter now."

"Did he treat you good, like you deserve?"

"Well, I … sometimes, most times."

"Was he a pig?"

"I wouldn't describe him as a pig."

"But, was he a pig? A big, how can I say, stronzo?"

"Stronzo?"

"How can I say? Asshole?"

"No."

Abriana took a big gulp of her wine. Bessy could see the wheels of her mind still turning over.

"Then a why you break up?" she said, after a while.

"He met someone else he liked better than me."

"He's a fucking stronzo!" she exclaimed, with a serious look of concern. But then she smiled and raised her glass. "You are a fine woman, Bessy. I like you."

They touched glasses. Abriana went to some length to explain every single thing on the menu but in the end, left the choice to Bessy. She chose the cross-cut veal shanks osso buco style with white wine broth and vegetables. Sticking with Milanese specialties, Abriana ordered La Piccata Milanese – fried slices of chicken with sauce and garlic mushrooms. A small bowl of salad was placed in the middle and the girls enjoyed their feast and the wine.

At the end of the night, there were more kisses and hugs between Abriana and the owner. After dessert, they called a taxi and waited outside.

"Where will you go, when you leave us, on your holiday?" asked Abriana.

"I haven't made up my mind, yet. Maybe Tasmania or Adelaide, or I might fly to Cairns." They got into the taxi and Abriana was the first out.

"Take care, you lovely girl. There someone special out there for you. I wish you luck and I want to come with you," Abriana said, laughing. She gave her a kiss on the cheek and a very long hug.

* * * *

Tom's foot healed quickly, helped by the salt water and the dry, hot conditions. He limited his bushwalking for a few days as it was uncomfortable to wear shoes. Paddo however did more walking than swimming and trekked over many parts of the Croajingolong National Park. An absolute highlight for him was taking a half-day trek discovering and learning about traditional Aboriginal bush tucker. He asked lots of questions and the Aboriginal ranger was very forthcoming and knowledgeable, highly skilled in the craft of finding food.

They spent a few nights in one camping area, then packed up and moved within the park to other sites. Plenty of time to explore the beaches and the rocks on the coastline meant doing just that at their leisure and they took naps in the early afternoons. The storm clouds moved in on a couple of days late in the afternoon but they didn't amount to much. Tom got sunburnt on his back and Paddo had to again remind him this wasn't the UK. Paddo was turning a nice bronze shade of brown, something he had never seen his skin do before, not even in India. They snapped off a few photos and both sent them to their mothers.

Late one afternoon, Paddo sat on the sand in seclusion watching the sunlight fade over the dunes. There was no other sound apart from the gentle rolling waves of the ocean. As he sent a photo to his mother from his phone, he realised that he hadn't sent any photos to his father. He thought about their last conversation and how his father had asked him to consider helping him with his businesses on his return. The answer was going to be a firm no.

* * * *

A little over a week passed and it was soon time to consider their next leg of their journey towards Melbourne. Both lamented the fact that the next stage would see them return to the built up urban world and wondered where a good place to stop would be for a few nights before the metropolis consumed them. Lakes Entrance, further south, seemed the front runner.

"It's a bit of a tourist place, I think," Paddo said. He added that it was near a 'little' beach. Tom was back in the driver's seat.

"When I say little, I was just pulling your leg," Paddo said.

"If you are going to pull my leg, don't touch my toe, please."

"I'm trying not to touch you at all, I hope you notice."

"Thanks, I appreciate that."

"Anyway, this beach near Lakes Entrance. It's called Ninety Mile Beach. It says here 'a stretch of golden sand separating Gippsland Lakes from Bass Strait.' I think it is where we should head."

"Is that right?" Tom said, as he overtook a semi. "Don't take one of your walks after lunch to the end of the beach and back, then, will you," he added.

"I reckon we find a camping spot and hang out there for a night or two."

"What's the weather going to be like?"

Paddo checked his phone and said it was going to be good, but there was some rain later in the week, and in fact the forecast was for quite a few showers. A lot more rain than they had encountered to date.

"That's fine. We will be in Melbourne by then," Tom said.

They set up camp in Lakes Entrance and after wandering around town and Paddo ensuring Tom was well fed, they took the Troopy, with some towels in the back, further down and around the coastline. Finding their way to Loch Sport, a small town on the beach, they had a swim and then travelled to the nearby town of Seaspray. After another swim, they explored The Honeysuckles and the Wild Dog Shore area before heading back to Lakes Entrance in the late afternoon.

Sitting in a bowls club not far from Ninety Mile Beach and sipping on cold beer, it was time to discuss the day's events. The club was near to what look liked a busy seafood café they had their eye on for dinner as a special treat and break from cooking back at their camp site.

"I can't say I would go out as deep as you did today," Paddo said.

"I didn't go out that deep," Tom replied.

"I think you couldn't touch the bottom a few times."

"I can't touch the bottom in the bath. In fact, a bath would be nice."

"None of those beaches were patrolled."

"I know," Tom said. "You think you have to tell me that?"

"I'd hate you to get into a rip. I am not coming in after you, you know that."

"I wouldn't expect you to."

"I would just get back in the Troopy and drive in the direction you were floating. I would go and get someone, after stopping for a beer."

"I think that's fair enough. I would just wade a bit and hope there weren't any sharks."

They looked at the menu and ordered some more beers, very comfortable with the spot in which they sat.

"Where are we going to stay in Melbourne?" asked Tom.

"Well, I was thinking one of the hostels in or near the city. I think we should stay in the city, close to the action."

"The action, hey," said Tom.

"Yep."

"What sort of action did you have in mind?"

"Just action. City stuff."

"Nightlife, you mean?"

"Not necessarily. I mean, being able to explore the city. The transport is good, apparently. The trams. I'm looking forward to seeing the trams. Maybe we can catch something that is on at the Melbourne Cricket Ground. Not the cricket. I would like to check out the Indigenous art at the gallery. We can split up a bit and meet back at nights, if you want."

"I don't mind. The art gallery sounds cool."

They decided to stay for dinner at the club that had an all-you-can-eat seafood smorgasbord. Tom tucked into some prawns, crab, fish and salad and Paddo did likewise, although in a smaller portion. After eating all they could, they took a slow walk back to their tent, climbed into their sleeping bags, still feeling the heat on their skin as the night air cooled around them. Asleep in seconds, they did not awake until dawn, with their snoring cancelling each of their own noises out.

* * * *

Bessy was counting down the days to her leaving her job for good. She had noticed that Lino was not interviewing anyone yet.

"Have you placed an advert yet?" she asked him, as he smoked a cigarette out the back of the premises.

"No, I have had a no time," he said.

"It doesn't take long. You can just make a phone call to one of the agencies. I can help you, if you like."

"Thank you, it's okay."

Lino had been preoccupied with some marketing material for the trade fair. He had some brochures printed along with menus, photographs and some cards to hand out. Also, there were several boxes of food, packaged and in jars that needed to be displayed.

"You will be able to set up the night before?" he asked.

"Yes, that's fine. How is all this stuff getting there?"

"We get Abriana's friend. He has truck. You go with him."

CHAPTER TWELVE

Warragul, 104 kilometres east-south-east of Melbourne

In the County of Buln Buln and the Shire of Baw Baw, Paddo and Tom were both out of the Troopy at what looked like the largest petrol station in Warragul. Tom had his mind on a snack, as usual, and Paddo was telling him that the town derived its name from the Aboriginal word for 'wild dog'.

Tom walked across the road and brought back a huge hamburger with beetroot. As he devoured it in the passenger seat, somewhat like a wild dog that hadn't eaten for several days, Paddo told him it wasn't easy working out the origin of the name 'Baw Baw'. He said it could be 'echo' but it might not be. Tom switched the radio on, his mouth full of food, incapable of adding anything to assist Paddo's quest.

All up they had spent almost a week in and around the Ninety Mile Beach area and were ready for a change. Tom wasn't exactly sure why Paddo wanted to take the short detour through Warragul, but told him it turned out to be a good idea as they had the best burgers he had yet eaten in Australia.

"I am pleased for you," Paddo said, without sincerity.

Soon they would be in Melbourne and Paddo said they should make it there in less than ninety minutes. It would be mid-afternoon and time for a cup of tea. That was something they agreed upon. Perhaps an English breakfast tea.

* * * *

Bessy was on duty. It was a Friday. Tomorrow was the first day of the trade fair. It would be her last afternoon at The Gourmet Pheasant. She still hadn't made any real plans about her break and figured she had time to get to that, once she finished work. Lino had told her that morning he had finally placed an advertisement for her position with an agency. He asked her to place a sign in the window saying 'Staff Wanted'. She remembered the sign that she had noticed years ago and when he suggested it, thought about how that simple sign had changed her life. The lunchtime crowd came and went. Sitting down with a cup of tea in the kitchen, she did up the sign pondering how the circles of her life had revolved and what might lie in store for someone, maybe someone like her, who might see it and cross over into the world of this little establishment.

Some fifty metres from where Bessy sat, Paddo and Tom slowly wandered down the path next to the road, chatting, and looking for a place to get that cup of tea.

"It's the first time I've really had a craving for tea," Tom said.

"Tom," Paddo said. He pointed. "See that sign up ahead? You might be able to get your stupid spatchcocks in there! What a tool you made of yourself that day, embarrassing us both!"

"Don't remind me!" Tom said. "Just remind me to eat."

"I'll remind you not to drink so much bloody beer."

The Gourmet Pheasant sign came closer into view.

"I always knew Melbourne would be more cultured than Sydney," Tom said, and they decided to continue in that direction.

At the precise moment that they entered the shop, to the ring of the tiny bell hanging at the top of the door, Bessy was sticky taping the sign in the front window. She didn't notice them as they walked in and sat down, each picking up a menu. She went into the kitchen and returned to the front. Only a few other customers were inside and they had already been served. She noticed two young men looking at the menu and grabbed a notepad and stepped out from behind the counter.

"Can I help you, gentlemen?" she said, standing nearest to Tom.

Paddo looked up and for a moment did not speak. There was something about the way she had said 'gentlemen' that struck him.

"Indeed," said Tom, almost turning on a poshness that he thought befitted the situation and civility of the address. "I shall have an English breakfast tea, and let me see, perhaps a slice of pecan pie, without the cream."

"Very good," she said.

Paddo was distracted by her rose-coloured cheeks.

Tom was thinking of his belly.

"And for you, Sir?" she said.

He had not really taken his eyes off her and had no idea what he wanted. He looked back down at the menu.

"Would you like me to come back?" she asked.

"Um, oh no, that's fine," he said. "The same is fine, actually no. I will have an espresso instead, please."

"And the pie as well?" she asked.

"Yes, that'd be fine."

Bessy left and Paddo leaned over to say something to Tom, but she returned before he could get out what he wanted to say.

"Sorry, Sir. Did you want the pie with or without cream?" she asked.

"With, I think," he said with a smile. Once Bessy was out of earshot he said to Tom, "Well, she is lovely, isn't she." It wasn't a question. It was a statement.

"Who?" Tom said.

"The waitress."

"Oh, yes, I guess so. I didn't notice. Where is she?"

"She's in the kitchen, I suppose. You don't notice much sometimes, do you?"

"I've noticed we are in Melbourne, what more do you want me to notice?"

Paddo shook his head and looked around at the displays. They waited without speaking for a period.

"Maybe it's been a bit too long for you, if you know what I mean," Tom said after a moment.

"No, I don't know what you mean."

"You will be looking up skirts next and I'll be having to bail you out of jail for indecency."

"If you mean I haven't had a shag for a while, you're right, but that has nothing to do with what I just said," Paddo said quietly, leaning in to ensure the other patrons did not hear his frustrations. "What are you bloody on about?"

"Nothing at all," Tom said without taking his eyes off the menu that he had picked up again and was studying. He then added that it seemed Paddo "had his chance" with "whatever her name was" from Odense, but had "passed it up."

"I never bloody 'passed it up' at all! It wasn't that sort of thing! She wasn't my type anyway."

"I wouldn't have passed it up," Tom said without hesitation, still looking at the menu.

"I know you wouldn't have. But it wasn't offered to you, understandably."

Tom sniggered.

Soon Bessy returned with the tea, then a moment later, the pie, then the coffee.

"Enjoy, and if I can get you anything else, please let me or one of the other girls know."

They both said thank you.

Paddo took a spoonful of the pie and thought about ordering something else, even though he wasn't hungry, just so he could have Bessy return to their table again and maybe, somehow, he could strike up a conversation. The thought crossed his mind how it would be very handy, just for once, if Tom was not with him. But there was nothing he could do about that.

Fifteen minutes later, Tom was reading *The Age* newspaper that he had grabbed off the shelf. Paddo picked up the menu again and decided to carry out his strategy. He was really quite full and he felt it was an act of silly desperation but he was going to try it anyway.

Tom could see through him and said, almost too loudly, "You just want her over here again, don't you?"

Paddo tried to make it quite noticeable that he was considering something more from the menu. He placed it in front of him as conspicuously as he could manage without looking absurd.

"You're pathetic," Tom said, looking over the top of the newspaper.

Paddo had decided on a slice of apple and blueberry pie. Bessy returned and he placed the order, very efficiently.

"Why didn't you have a crack?" asked Tom, attempting to provoke him.

"Shut up," he snapped back. "Keep your voice down, will you?"

"Righto," he said and returned to his paper.

"Besides, I will think of something to say when she brings me the pie or tart or whatever it is. Maybe ask for some directions or something. You know, act like I'm a dumb tourist."

"You will be able to pull that one off without even trying. Don't even speak, just sit there. That should do it."

Paddo was not at all in the mood to tolerate Tom. He seriously needed a break from him. At least they were in the city now; he could lose him for a day or two.

"Don't make yourself sick, son," Tom added, patronisingly.

But when the apple and blueberry pie arrived, it wasn't Bessy who brought it to him. It was one of the other girls. The slice of the pie was massive. Paddo looked mortified.

"Thank you," he said. He didn't mean it.

"Serves you right," Tom said. "Tuck in, now."

After two mouthfuls, he offered some to Tom.

"I'm not helping you," he said and returned to his paper. "You'll have to suffer through that silly mistake yourself."

Paddo sighed and squirmed in his chair uncomfortably as he placed a tiny mouthful into his mouth. It would be embarrassing to leave most of the pie. But his demeanour improved following Bessy's reappearance behind the counter. He stole a sideways glance and considered his next move when, all of a sudden, Bessy removed her apron and hugged one of the girls. It was a hug that lasted a long time. A really long time. Paddo watched her arms stretch around the girl and wished, just for that moment, it was him. Then, in an all too fleeting moment, Bessy vanished out the front door. The door slowly drew to a close, with the sound of the tiny bell above it ringing in Paddo's lonely ear.

"She's gone," Paddo said.

Tom lowered his newspaper. "Who?"

* * * *

It would be an early start for Bessy the next day. Lino had told her to be at Docklands no later than 7 am. She would receive a phone call from James, Abriana's friend with the truck. All she needed to do was help James with the stock, he explained, as the site inside the centre had already been set up. All went smoothly to plan and by 10 am, when the first set of customers entered the centre, Bessy had everything set up nicely.

The trade fair was a sizeable gathering of mostly small but some larger food and beverage providers, including retailers and wholesalers. The city of Melbourne was the chief sponsor, although some wholesale suppliers took the opportunity to also pay for some of the centre's hire costs and obtain larger advertising privileges to increase their profile. Many of the restaurants, cafés, delicatessens, Asian supermarkets and small specialty food shops that were in and around the immediate heart of Melbourne had a presence. Bessy thought the atmosphere was wonderful and wanted to be able to wander around and chat to all the people behind the stalls.

* * * *

Paddo and Tom woke up earlier than they had hoped. The backpacker hostel was almost full and the morning noises soon had them awake and thinking about breakfast. They had decided to "chill", in Tom's words, for the day and perhaps even the next and just go with the flow of wherever their legs might take them. They had a pile of city maps and information, and felt there would be no difficulty in occupying their time.

"I think we need to be disciplined today," Tom said, sipping his morning coffee on the edge of his bed.

"About what?" asked Paddo.

"About doing hardly anything, just chilling."

"Fine with me, as I said. I do need to go and work out a better parking deal though, at some stage. The place we have is costing almost as much as this room per day."

"Good idea, I'll leave you to do that."

"Gee, thanks."

By mid-morning, Paddo had done what he set out to do and caught a bus back to meet Tom in the city. He had found a secure, long-term parking facility quite a way out of the city centre and it was considerably cheaper. He had to commit to laying down a payment for at least ten days. He didn't check it with Tom but figured rightly that Tom would agree, as they would not need a car in Melbourne much and a ten-day stay was the minimum amount of time in front of them.

They met up in Federation Square. Then, they crossed the Yarra River to get to the National Gallery of Victoria. Tom impressed Paddo with his eye for art and his enthusiasm for searching out and finding the Aboriginal art that Paddo was so keen to see. The photography course had given him somewhat of a photographic eye and a broader appreciation for visual art than he once thought he was capable of possessing.

Paddo expressed that the next item they should put on the agenda, not necessarily today, owing to Tom's insistence that they 'chill out' but soon, was the theatre.

"I forgot you were somewhat of a thespian," Tom said.

It was here, in front of the gallery, that a decision was made that could easily have gone either way.

"I want to go to the botanic gardens," Paddo said, after they exited the gallery.

"Now?"

"Maybe," he replied, looking at his watch.

"We could if you want. It's a nice cool afternoon. I'm happy to, if you are." Tom looked at the sky. The forecast rain had not yet arrived.

Paddo scratched his head and from where he stood he could see the gardens. He reached into his back pocket and pulled out the map he had picked up from the hostel. He stood there looking at it for a while. Tom kicked a stone around and checked his phone. Paddo studied the map closely and after a while said, "I think we should do that tomorrow."

"The park, you mean?"

"Yep, the gardens. The Royal Gardens."

"So, what do you have in mind, instead? Back for an early night?"

"Sort of. I wouldn't mind checking out Docklands. It's not far from here. We can walk."

Tom had instructed himself to chill and go with the flow. So, anything moderately suggestible was going to be just fine.

"Sounds good to me. Lead the way, McDuff."

It was approaching 4 pm when they got to Docklands. They wandered around and posed for some photos. Tom took a photo for two Japanese girls who spoke very little English but gestured enough to allow Tom to take their snap and hand their camera back, after checking he was satisfied with what he had taken. Paddo took a photo of Tom taking the photo. Without a word to each other, they casually wandered into the large trade fair, which just seemed like the natural thing to do. People were walking in and out and many of those walking out had show bags.

"There's a craft brew place over there," was the first thing Tom said. Paddo nodded.

As they got closer, Tom said something about a sign that said the fair was open until 9 pm.

"This might be the best place to get a bite to eat," he added.

Paddo was at cruising speed and stopped to chat to various stall-holders. Tom did likewise. It was busy but hospitably so, without hustle. There were two levels and on the upper level there was a space to sit on some high stools and enjoy an ale with a view to the lower level. They decided to go up to that level, order a craft beer and consider what they might want to eat.

"The choice is too much," Tom said, pleased to have it.

"It's pretty cool," Paddo said.

Tom looked at the photos on his phone and showed some to Paddo. But Paddo seemed distracted.

"There she is!" Paddo said with an excitement that seemed out of the ordinary from the last several hours they had just spent together.

"There who is?" he asked, putting the phone back in his pocket.

"That girl! That girl who served us at the café yesterday, The Pheasant place."

"Oh, for Pete's sake, man! Stop it already," Tom said.

"It's definitely her," he said, extremely pleased with himself.

"I can't see her, where?"

"Down there, just near the sign. You can see the sign, can't you?"

"I suppose."

Paddo took an almighty gulp of his beer. It almost took half the tall glass.

"You're not contemplating some Dutch courage, are you?"

"My word I am."

"You're going to pay her a visit down there, are you?"

"I'm going to walk down those stairs and casually wander over to her stall and talk to her, yes."

"You are going to stalk her at the stall, are you? And compliment her on the apple and blueberry pie, even though you walked out leaving half of it?"

"As a matter of fact, yes. It's not stalking her!" And with that he downed the rest of the beer in his glass and walked away.

"What am I supposed to do?"

He turned. "Wait. And get yourself another beer."

Tom watched Paddo walk down the steps and across the floor. He had a nice view but no sound. He figured he could try and work out what they said to each other by their body language.

There was no one in front of the stall and Bessy had her back to the front, putting some money in an envelope.

Paddo made as much noise as he could while he looked at the display and then fiddled with the stock in front of him. He picked up a jar of truffles and twirled it in his hands. As Bessy still had her back to him, he picked up a packet of dried figs and pretended to accidentally drop the packet.

Bessy was concentrating and the noise of the hall was such that she likely didn't hear any of this. It had been a long day and she was looking forward to chilling out, herself.

Tom looked on and laughed when Paddo turned around and glanced at him.

"You have some lovely things here," Paddo said, eventually. He made sure he said it in the best tone of voice he could muster, while at the same time readying himself to exude a calm confidence.

Bessy turned around. "Thank you. There are some lovely things," she said.

"Yes. I was just admiring the truffles there. And the figs, they look interesting. Where are they from?"

"I think they are local. Grown in East Gippsland, I think." She picked up the packet and looked at its label.

Paddo found it hard to take his eyes off her and noticed his heart pound a beat faster. *That's odd*, he thought. *Carry on*, he silently counselled himself. She was even more beautiful today.

"Actually, now that I think of it," he said. "I was in your store – sorry, café – yesterday, I think."

"Really?"

"Yes. Let me think." He took a look at the sign above which meant stepping back a notch. "Yes. My friend and I stopped in for a cup of tea. Well, I had coffee and pie."

"Right," she said, not really recalling it.

"The food was really nice."

"Thank you."

He had broken the ice. The next step would be crucial and he had no idea what that was. He most certainly couldn't come out and say what he wanted to say, which was something like, 'What are you doing after this?'

"Today was the first day of the fair?" He thought that was a decent question until he could think of something better.

"Yes. It finishes up tomorrow."

"How's the day been? Has it been busy?" He looked behind him for any customers. "Sorry, I am not interrupting you closing, am I?"

"Oh, no. I'm here for another few hours yet. It's been good. Fun." She smiled.

"My friend, Tom and I have only been in Melbourne for two days. It's nice to wander around this place."

"Do you like what you have seen so far?"

"Yeah, I think it's great."

Just at that moment another couple approached the counter area and started to pick up some things. Paddo decided timing was everything.

"Well, I might come back tomorrow and buy something. The figs, perhaps. They really look great. Will you be here?" This was a risky question but he had decided risk time had arrived and he had nothing to lose.

"It will just be me," she said, as an observation more to herself, given Lino had not rostered on any help.

"Lovely, might see you then," he said and smiled as he walked away.

He bounced up the stairs, repeating those words in his head: "It will just be me."

Tom had gone from the spot where he had been sitting. Paddo went to order a beer and found Tom at the tap in front of the craft brewer.

"How did it go?" asked Tom.

"She's gorgeous."

"That's not what I asked. I know you think that."

"Let's go after this. I need to research everything there is to possibly know about truffles and figs."

CHAPTER THIRTEEN

"I wish you the very best of luck today," Tom said next morning as he ran a brush through his blond curly locks and looked in a mirror, checking how his sunburnt face was peeling. He had already told Paddo that today would be their first day apart and he would get up to his own devices. This suited Paddo perfectly. "I think you'll need all the luck you can get." He grabbed his wallet and put it in his pocket. "Don't fall in love," he added and left the hostel.

Paddo had no intention of falling in love, but he did want to ask if he could go on a date, on an outing, anything that may involve some company with this girl that had occupied his mind since he last laid eyes on her. This was not going to be easy, he realised. No social setting would magically present itself that would happily facilitate his desire. He would have to manufacture the outcome, somehow. And timing, timing would be crucial, he kept reminding himself.

If he turned up too early in the day and made an appearance, he thought he would appear too eager. If he left it too late, she might leave early and his opportunity would be lost forever. Then there was the question of how he would convert buying something into actually asking her out. "Hi. I'll have that jar of truffles and by the way, what are you doing after work?" That simply was not going to work, he figured. He smiled to himself, realising that he had set himself an unusual challenge as a means of getting a break from Tom.

Swimming and bushwalks were great fun, but now it was time for something else. He said these words to himself as if to psyche himself up, but he could not take himself seriously. Best not to take this seriously at all. That was the best advice he could give himself, and he settled on it.

He wandered out just before midday and got some lunch. By then he had decided that about 3 pm was the ideal time to put his plans into action. Of course, he had no idea what was going to work and what wasn't. He couldn't remember a time he had been the one to initiate things. This was perhaps a first.

He walked into the pavilion at 2:45 pm. What if she was gone? He put that out of his mind quickly and thought, so be it. He deliberately took the long way around to see if he could see her from the craft brewer on the upper level where he had first seen her. When he got up there it was uncomfortably crowded and he had to almost push his way through to the railing to see.

She was there. But something didn't appear right. A man appeared to be berating her. His hand gestures were sharp and angry. Staring down at the scene for a moment and taking it all in, Paddo wondered if this was an argument with a boyfriend or at least someone who knew her. Regardless, she looked uncomfortable. This was not expected and his plans went into disarray, even though they consisted of no more than a conversation about figs and English truffles, and saying intelligent things that he had gleaned from his research the night before, as if he had known such things all his life.

Wandering down and getting in earshot seemed the right thing to do, if for no other reason than to check this nasty fellow out.

"I fucking don't think that's right," he heard the fellow say. Paddo had determined this man looked like, and indeed was, an arsehole, whoever he was.

"I can't add anything further than what I have said to you," Bessy said, bright red in the face.

"Well, that's not good enough, and that is what I have said to you!" The fellow turned up on his toes.

"I can't reach him now, as I have told you. You are best to ring him at the shop."

Paddo saw she was flustered and shaking. He moved closer but not up to the counter.

"If you don't do something about my bloody money now, *and I mean now*, I am going to upturn this stall!"

Paddo noticed that the man's teeth were gritted and he moved next to him out of instinct now. "What's the problem?" he asked him, not even looking at Bessy.

"Who the fuck are you?"

"My name is Patrick."

"Well Patrick, it's none of your God damn business!"

"I don't like the way you are talking to her."

"I don't give a hoot what you like!" He turned back to Bessy as if Paddo didn't exist.

Paddo looked at Bessy and realised he wasn't helping. "I *asked you* what the problem was."

The fellow took a step back, sniffed and looked at Paddo. "The problem, if you need to know, is her fucking boss, who is an incompetent deadshit, owes me money and I'd like to be paid."

"I told you what to do," Bessy said.

"I don't think this is appropriate. To be speaking to this young lady here about it," Paddo said.

"Look. Who are you to tell me anything! I have run out of patience. I'm going to fucking turn this stall over, if I don't get my money."

"I think you should calm down and pay attention to what you are being told," Paddo said.

The man's fist hit the table and stock went flying. Paddo grabbed him by the arm and the fellow turned and threw a punch that connected right above Paddo's eye and sent him hurtling into the stall next to them. It didn't knock him off his feet completely and he staggered for a split second, with his arms out. He was not as big as this fellow but he rushed at him, tackling him around the waist and wrestled him away to the floor, barrelling out into the stream of people wandering in the middle. There they stayed for a few seconds in a messy, clenching wrestle until two burly security guards appeared, dragged the fellow off Paddo and quickly restrained him.

Paddo was shaking and by now, Bessy was crying. The security guards had been watching, tipped off by the stallholder next to Bessy. They had timed their intervention and were apparently on their way when the fellow hit Paddo. A CCTV camera pointed exactly in the direction of the stall. A crowd gathered but as soon as the other fellow was led outside, it quickly dispersed. A lady came over and talked to Paddo and gave him a cloth to stop the bleeding above his eye. She had a name tag and looked like she had some official role in the fair.

One of the security guards returned and said they would call the cops if he wanted. "You should report him, mate," he said.

"I don't …" He was still shaking. "Ask them to come, for her protection, but I'm not interested in charges. Maybe, I don't know."

The police were outside already and were soon inside talking to Paddo. He told them what happened and said he just wanted to go. The officers then approached Bessy.

"He told me he was owed lots of money by my boss. He didn't say how much. I tried to call my boss who owns the business but I got no answer. I told this guy he had to take it up with Lino but he didn't want to know. I asked him to leave and that I couldn't do anything. I just couldn't!" She had stopped crying but she too was shaking.

The police took down Lino's number and address. They thanked her and told her she should go home, if she could. Soon the police were gone and so was all evidence that anything had happened, except for a disordered stall, and Paddo's emerging black eye. About twenty minutes had passed since Paddo had made his move, a move that had focused upon his timing being everything.

He still held the cloth to his head. The bleeding had stopped and it was only a small cut.

"I am so sorry," Bessy said to him. "I don't know what to say, how to thank you."

Paddo smiled. His face was throbbing now. The punch had landed well. The cut was most likely from the fellow's ring but his hand was large and had connected with his whole eye socket.

"Hey. I've still got all my teeth," he said. He stopped shaking.

"You were here yesterday, weren't you?" she said.

Paddo nodded.

"Oh, I am so sorry. He was such a bastard. I've never seen him before. Such a temper."

"I reckon."

"Look at your eye. Let me see." She moved right up close to his face, standing on her toes. Paddo obliged by bending down a fraction.

"You need to get an ice pack on that," she said in a worried tone.

"It's fine."

"No, you need to contain the swelling." She looked around. "Look. I am going to make a call, and then I think I'm going to shut up shop here. They have extracted enough from me. Give me a second."

Bessy grabbed her phone and tapped out some numbers. She paced around the stall as she spoke. Paddo watched her but he also tried not to watch her too much. He started to think what he would tell Tom and how Tom would react.

Bessy seemed pleased when she had finished her call.

"How did you go?" he asked.

"Good, I think. I should have called Abriana before. Abriana owns the place with her husband. She has told me to go home and she will call me later. I told her what happened."

"What about the stall?"

"Yes, well, she said the guy who helped me set up is going to be here in ten minutes. He's going to collect it. I suppose I should wait," she said, looking at the items on display.

"I'm happy to wait with you."

"Okay, and then I'm going to take you home with me so I can put some ice on that."

"Oh, that's not necessary. I mean, that would be, well, I…" He thought he'd better be careful.

"I insist. What you did for me was amazing. If you hadn't been here, I don't know what would have happened. I'm Bessy, by the way," she said, smiling.

"Paddo. I mean, Patrick. My friends call me Paddo."

"You're English?"

"Yes."

Bessy's phone rang. She talked for a moment and then hung up.

"My help is out the front now. He'll be in here soon."

"Okay," Paddo said. He wanted to call Tom. But decided that could wait. "I might find a bathroom and clean myself up a bit."

"Good idea," she said and returned her attention to the stall.

Paddo left for the bathroom. He was interested to see how he looked and expected the worst.

James arrived and Bessy helped him carry out several boxes full of stock.

"Let's leave the brochures and signs. I will be back later to get them," he said.

Bessy was eager to get out the door and, once and for all, end her employment. It had seemed like it had been a very long two days. She collected the small amount of cash and gave it to James, as Abriana had instructed her to do. There was no computer terminal and she had just been manually recording the sales.

Paddo wandered back to find no one at the stall but soon Bessy returned along with James for one more run of the stock out to the truck.

Eventually, Bessy said, "Ready to go?"

"Yes."

"I don't live far."

"That's fine. You sure you're okay?" asked Paddo.

"No, but it doesn't matter," she said with a laugh.

"I really appreciate this. I could just go back to the hostel, it's not far."

"Is that where you are staying?"

"Yes. We've been there a few nights now."

"Is it the one down near the fast food chains, sort of in that direction?" she said as they walked.

"I think so. No, maybe, wait. I don't know." He felt a tad dizzy and his adrenalin was still pumping.

"How's your eye feeling?"

"I can see, that's the main thing."

"Well, it looks sore. I expect you are going to get a nice shiner."

They crossed over various intersections and waited at traffic lights and eventually arrived at Bessy's building. She seemed on a mission to repay the good deed. Paddo could see that was her focus.

"Sit there," she said as soon as they got inside. She pointed to a chair next to the dining table.

Apart from the single bedroom and the bathroom, there wasn't a spot anywhere they could not see each other. She opened the freezer and dug around for a moment and then returned to the chair with a packet of unopened frozen peas. "It's not ice but this will work." She pressed them against the corner of Paddo's face and he flinched. "Now, hold that there," she ordered. He dutifully obeyed.

She then went into her room and returned with a red first aid packet. Sitting down, she emptied its contents on the table. Out fell bandages, band aids, scissors, pain killers, a small bottle of antiseptic and some things that Paddo could not identify.

She found what she wanted, set it aside and returned to Paddo. "Let me have a look at that cut. I don't think it needs stitches."

"No, it's fine, really," he said.

"You can't see it."

"That's true," he stood corrected or, more accurately, sat. He never felt so delighted to be corrected in his life.

"I'm going to dress it though. Just keep holding the peas on your eye for a moment."

She eventually returned to his side after running a cloth under warm water.

"Now, just put the peas down for a minute." She bathed the wound until she was satisfied it was clean, then dried it before brushing the cut gently with antiseptic.

"Thank you," he said, holding his head perfectly still. Now the peas were off his eye, he could feel he had been perspiring under his clothes. With Bessy so close, he could smell her perfume and became concerned she would notice that he didn't smell the best.

"I'm just going to let that dry for a second," she said, stepping back. "How long have you been in Australia? Did you say you are travelling by yourself?"

"It's probably been about six weeks now. I'm travelling with a friend."

"Where have you been so far?"

"Well, we met up in Sydney initially then stayed there for a while, bought a car, if you could call it that, and made our way down the coast camping and hanging out."

"That sounds fun."

"Yes. It's been really cool."

"Okay, let's get that bandaged."

Bessy lay two strips of bandage across the wound. "That should do it," she said.

"Thank you."

"Would you like a glass of water?"

"Yes, please. Back to work tomorrow?" he asked.

"No, thankfully. Today was my last day. I am now officially unemployed."

"Really, so that means I can't come and see you at The Pheasant?"

"Afraid not."

"You have something else arranged, another job lined up?"

"No, I um, quit with a holiday in mind. Though I have no idea what I'm doing."

"That sounds like us. I mean my friend, Tom and me. We have nothing planned."

"Yeah? Does that work for you?"

"Well, sort of. We have a rough plan, but it's hardly a plan. At the moment, we're just checking out Melbourne. We might continue west but we haven't really spoken about it for a while."

"That sounds really cool."

"Well, sounding cool and it being cool are sometimes different. It all sounds great but travelling each day together has been a bit tough at times. But, no, we're enjoying being a bit fancy-free, footloose, what's the saying?"

"Yeah, I know what you mean."

He finished his glass of water and she refilled it from the jug in her fridge. For a few seconds they didn't talk at all.

"Should I put the peas back on?"

Bessy laughed. "That's probably enough."

"I should be letting you get on with your afternoon."

"It's fine." Now, she was showing signs of someone coming down after a big day, maybe a big several years. She looked and felt tired. "I'm just gonna crash, I think. I feel like I could sleep for a week," she said, laughing again.

"I'd better go. You've been very kind." He paused, then rose to his feet, placing the peas on the kitchen sink.

Bessy experienced her adrenalin rush almost an hour and a half ago now. She thanked him again and asked if he was right to walk and offered to walk him back.

"Now, that's ridiculous," he said.

She opened the door for him. He opened his mouth, about to say something, summoning courage to ask her what he wanted to ask her, but before he could do so, she said, "Bye."

In the hallway, he stood for a moment looking at the closed door. *You just walked out and now you're standing outside her apartment, you fool.* If the motto for the day had been 'timing is everything' then the time is now. With a wry smile, he knew what he had to do and turned around and knocked on the door.

He knew she would know it was him but his nerves had long gone.

The door opened and she smiled. "Yes?"

"Can I take you out for dinner tomorrow night? Well, that's if you can put up with being seen around this city with someone who looks like a thug with a black eye?"

"Sure," she said with a smile, more quickly than he expected. "Wait a sec." She ran back inside and when she returned she shoved a piece of paper into his hand. "See you then." And she was gone.

Paddo unfolded the paper. It had 'Bessy' written on it and her number. He put it in his pocket. He felt like sprinting out of the building but wisely, decided against it.

CHAPTER FOURTEEN

When Paddo got back to the hostel, he found Tom reading on his bed on the top bunk. He decided to have a shower and left quickly without saying a word, leaving Tom to continue with his reading.

He returned to their room to find Tom sitting in the chair in the corner. Now he was looking at his phone. "Hello," Paddo said.

"Hi," he said, not lifting his head.

Paddo sat on the bottom bunk. He stared deliberately at Tom. "Have a nice day?"

"Fine," he said. They still hadn't made eye contact.

He waited for Tom to ask about his day but as it never came, he stretched out on the bunk. He sighed as his head hit the pillow and fell asleep. A deep sleep, almost as if it involved missing time. The sun had only just set.

Sometime later, he awoke, confused about where he was. His first thought was to wonder why his eye and the whole side of his face was hurting. But then he remembered. He looked at his watch. 11:32 pm. He got up and had a drink of water. He noticed that Tom lay on the bunk, facing the wall. He looked like he was asleep. Paddo climbed back into bed.

"What happened to your eye?" Tom said.

Paddo heard Tom roll over onto his back. Despite Tom's small frame, the bunk bed sagged once he had done so. "I thought you were asleep," replied Paddo.

"I just got in."

"How do you know?"

"You were sleeping on your back by 8 and I noticed it then, just before I went to the pub. Looks pretty nasty."

"It's fine."

"So, either she had a boyfriend or she didn't appreciate your advances, huh?"

"Yeah, that's it." Paddo was not really in the mood for Tom's wisecracking.

"So, you saw her?"

"Yes."

"And?"

Paddo exhaled. "Can we leave this to the morning?"

"Sure." Tom rolled back over.

Tom was first up the next morning and was making a lot of noise. Paddo stuck his legs out of the bunk and sat up scratching his scalp. He touched his eye to feel the swelling. "Does it look as bad as it feels?"

Tom was shoving something into his bag and took a close look. "Yep. It certainly does. How's the other guy look?"

"Hmmm," muttered Paddo.

"Are you going to tell me what happened?"

Paddo told him.

"Well, you timed it well. You said timing was going to be crucial. Wasn't that the word you used?"

"I'm going to take her out tonight."

"What, with that face?"

"I'm going to get some breakfast. You coming?"

"Sure."

They went across the road and ordered bacon and eggs. Tom felt like a full English breakfast and ordered two sausages and mushrooms as well. Paddo ordered a double espresso to kick charge his body, feeling it needed more rest.

"Where are you going to take her?"

"I don't know yet. Somewhere nice."

"What's her name?"

"Bessy. She's nice. You'd like her."

"Don't fall in love, son."

Paddo shook his head. "Just eat and drink your coffee, would you?"

"Well, I discovered something yesterday that I want to do today," Tom said, as he cut his sausage up.

"What's that?"

"I have to make a call to arrange it. Tell me if you want to come."

"Well, what is it?"

"It's a tour of the iconic sporting venues. It's in a small group. They take you to the MCG, Rod Laver Arena and Flemington."

"Tell me what they are again."

"Didn't you say to me you wanted to see something at the MCG? Or was that me? Anyway, the Melbourne Cricket Ground, the tennis stadium complex, where they play the Australian Open and the race-course where they run the Melbourne Cup, which, probably with Ascot's races and the Kentucky Derby, is one of the world's most famous horse races."

"Are the cricket, tennis and horse races on today?"

"Of course not."

"Then what's the point of going?"

"Never mind. Look, these places have small museums or similar, I think, and they take you into the special areas that you can't go into if the events are on. Like dressing rooms and locker rooms and parts where they have old things displayed. It's like going back stage at Wembley."

"Hmm. I'm not sure. Going back stage when the band's not there?"

"It's not compulsory, old son. Maybe you should just give your head a little rest today."

"How long does it go for?"

"They'll pick us up at 10, right out front and drop us back here at 4."

"I think I might leave you to do it. You can tell me all about it. You are more into those things than me, especially the cricket."

"That's fine."

They finished breakfast and Tom was soon out the door.

Paddo was pleased with his decision. He would rather spend his money on a good restaurant but he felt a little like he had let Tom down. There was no doubt Tom would have a good time regardless and entertain as well as be entertained. He decided to book a restaurant and take a punt that it would have food Bessy might eat. There was far too much choice, he considered, with even the most moderate of research. He called her at noon and said he would pick her up at 6:30 pm, if that was alright. She told him that was fine.

It had rained lightly all day but the heavier rain expected had not eventuated. Tom wasn't back when Paddo took a taxi to Bessy's apartment. He asked the driver to wait when he got there but told him he could leave if he wasn't back in five minutes and he was knocking on Bessy's door a little after 6:30. When she opened it, she smiled and asked him to come in.

Dressed in black jeans, with a grey shirt, black cardigan and black boots, she also wore a necklace and silver earrings. Her hair was out, falling to shoulder length. Paddo thought she looked beautiful but was careful not to say too much, too soon.

"You look ready. There's no rush," he said a little nervously.

"We can go," she said, grabbing her bag.

They got into the taxi. Bessy leant over and looked at his eye. "It's coming along as I expected," she said, with a smile.

"It's fine."

"I'd say give it a few days yet before it really turns black."

"Did you have a nice day?" he asked.

"I did. I got up late. I must have had ten hours sleep. I cooked myself a big breaky and haven't eaten since. I'm starving!"

He liked that nearly everything she said to him was with a smile. It seemed she was happy and he was hoping not only that was her normal way, but she was happy to be out with him. He felt comfortable, despite being a little nervous that he was sitting next to her in the car.

"That's great. I hope you like this restaurant. Maybe you've been there. It's an Italian restaurant not far from here."

"I've only been to one Italian restaurant and that was in Carlton," she said.

"This one isn't in Carlton." He told the driver the address. "You look so lovely and I look like a boxer or maybe an Aussie Rules player." He was relieved in a way that he was able to give her a compliment without sounding like he was coming on to her, even though that was exactly what he felt an overwhelming urge to do.

"Oh, thank you. You'll fit in around this town, don't you worry. I will tell anyone who asks whatever lies we can think of. You look the right age and height for a Collingwood player. You can be a Collingwood ruckman for the night."

"Yeah. What does a ruckman do?"

"In Aussie Rules a ruckman contests the centre bounces and stoppages and boundary throw ins. They cop elbows and arms in the eye all the time."

Soon the driver was ready to collect the fare and Paddo handed him cash.

"Here. Take this," she said to Paddo, handing him some notes.

"No. You keep that. This is my shout tonight. Think of it as a 'welcome to your holiday' night. And, a thanks for patching me up."

The early evening light had completely faded and it was dark by the time they got out of the taxi and walked into the restaurant. The first thing Bessy noticed was how elaborately decorated it was by comparison to where she had been with Abriana. It looked classier.

"This is lovely," she said, as they had their chairs pulled out for them by a man dressed in a white shirt and thin black tie. Paddo knew the importance of first impressions and decided the higher end of the market might be in order but not too high, and not because he wanted to save money, but because he didn't want it to be too exclusive and over the top on a first outing.

"I hope you like Italian. I figured that even if you didn't really, there's usually something on the menu that appeals to most people."

"I love Italian."

For the next two hours, they enjoyed a three-course meal and a bottle of red wine from a local Victorian vineyard. Bessy noticed the prices were roughly double that of the other restaurant she'd been to.

Paddo asked whether she was from Melbourne originally and then naturally encouraged her to tell him about Jeparit and growing up there, when she mentioned it. He listened with his usual genuine interest, conscious of trying to ask just the right number of questions.

He told her about growing up in Norwich. At the right moment, he explained that his family were "well off" but he didn't "care as much about money," at least not as much as they did.

Bessy nodded. She had never heard anyone talk about 'caring' about money, either a lot or at all. She was very aware that people wanted it, particularly given the events of the previous day. "I don't know if I *care* too much about money or not. I guess because we never really had any, I don't know the difference."

Paddo smiled.

"Did you do any more thinking about your holiday?" he asked.

"Not really. I think I'm just going to hang out for a little while."

He told her a little about Tom.

"He sounds like a good guy to travel with," she said.

"Yes. He is. He can be a little full on at times and there is usually never a dull moment. But we have got to know each other pretty well, in a relatively short time, I guess. And I'm sure I'm not Mr Perfect to travel with."

She looked at him and thought he looked pretty perfect to her, even with his shiner. But then Josh appeared in her mind and she reminded herself there was a time she thought he was perfect. She pushed thoughts of Josh aside.

"No one's perfect, thankfully," he said, at that very instant.

"I've noticed," she said. Then adding, as if to make sure she was included, "I think if we were all perfect, it would be a bit boring."

"I agree."

"That fellow yesterday. I think he was a perfect bastard," she said. She rarely swore at the best of times but could find no other word to describe that man.

"Yes, but he didn't have a perfect left hook. He could have connected even better."

"Enough to give you a perfect black eye."

"That's for sure. It's not perfect yet. Like this wine, it will take a little while to show its true colours."

"Yes, let me see." She moved in closer to him across the table. "I can see a shade of purple, or is it mauve – maybe lilac – in there already. A hue of chocolate brown perhaps, with overtones of charcoal black."

The black eye was giving her ample opportunity to look deeply into his eyes. She noticed he had blue eyes that made a very handsome contrast with his dark hair and tanned skin. As the wine was starting to take effect, she started to realise for the first time that she was on a date. How could this be? Even though the question was apparent to her, she felt warm and happy. Even during the day, she had given very little thought to tonight as a date, or Paddo, for that matter. Sure, she knew he was going to arrive and they were going to go out. But it wasn't like she focused upon it. But now, it seemed things were a bit different. This man, he liked her. She felt her confidence rise again.

"Tell me why they call you 'Paddo'."

"Only if you tell me why you're called 'Bessy'."

"You first."

"My surname is Paddington-Smythe. My mother and father call me Patrick and so does my brother. But when I was at school, someone started referring to me as Paddo and I got stuck with it, I guess."

"Would you prefer Patrick?"

"It doesn't bother me either way."

"What would you like me to call you?"

"Anything, I don't mind. Just don't call me late for dinner."

She smiled. It made her think of her mother never calling anyone for dinner, except her father.

"Well, I was named Beatrice," she said. "Beatrice May O'Halloran."

"That's lovely."

"I never liked it. I got my friends at school to call me Bessy and one of my sisters called me that anyway."

"And your mother called you Bessy?"

"Yes."

"Does she live in Jeparit?"

"No. She died."

"Oh. I'm sorry."

"That's fine. It was a good few years back now."

"And your father?"

"He died when I was a kid."

Paddo could see in her eyes something that moved him, just momentarily, when she said that.

He touched her hand which was resting on the table. She felt his warmth. She wiped a tear from her eye that had unexpectedly just trickled out. Surprised at her reaction, she felt a fool. After a moment, she smiled at him and said, "I will be back. Please excuse me."

She went to the bathroom and looked at her makeup. She blew her nose and cursed herself. She felt annoyed and embarrassed. Alcohol sometimes made her emotional and it always seemed it would hit her out of the blue when she least expected it. She had grown tired of her past upsetting her. It was something she wanted to overcome. She returned to the table.

"This has been beautiful. Thank you so much," she said.

"Would you like to go and get a coffee somewhere?" he asked.

"Maybe a cocktail," she said, surprising herself.

"What about if we combine the two and get an espresso martini? Have you had one of those?"

"No. I don't think I have. It sounds wicked."

They walked across the street and around the corner and found a wine bar that was very long and narrow. Sitting down at a space at the bar at the very end, they ordered the drinks. They talked some more about Melbourne and the nightlife. He told her about his interest in theatre and some of the plays he had been involved in. And he told her more about Norwich. She could tell he missed it, despite the fact that he was having the time of his life in Australia.

"It sounds so beautiful there."

"I do love Norwich. It's a pretty cool place, especially if you are into the arts."

When the time came to leave, they returned to Bessy's flat in a taxi. It was about midnight by the time it pulled up outside of her building.

"I don't think we need more caffeine," she said, as the driver brought the car to a stop, "but you're welcome to come up for some water."

"Okay," he said.

They both knew that water was not the highest priority. Not long after sitting on the couch, he asked a question. "I am going to catch a cab very soon," he said, "but before I do, would it be okay if I kissed you?"

She looked at him. "You are a very formal gentleman sometimes, aren't you?"

"I suppose I am. Does it bother you?"

"Yes."

She then leaned in and kissed him. As she touched his lips, she thought for a second, *what am I doing*? But that soon gave way to, *why can't I stop*?

But she didn't want to stop. And neither did he. But they both knew that they should. It was perhaps the very first thing, the very first thought, they had in common.

"I'm going to go now," he said. "But I will call you tomorrow. I want to see you again and then again, if that's okay. But tonight ..."

"Shoosh," she whispered and continued to kiss him.

Eventually, he took hold of her hand. He noticed the ring her mother had given her. He kissed her hand gently, then holding her cheek in the cup of his hand, he kissed her again on the lips. He got up and let himself out.

She rested her head back on the couch feeling warm and, it seemed, cared for, again.

* * * *

The next morning Tom was very keen of course to hear how Paddo's night had gone. He was equally keen to tell Paddo all about his day. They decided to get lunch in a pub and have a few beers but not too many. Their plans not to have too many almost never worked but that never stopped them from trying.

"I'm only having a few," Tom said. "But remind me of that, if I forget."

This time, however, Paddo had a huge incentive to be disciplined. He had made a promise to Bessy to call her.

Tom had been very impressed with the tour and rattled off a bunch of names and events that Paddo had never heard of before but he nodded as if he had.

Tom could see that Paddo was otherwise occupied in his own thoughts. "You know we're eventually going to leave Melbourne, don't you?" Tom said.

Paddo looked at him. He felt Tom was almost treating him like a child. "I know that. But can you let me enjoy the moment, please?"

"When do I get to meet her?"

"When I decide. Anyway, you met her at the shop."

"I didn't get to kiss her."

"And it will depend upon your behaviour."

"Goodo! I will try to be on my best then."

"I'm going to see if she wants to go for a walk in the gardens today."

"Can I come?"

"No."

"You promised you were going to do that with me."

"I never promised."

"Yes, you did."

"Best get over it."

At about 3 pm Paddo rang Bessy and suggested the botanical gardens. Yes, she could meet him there and yes, what a wonderful idea, she said.

They walked around for a couple of hours and Bessy impressed him with her knowledge of Australian native plants, giving him both the common and the scientific names. He'd never heard of a Powderpuff Lilly Pilli or a Lemon Scented Gum Tree. Paddo mentioned his interest in Aboriginal names for places and he too impressed her with the things he had already picked up. They got a cup of tea and cake inside the gardens before the café closed.

She invited him for lunch at her apartment the day after next.

When he got back to the hostel, he told Tom.

"This is getting to be a habit," Tom said. "I'm going to have to get a hobby."

CHAPTER FIFTEEN

Bessy awoke and instantly knew the day would be different. Unlike several days ago, Paddo was firmly in her mind. Sandwiches for lunch were just not going to cut it. Salad was not quite special enough, although perhaps the right salad might, with seafood.

Paddo arrived at 12 noon as he had been instructed. He brought flowers and Bessy gave him a kiss on the cheek and told him they were lovely. One of the things she had been allowed to keep from Jeparit was one of her mother's vases. It was the first time she had placed anything in the vase.

She placed the salad on the table. It was a mixture of English spinach leaves and rocket with Spanish onion, haloumi cheese, eggplant sprinkled with herbs, roasted red and yellow cherry tomatoes and toasted pepita seeds. She had made a lemon and olive oil dressing and placed it in a jar, ready to pour just before serving. Her skills in the kitchen had developed into something she was proud to display.

A bottle of chilled white wine in the middle of the table completed the setting. She had marinated two salmon fillets in basil pesto with pine nuts and a dash of chilli and fried these up. Soon they were enjoying the fresh food and the fine wine and talked more about the gardens and Norwich and Jeparit and Melbourne.

When there was half a glass of wine left in each glass, Bessy went to wash up. She ran some water in the sink and plunged a plate into it.

Paddo came up behind her and put his arms around her and kissed her on the side of her neck. He lifted her brown hair up and kissed her softly all the way around to her cheek. She closed her eyes and let go of the plate into the water. He reached around and turned off the tap. He lifted her up and kept kissing her.

"Is it …?"

"Shhh …"

Inside the bedroom, he laid her on top of the covers and they kissed. Without speaking, she slowly got up and pulled the sheets free, undid her top and then let her skirt drop to the floor. Paddo removed his shoes, jeans and shirt then they embraced each other. She was shaking but he moved slowly. He kissed her more and she ran her hands up and down his arched back, then through his hair. He kissed her breast.

She felt herself too ready and when it was time, she tried to stay in the moment. But that only lasted for a minute and she tried hard not to let herself go but then she did, and then again. Sighing and breathing heavily she whispered, "I'm sorry."

Paddo whispered back, "Don't be," and then lost control.

He held her and they made love again and then again.

* * * *

More than a week later, the storm that had been threatening to unleash its fury, struck, not outside the hostel, but inside. Paddo had taken Bessy to the theatre twice, once during the day.

"I had to go and renew that bloody car parking thing today. Wasn't that supposed to be your job? It took me half an hour to convince the guy I had *your* bloody authority to do it," Tom said to Paddo. "What a joke! I told him I owned the bloody thing."

"I told you that was on my agenda."

"Well, there has been a lot on your agenda of late."

"How long did you renew it for?"

"Three days. Which is about the time I think we should be leaving Melbourne, as *planned*." He refused to look at Paddo as he sorted his laundry in a huff, with clothes strewn out across the floor of their room. The room was in a total mess.

"I'm not going to be ready to go then," Paddo said.

"Ah, and I wonder why that might be?" Sarcasm wasn't Tom's usual style, being the lowest form of wit. But he wasn't in the mood to be funny. "I have no idea!"

"Give it a break."

"Give *me* a break! I told you specifically not to fall in love and what do you go and do!"

"I'm not in love."

"Bullshit!"

"Keep your voice down!"

"Who is going to hear me, my mother? Besides, surely you're over this bloody room. I know I am," Tom protested, picking up a pair of shorts in dire need of a wash.

"I'm over you whingeing." Paddo got the broom and started sweeping the floor, pushing a pair of underpants out of the way across the floor to Tom's corner. Tom left them on the floor and sat in the chair.

"Look, I just think you need to get a grip. Yes, she's lovely, but ..." He looked at Paddo without finishing his statement.

"But what?"

"Well, all I'm saying is, you need to do some thinking."

Paddo knew he was right about having to do some thinking. The problem was thinking and logic and rationality were enemies of emotion and love and spontaneity. He heard himself say that word 'love' in his head.

Tom looked at him. "Talk to her," he said. He then got up and left.

Paddo had arranged to meet Bessy for breakfast the next morning. He thought carefully all night and hardly got any sleep. Tom got home late and had been at the pub, yet again, and was still asleep by the time Paddo left the next day.

"Look, I've been doing some thinking," Paddo said to Bessy, as he sipped his coffee.

"Yes. About what?" For a moment, and for the first time in a long while, Josh entered her head. It was something about the situation that reminded her of that terrible afternoon which now seemed a lifetime ago.

"About us." She started to get slightly worried.

"And?" She was having an English breakfast tea, which Paddo had introduced her to and now she was quite happy to order almost each time.

"Well, you met Tom the other day. Do you like him?"

She laughed. "Yes. He's a bit of a funny one but yes, why?"

"Well, let me ask you this."

"Yes."

"Have you made up your mind about your holiday? Your trip?"

"No. Not really."

"Tom and I bought that car, the Troopy I told you about."

"Yes. It's in storage, isn't it?"

"We have it in a long-stay carpark. It's costing us a fortune. I don't really care how much it is costing but Tom is a bit upset. Plus, we are a bit over the hostel and all. And it's like, Tom wants to go and explore and well, that was the plan, as I mentioned. He's ready to move on from Melbourne. It's probably not a bad idea."

"I know those car parking places can be expensive."

"Well, I don't know what you think about all that."

She was trying to work out if this was a goodbye of sorts.

"I can't … I wouldn't stop you. You know that. We have only known each, for what …?"

"That's the thing," he said.

"What thing?"

"That we've only known each other for a ridiculously short space of time."

"It's true," she said.

"But," he paused. "I feel like I've known you a lot longer and well, I don't know how to say it, but I want to keep knowing you, if that makes sense."

"What are you thinking?"

"I want you to come with us, with me. With me and Tom."

"Whoa!"

"Yes. I know, whoa." He sat back in his chair and smiled.

She sat back in her chair.

"Look, he's not the worst guy. In fact, he is very easy to be around, once you get to know him a bit. And well, you don't have anything planned, so in that way, it's perfect."

"I thought we agreed, nothing is perfect," she said.

He was relieved that was the first thing she said, rather than an outright no.

"Oh, God! I don't know," she added.

"I don't expect you to decide now."

"Gee, thanks," she said, smiling.

"In fact, I haven't even told Tom about this." He breathed in through his teeth with a distant look, partitioning the conversation he would need to have with Tom to a compartment in his mind for later. But not too much later. Something had to give and he decided it would have to be Tom.

"No? That's a bit of worry."

Bessy was relieved he wasn't saying goodbye to her. But what he was proposing was wholly different. She was grounded enough to know she would need to think. But not necessarily think too much.

"Oh, he'll be fine. I'll tell him. He'll be absolutely fine with it. It's more that you are comfortable with it."

"Will he listen?"

"You coming along is not going to change a thing."

"Really?" She laughed.

They both laughed.

* * * *

It had been more than a year since Bessy had heard from her girlfriends from Jeparit. That made her sad. Sophie had moved on. She *could* mention the decision she had to make to a handful of others she didn't know that well. No, it would have to be Abriana to talk this thing through with. She called her that afternoon.

"Can you meet me for coffee, tomorrow afternoon? I need to talk to you."

"What is it my dear?"

"Can I tell you then?"

"Of course. Where?"

They met at an Italian coffee shop in Carlton, around the corner from where Lino and Abriana lived.

"So lovely to see you my lovely." Abriana gave her a huge hug and kisses on both cheeks.

"How's Lino?"

"He's stressed, as usual. That bastard who caused all that kerfuffle when you were at the fair. I am so sorry dear. The *stronzo*, he is suing us. I donta know how the bastard is on the street. We owe him nothing but he is a screwing with us. 'Scusa my language."

"Well, I'll testify in your favour, you know that."

"Of course, my dear. What is going on in your life? You sounded worried."

"No. Everything is fine. It's too fine."

"It's a too good?"

Bessy laughed. "I have met someone. A man. You told me I would, I just didn't expect it to happen that quickly."

"That's a wonderful dear! Oh, that's so …" Abriana threw her hands up and hugged her across the table, knocking over an empty cup.

The coffee arrived. Then Abrianna asked, "But what's a wrong? Why the concern? Is he a pig?"

"No, no, no. He's beautiful."

"Well?"

"I've only known him for little under, I don't know, two weeks, and he wants me to go away with him, travelling, in their car. He's English. He's been travelling with a mate who's also from England. They've been like, travelling together, and it would be just the three of us. I wanted to talk with you, before I said yes."

"This other man, is gay?"

Bessy laughed again. "No. They're mates."

"Huh, you like this man?"

"He is so wonderful, Abriana. He's the one that bastard punched. He was there. That's how I met him."

"Ah," she said, as if it came from the depths of her shins.

Bessy waited but she knew Abriana enough now to know exactly what she was going to say and, secretly, what she wanted to hear. Abriana was a good ten years older.

"You live once only, this life, my dear. You go with this man. He sounds good man. You take chance, you canta lose. Only gain."

* * * *

An icy silence in their room in the hostel had ensued for most of the evening. Tom took off his shoes and pants, slipped on his sleeping shirt and went to climb into his bunk.

"We can leave in two days," Paddo said, sitting on the edge of the chair.

Tom stopped and turned. "You're joking! Well, that's great! Brilliant news."

"Yep. I thought you'd be happy. I'll pick up the Troopy in the morning. I want to give it a good clean, inside and out."

"Sounds good. How did Bessy take it?"

"Very well. I spoke with her tonight."

"Well, that's doubly pleasing, isn't it?" Tom was amazed, standing there in his underpants, finally thinking Paddo had come to his senses.

"I think so. She's excited."

"For you?"

"Yes. For us, really."

"Oh, that's nice. She's a great girl. I'm glad you had a good time with her. You're lucky to have met her, you know that?"

"I certainly do. And I'm glad you think that. That you like her."

"Look, I always have." Tom grabbed Paddo's shoulder, shook it, and then gave him a pat on the back. "Well done, son." He turned and put one foot on the ladder leading to his bunk.

"Brilliant, because she's coming with us."

Tom stepped down. "What did you say?"

"I said, I have asked her to come with us, and she thought about it and said yes." Paddo sat back, stretched his legs out from the chair, crossed them and smiled.

"You asked her to come with us, just like that? What! Without asking me?"

"That's right. You've been dead right about everything so far. Dead right."

"Well, hang on just a minute."

"Why?"

Tom didn't quite know what to say.

"What's wrong?" asked Paddo.

"It's just that ..."

"What? Two's company? Three's a crowd?"

"You have known her for two bloody weeks, man!"

"I know that. You don't need to tell me." Paddo drew his legs back and sat on the edge of the chair again.

"What if she's ...?"

"What?"

"If she, I don't know, can't cope or something."

"Can't cope with you, you mean?"

"Or you."

"Well then, she's a free woman. She knows she can bail at any time. She can hop on the nearest train or bus. It's going to be no different from what we've already done. It'll be fun."

"She's your girlfriend."

"So?"

"What about sleeping?"

"I plan to sleep. Do you?"

"You know what I mean."

"She is going to bring her own tent. She has her own money. If we camp, we can still use one site. If we're in a hostel, like this joint, she will be in a separate room. If it doesn't work out, we're all mature enough to do something sensible about it."

Tom scratched his head. He jumped up onto his bunk. Paddo waited for him to get anything else out in the open.

"Look. I know it's a bit of an ask," Paddo said.

"A *bit* of a bloody ask?"

"Yes. I do. And I understand how you might feel. I do. But, if I thought it would be a disaster, I'd tell you. But I don't think so. I want to take a chance on this. I am asking as a friend, let me."

Tom pulled the blanket over him. Paddo climbed into his bunk and switched the side light on. He pulled out a map.

Tom had his side light on and flicked through some pages of a magazine he'd pinched from reception. After a while, he said, "I'll give you my decision in the morning. Goodnight," and then he switched the light off.

* * * *

Paddo was up early. He wasn't proposing to hang around for Tom. If they were to leave tomorrow, then he needed to get plenty of things done. He almost felt like writing a list. Bessy may not be ready to go but they could always delay things. No one needed to be anywhere urgently.

He pulled his belt around his pants and was getting ready to head out the door when his phone rang. It woke Tom.

"Hello."

It was his mother.

"Oh, hi Mum. No, no it's fine. I'm awake."

He listened and then said, "Yes. I'm fine. Is everything okay?"

He listened some more.

"When is it?"

Then, "Are you sure?" Then, after a while, "In Melbourne."

Miriam was doing most of the talking while Paddo listened carefully. After a while, he said, "Why?" and, "When?"

It went on like that before he said, "Last week? What? Since when? I mean, I don't…."

Tom was now wide awake and curious.

"Well, that's …" and, "Yes. I think so. What did Dad say? How is he?"

After a little while, Paddo shook his head and said, "Wow! Oh Mum, it's going to be fine. He's fine. Don't worry. Don't worry about it at all. Yes, I agree, but it's all good."

After more of this for a good ten minutes, Paddo told her that, "He would try," but they were, "Hitting the road again." Finally adding, "Okay, Mum. Love you, say hello to Dad. Bye."

He hung up and started to lace up his shoes, thinking about the call. Tom leaned over the bunk. "Is everything alright?"

"Yes. It was my mother."

"Is she okay?"

"She's fine. She had some news for me. About Roger. My brother. And she was telling me about the general election coming up. And how I needed to vote."

"What's the story with Roger?"

"He told Mum last week he was 'coming out'. She thought he said 'going out' and asked him 'where?' He said, 'No, Mum, I am gay.'"

"What, your brother is gay?" He was sitting up on the bunk now. "Not that there is anything wrong with that," he added.

Paddo scratched his chin and smiled.

"Did you know?"

"No. I never really considered whether he might be or not. I mean, we were never that close. I haven't really seen him much, for a while now. I don't think anyone knew, maybe, like family. He's always kept things close to his chest."

"What did your mum say?"

"She said she didn't know what to say. He came for the weekend and my dad was there. I think he was fine. It's cool. She just didn't expect it. It was a shock."

"Is he in a relationship?"

"Apparently."

"Oh well, that's nice for him. So long as he is happy."

"It's with Henry."

"Really? You're kidding! Good old Henry."

"Yep."

"He didn't bring him last weekend. My mum is worried that the next time he comes to Norwich, they will want to sleep in the spare room with the double bed. I told her to run with it. Make both rooms up, let them make the choice."

"Good advice, son."

"She's worried that I need to vote. The Tories have announced a general in six weeks' time. She thinks it's going to be close and wants me to vote for the Tories by postal vote."

"You're voting for the conservatives?"

"No way. I'm not voting at all. I'm not that interested. She reckons it could be a hung parliament."

Tom jumped out of the bed from the top bunk. "If it's going to be a hung parliament, I've always said that hopefully, it will be a well-hung parliament. The last thing Britain needs is a bunch of half-cocked pollies."

Paddo shook his head. "I'm going to get the Troopy. See you around ten."

* * * *

Bessy was excited. She was also a tad nervous. But she was not over-whelmed. Something good had happened to her and she was going to take her chance and trust her instinct. She told Paddo it would take her a day to pack. There would be no overthinking. Abriana, she decided, had given her good advice. One thing was for certain and that was Abriana would never hold back with an opinion.

She checked her bank account and figured she could allow herself two months, without too much trouble. A single person tent could be bought cheaply and as the weather was warming up, she could get away with leaving a lot of clothes behind. She got off to a slow start in the morning and Paddo interrupted her with a phone call.

"I've picked the Troopy up and I'm going to take it for a clean. I might swing past this afternoon. How's your packing going?"

"Slowly."

"Take your time. We don't have to leave tomorrow."

"I should be right."

"I've noticed there's a big camping store on our way when we head west. We can help you choose some stuff. I wouldn't mind getting some gear there too."

"That sounds great. How's Tom?"

"Good. I told him last night."

"And?"

"And I'll be seeing you this afternoon. Bye."

Paddo found a thirty-minute parking spot in walking distance from Bessy's apartment. He asked her to come down and inspect the Troopy.

"Not a bad thing, is it?" he said, standing by the side of the curb. Bessy didn't know anything about cars. But she had a driver's licence. Never before had she seen such a vehicle.

"It looks a bit like an army truck," she said.

Paddo rubbed some dirt he'd missed off the bonnet with his hand and some spit. "Yep. She's a beauty. And look how much room there is in the back."

They wandered around it and Bessy seemed impressed.

"Do you have surfboards?"

Paddo said no but he pointed to the roof racks and said they could get some. They decided he would try to get the same parking spot tomorrow about 11:30 am and they would leave at 12 noon.

"You know, it's a mystery tour and the laws of democracy will apply?"

She laughed. "Are you sure it's not a destiny tour and an autocracy?"

"No. I'm not." He smiled and kissed her. He jumped in and cranked the old engine over, starting on the third go. She watched him drive away and wondered if the Troopy, or perhaps her decision, was going to backfire.

CHAPTER SIXTEEN

M8 Western Freeway, near Melton 12:27 pm

"It seems to me, people," Tom said, driving and glancing at Paddo who sat in the front and Bessy, in the back, "that we have some decisions to make. Pass my sunnies to me, please. Firstly, quite frankly, and I think most importantly, is to decide whether to have beetroot on our hamburgers or not. My vote is yes but I think it should be left to a conscience vote, personally. Secondly, and less importantly, but perhaps best raised sooner rather than later, is to decide where we are going exactly. Because I have no idea."

Paddo looked at Bessy and raised his eyes. "Whatever you do, Bessy, take my advice. Never encourage him. I think stopping at the camping store coming up here on the right in a minute is a good idea. It's roughly 300 kilometres to Adelaide. Camping along the way seems good to me, but I'm open to any suggestions."

"What about Jeparit? It's kind of on our way if we are going to Adelaide. What do you think, Bessy?" asked Tom.

"Oh, I don't think we want to go there," she said.

"Why not?" Tom asked.

"I just don't think you would ... there is not a lot to do there. I'm not sure there is anything there that might be appealing to tourists."

"I'd like to see where you're from," Paddo said.

"Let's leave it as an option, maybe. We can always decide later," Tom added.

They pulled in to the camping store and spent a good half hour there. When they returned to the road, the conversation turned to the Grampians National Park. This was a place one of the staff in the store had chatted to Tom about, whilst Paddo and Bessy looked at tents and various other things. As Bessy decided on a tent, Tom took the opportunity to find out all he could about the Grampians and where might be a good spot to pitch the tents.

"You might be interested to know, Paddo, it has some of the country's best Aboriginal rock art sites," Tom said. Paddo pulled out his map and his phone as the Troopy wound its way through the traffic.

"We could be there by this afternoon," Tom said.

Paddo passed Bessy the map and continued to look at his phone, thoroughly ensconced in research, occasionally looking up at the cars in front as Tom kept focus on the road. "It says here you have the option of bush, forest park camping sites or motor home/caravan sites," he said.

"Bush sites sound good," Bessy said.

"I agree," Tom said.

It wasn't long before Tom's attention turned to food and they stopped for lunch. Paddo had noticed that when Tom was in control of the Troopy, he offered no choice about where to stop. Instead, he would park as close to a hamburger or fish and chip shop as possible and say something like, "Well, we may as well eat here," as he pulled up outside. Today was no different and he ordered a deluxe burger with beetroot. Bessy got a salad sandwich and so did Paddo, although they had to walk across the road to a small supermarket that sold packaged sandwiches.

It wasn't long before they were setting up camp well into the Grampians. The rain that had come into Melbourne had long since been left behind and was moving in the opposite direction. The weather was still cool of a morning and the conditions under foot were moist, following a decent soaking of rain. They found a camping spot that allowed wood fires but most of the wood was wet. By late afternoon, Tom had secured a decent fire and they were all set to try out some new cooking equipment.

The backdrop of the cliffs near the clearing they had settled upon provided quite a spectacular setting. Paddo positioned Bessy's tent nicely opposite the larger tent that Tom had set up. Bessy had not been camping since she was a small child. They cooked some small steaks that Bessy had wrapped the night before and she made a salad to go with them. With the crusty bread that they got at the supermarket, they went to bed with their hunger well satisfied, after chatting some more around the fire. Tom and Paddo went to bed very happy to be out of the city and once again to be camping in a national park. Bessy liked her new tent and slept soundly, snuggled in her warm sleeping bag.

The next day they went for a long bushwalk in search of creeks, waterfalls and rock art. By lunchtime, they had come across all three. They swam in the shallows of several creeks and in the deeper water of one of the waterfalls. They met and talked with other campers, and in the middle of the day, swam with a couple who had three young boys aged six and under. Bessy helped the mother as she tried to get all three boys out of the water for a bite of lunch, while Tom and Paddo sat on the rocks and talked to the father.

It was a hot, dry, sunny day with very few clouds in the sky. It had been an almost perfect start to their journey together with the exception of one minor mishap. Five minutes from the camp site, on the way back, Tom stumbled into a bull ant nest. At first, he wasn't aware that he had landed on the nest but then he noticed the first nasty bite on his leg, followed by several others on the back of his calf, then one on his inner thigh. When he felt the first bite, he had dropped his towel right into the nest and when he put the towel back around his neck, an ant bit him on the chest. When he realised what he had done, he yelped and jumped up and down, then gave himself a somewhat urgent shakedown.

As he was quite a way in front of the other two on the track, his actions warned the others to detour around. At first, Paddo was confused by Tom's movements. He thought he was trying to perform some sort of dance – an Aboriginal tribal dance perhaps – but then realised with horror what was happening and was very thankful it was not him or Bessy who'd been so unfortunate. As Tom stood to the side of the track cursing, Paddo took a closer look at some of the ants that seemed about an inch long. Bessy told him to keep clear, as once disturbed they might jump.

When they got to the camp, the stings were peaking and Tom was speaking to himself in colourful terms. Paddo felt awful but was unable to avoid a tiny laugh.

"Paddo, that's not very nice," Bessy said, as she went into her tent, quickly returning with her first aid kit.

Tom sat in one of the camping chairs and pulled off his hiking boots, socks and shirt. His face was red with sunburn and fluster, and he was in some considerable agony. When Paddo asked him if he wanted some water, he said, "Not fucking right now." All in all, he must have had a good dozen bull ant bites on him, with the one on his inner thigh smarting the most.

Bessy pulled up a chair in front of Tom and said, "Here, rest your leg on mine."

Tom obeyed immediately. She examined the huge welts then pulled a tube of ointment from her kit, squeezed a generous amount into her hand and rubbed it on various parts of his leg.

"There's an evil one on my chest as well. It's killing me!" Tom said, eyes shut tight for a moment as he shuddered.

"Hold your hand out," she said. She then squeezed some ointment into his hand. "Rub it in gently for a couple of minutes. It's not going to work for a while and it will eventually calm the bites down a bit, but only time will do the trick."

"Great, thanks!" replied Tom, shaking his head and breathing heavily. Tom covered his chest with the ointment, then grabbed the tube and found the bite on his inner thigh. He gave it a generous coating. Bessy reached into her kit and pulled out a small box of antihistamine.

"Now these will make you drowsy," she said, passing him the box. "But they will help with the redness and relieve the itching, which you are likely to get later. You might want to avoid scratching them, although it'll be hard. If you scratch them and take your skin off, which is easy to do, they can get infected. So, remember, you don't want that."

"I don't care about the bloody drowsiness or the itchiness right at the moment, they're still killing me!"

Paddo gave him a bottle of water. Bessy told him to take one now and maybe one later tonight.

The late afternoon sun soon vanished over the cliff face without them noticing and they settled around the fire that Paddo had built. The bites had backed off after about half an hour and Tom read several brochures about the Grampians and sipped on tea that Bessy had made in a billy over the fire. They all felt tired and tried to work out from the maps how many kilometres they had walked. After an early dinner, Tom dozed off in his chair until Bessy woke him and encouraged him to go into the tent and into his sleeping bag. He muttered something which sounded like a thanks and quickly resumed a deep sleep.

Bessy and Paddo chatted quietly around the fire. They had chosen a spot where they could not see or hear any other campers. With a cup of tea in their hands, they walked to a spot nearby where there was a larger clearing and gazed at the brilliant stars in the sky. The Milky Way spread its wonder from one side to the other in all directions. They sat in the middle of the clearing where they held hands and kissed. When they returned to the camp, Paddo cosied up next to her in her tent until she dozed off. He returned to a snoring Tom and fell asleep.

By the next morning, it had turned overcast and drizzly but showed signs of clearing, with patches of blue sky in the distance. Tom was the first up and Bessy lay awake hearing bird calls in the distance and the movements around the camp. Tom had set up the gas stove and was boiling water.

Bessy emerged from her tent with a jacket over her. "How're your bites this morning?"

"They're a lot better. A bit itchy, as you said. That's all. Nasty little buggers."

"Good. That doesn't last long. I will leave you with the cream today and that will help."

"Thanks. The antihistamine sure knocked me out. I didn't even take the other one. I had the best night's sleep I think I've ever had."

Paddo didn't rise for another half an hour. Tom and Bessy sat chatting about Jeparit and decided to suggest visiting there to Paddo.

Enough light rain had fallen to wet the tents. That meant packing them wet, which Paddo suggested was far from ideal. But it now seemed somewhat unavoidable, unless they decided to wait or stay another night.

"We can dry them out later," Tom said.

By 10:30 am, the Troopy was almost packed. They aimed to stop in Horsham for an early lunch, as they had only had a small breakfast. Tom was happy to drive and let Paddo entertain them with his research. Paddo had already noted that both Horsham and Jeparit were on the Wimmera River.

Bessy had picked up on the fact that both Paddo and Tom were curious about where she had come from and wanted to see her little town. For her part, it was now so close that she was willing to make an unexpected return.

On the way, Paddo said that he was glad Tom had asked what 'Wimmera' meant even though he well knew he hadn't. "It means 'throwing stick' but seems to be an adaption of an Aboriginal word meaning that."

Bessy noticed that it was Paddo who was interested in Aboriginal names and he entertained himself by giving answers to Tom's non-existent questions, substituting Tom's silence on the topic with his own fake dialogue, to get a rise from him.

They made good time and at Horsham, Tom found a car park in front of the performing arts centre. Paddo looked around to see if he could spot a hamburger shop and was surprised that there wasn't one in sight. They got out and wandered for a while, taking a walk along the river before settling for lunch at the RSL club, which in the end didn't turn out to be an early lunch at all.

The hour drive through to Jeparit took them in parts right beside the river. At one point, they were tempted to detour to the west and go into the Little Desert National Park but by the time they had given this idea any serious consideration, they were past all the turn offs.

Both Paddo and Tom encouraged Bessy to talk about Jeparit and her time there. She felt the journey into her old town was an unexpected reality now and was curious herself how she would feel when they pulled into the main street. At first, she was reluctant to say much but they were eager to hear whatever she had to say.

By now, only an occasional car passed the Troopy travelling in the opposite direction. Bessy told them the post office opened some time in the late 1880s and for the first couple of months, the town was known as Lake Hindmarsh. She asked if they had heard of Sir Robert Menzies, 'the town's most famous son', who was born there in 1894. They hadn't and she told them that he was Australia's longest serving Prime Minister, by far. Paddo admitted he was a bit embarrassed that they hadn't heard of him.

They drove into town and Bessy directed Tom to stop near the park. They all piled out and Bessy took them over to the spire that stood on the corner of the park. It was the Menzies Spire. The plaque informed them that it had been erected in 1966. They strolled around the park. Bessy started to talk about her mother but then turned the conversation to the weather.

"It gets seriously hot here," she said. The park was dry and dusty, and they were the only people walking around.

"One of my earliest memories is seeing my mother sit on the veranda with her feet in a square bucket filled with ice to cool her down. We didn't have a phone for a while. We eventually got one but Mrs Frost, who lived across the road, used to take messages for my mother on her phone. I can remember seeing my mother walk over to Mrs Frost's house in bare feet, her feet fresh out of the bucket and then walk into the house."

"Is there a school in town?" asked Paddo.

"I went to primary school here and to high school in Rainbow, which is down the road a bit that way."

They drove to the supermarket and bought some drinks. Bessy recognised a girl she went to school with at the check-out and said, "Hi". She also saw Mrs Ebsworth from her street buying sausages but Mrs Ebsworth didn't see Bessy. After getting the drinks, Bessy found herself quite keen to get back into the Troopy. She guided them to her street and showed them the house she grew up in. They didn't stop at first but then

Tom pulled up further along the street, did a u-turn and parked opposite the house. Bessy didn't think much had changed, except it looked like some trees had been taken down in the backyard and one really old eucalyptus tree from the front. There was a car parked in the front yard. She mentioned that the house needed painting again.

They stopped at the pharmacy for Tom to get some anti-itching cream to reimburse Bessy's generosity. He had used a good portion of the tube she had given him and he thought they may need some more. "You never know what other nasty little blighters are out there," he said.

After getting some cash they stopped by the Wimmera Mallee Pioneer Museum. Here they were greeted by several lovely, elderly gentlemen and Bessy recognised one of them but she didn't think he recognised her. The men were very proud of the museum. Paddo was impressed with its collection of old farm machinery and said so. Tom enjoyed the intricate displays and collections of photographic memorabilia. On the way out, Tom asked one of the gentlemen if he could take a photo of the three of them in front of the museum and of course he was more than happy to oblige. Next, they took a short drive out to the golf course and back. Bessy told them about getting paid to collect golf balls there when she was a child. She said that she often used the pocket money to buy yabbies. "You could get ten for three dollars and my mother would eat eight for lunch and I would have two." She held her finger and thumb out to show them that the yabbies were about four to five inches long.

Tom drove past some of the local hotels and suggested they go in for a beer. "I'd sooner not, if that's okay," Bessy said.

Paddo and Tom both said, "That's fine," almost exactly at the same time and the conversation turned to where they might stay overnight. Bessy told them to drive past the hotels and soon after they noticed a caravan park called 'Sir Robert Menzies Caravan Park'. Tom asked if everything was named after 'Uncle Bob'. For no other reason but to shop around, they decided to make their way to the Four Mile Beach camp ground on the southern shore of Lake Hindmarsh, about five kilometres from Jeparit. Rather than driving again, they headed straight to the showers, before setting up camp.

Paddo was excited that the evening was shaping up to be clear and that the night sky might give even more spectacular views of the Milky Way. After dinner, they strolled around the lake for a while. The night sky was not quite as brilliant as Paddo had hoped but he was only mildly disappointed, as he had already witnessed far more of the night sky than he had ever seen in the UK.

They were enjoying each other's company a lot it seemed and found it easy to be around each other. Once again, the day had been long and tiring, and by 9:30 pm they were in their tents, ready to fall asleep. Each of them gave some thought to what tomorrow might bring, before they dozed off. Bessy was happy she had returned but was happier with the knowledge that the next day and each day after that, for the time being at least, she would visit places she had never seen. She loved the way the boys listened to her. And how they both were very courteous, thoughtful and respectful. In the space of three weeks, her life had taken a new path. She was very happy not just for herself, but for Paddo and Tom.

As she closed her eyes and listened to the crickets, she thought about how she would have loved to have come back to Jeparit to find her mother still living in the house. She allowed her mind to wander, to imagine that very thing. Walking into the backyard and then through the back door, with Paddo in toe and saying, "Mum, here is the handsome man I met in Melbourne I told you about – he's from England, you know!" Then seeing her mother's expression when she saw Paddo's face, and what she would say, and then cook, and then do. And later saying, "Mum, I have become a woman. Aren't you proud of me?" And she would say, "Yes, yes, I am dear. And, isn't he a fine young man."

CHAPTER SEVENTEEN

The next morning, they had to make a decision about which route they would take to Adelaide. As they discussed this, Bessy directed Tom to drive past the little Lutheran church in Jeparit. She told Paddo and Tom she was not religious but had enjoyed going to church there as a child. Paddo told her about Norwich Cathedral and that there were many little churches in Norwich. Soon they were on their way out of town heading south, taking the A8 National. This route would take them a little over four hours instead of close to six hours if they travelled north and skirted around Wyperfeld National Park.

A silence fell as they exited the town. Bessy knew she may very well never return.

By the time they had reached the border with South Australia and were on their way to Bordertown, the conversation had taken a lively turn. Tom said he was considering his future career. Paddo was especially interested in what Tom might have to say, as he had never heard Tom discuss this subject before.

"I think that if I can combine my interest in photography with my natural inclination to stir the possum, I might find something I can do," he said. "I don't want to be bored."

"I don't know what photography and stirring possums has got to do with anything. Could you be a little clearer? Maybe you should just concentrate on the road," Paddo said, taking a swig on a bottle of water.

"Look, I'm not going to be happy doing the mundane. I need some controversy to keep me active, motivated."

"Politics," Bessy said. "Though, that's nothing about photography."

"No, I couldn't bring myself to lie like that. I mean lies are alright, I think, when needed and if they are necessary or called for. But not like politicians tell lies. Lying like that is just wrong."

"A police officer?" asked Bessy.

"Oh, no. I would get too frustrated and want to break the law too much." Tom was enjoying having the focus on him.

"Well tell us then, Tom. What is it that you think you might go into?"

"I've given it some thought and I'm thinking of becoming a PI – a private investigator. I could use my photography skills to surreptitiously take photos, specialising in working for wealthy, soon-to-be ex-wives who might pay me handsomely. I could set my own fees."

"It can be dangerous work, Tom," Paddo said.

"Oh, that wouldn't bother me."

"It would bother me," Bessy said.

"It's not everyone's cup of tea but it would be a service, of sorts. I could be of service."

Some rain arrived and the noisy windscreen wipers curtailed conversation for the next few kilometres. Tom was very happy to be driving at a comfortable pace and chatting about himself.

"Have you anything in mind, Bessy, about what you might want to do?" Paddo asked.

"Yes. I've decided I don't want to be a private investigator."

Paddo and Tom laughed.

"Seriously, though," Paddo said.

"I've thought about nursing. I don't know, really."

"I think you'd be very good at it," Tom said.

"I agree," Paddo said.

They pulled in to a service station and Paddo got out and filled up. The smell of diesel was in the air, exacerbated somewhat by the smell of it already embedded in what was left of the thin upholstery in the Troopy.

Tom turned to Bessy in the back. "My sister is a nurse in London. She works at St Mary's Hospital in Paddington. I hope I never go there, you know, unless I'm picking her up for a night on the town. It's so enormous. What a history inside those walls."

"I think I would like to work somewhere like that," Bessy said.

"She said to me once, the hardest thing about the job is getting close to someone – a patient, I mean – and coming in to work the next day to find them gone."

"I know that feeling," Bessy said.

Paddo arrived back with a packet of jelly snakes and they were soon counting down the kilometres to Adelaide, arguing about which colour snake tasted the best. Bessy expected Paddo was going to take his turn and discuss what he might consider career wise, but the colour and tastes of the snakes seemed to be more important. When he started researching hostels and camp sites on his phone, she decided not to press him.

"You know, Adelaide is known as the city of churches," Paddo said.

"And you're from Norwich!" Tom said.

"Seriously, in Australia. Or sorry, 'Oceania' anyway," replied Paddo.

"Something different then," Tom said, a little sarcastically.

"It's not going to be like Norwich, Tom."

"I'm looking forward to the wine," Bessy said. She then offered some observations about the Barossa, McLaren Vale, Coonawarra and the Clare Valley, as examples of some of the great wine regions in the world all being 'a stone's throw' from Adelaide. She had come to know a little bit about the wine regions because The Gourmet Pheasant had served wine and had some fine selections from each of the main regions in South Australia.

"I've never really tried a lot of wine," Paddo said.

"Well then, we will have to fix that, won't we, Tom?" said Bessy.

"Fix him up, we shall," Tom replied.

Paddo of course was interested in the name 'Coonawarra'.

"Here, let me do the research on that," Bessy said, grabbing Paddo's phone from him.

After discovering it meant 'honeysuckle' in Aboriginal, they decided the limestone coast region in the Coonawarra was perhaps the least 'do-able' as a day trip from Adelaide.

"You realise if we don't go there, we are missing out on the Cab Sav region."

"The Cab Sav?" asked Paddo.

"Cabernet Sauvignon," Bessy said. "You really are a novice when it comes to wine, aren't you?" They had fun discussing what each wine growing region was famous for and tried to work out the differences between the grape varieties, eventually deciding the best way was simply to drink the wines.

It was a little after 2 pm when they arrived in Adelaide for a late lunch and found a car park not far from the central part of the city. They had already started to notice the churches. Tom had a craving for pizza and this time, his craving was shared by the others. They soon found a small takeaway pizza shop. Tom was amazed that shark was one of the toppings and he decided to order a shark pizza with red onion, baby capers and cheese. Paddo and Bessy shared a more traditional Italian pizza, after some discussion whether anchovies were to be included and that the world could be divided neatly into those who liked them and those who didn't. They differed on the point and so they were excluded.

After a stroll around parts of the city they all agreed camping was certainly an option, questioning whether they should do that again or check into a hostel. After Bessy had commented about having done the 'camping thing' of late, the hostel option won the day. They were soon buoyant with their choice of one in Glenelg, right near the beach. It was in a beautifully restored Victorian era villa, and with a bar downstairs. The sun glistened over the deep blue ocean and the tram right into the heart of Glenelg was nearby.

The only frustration for Paddo and Bessy was separate rooms. After they returned from a walk together on the beach in the late afternoon, they had arranged to meet Tom at the bar for pre-dinner drinks. "Would you be okay if Bessy and I took the Troopy for a couple of days?" asked Paddo, a little nervously but confident there was nothing he could not suggest to Tom.

Tom had just returned to the table with three glasses of Cabernet Sauvignon.

"Where are you going?" he asked, taking a sip and frowning.

"Maybe the Barossa and if we could fit it in, Clare Valley," Bessy said.

"You know there are tours, where you can get picked up?" Tom said. He had seen some brochures already in the hostel and hadn't studied them closely but was entirely confident that he was in fact right.

"That's an option, maybe we should do that," Bessy said, looking at Paddo.

"I don't mind, it just leaves me without wheels, is all," Tom said. They were pleased he had responded with flexibility and some rationality. They decided to look into the tour option tomorrow and discuss it further then.

"This Cab Sav, it's chunky," Paddo said.

"Bold and deep, I believe, is the more accurate description," Bessy said, putting on her best cultured tone.

* * * *

By 2 pm the next day, Paddo and Bessy were packed and ready to be collected by the tour operator for a three-night tour of the Barossa and the Clare Valley. The package included six wineries, all meals and accommodation. Paddo had insisted on paying the entire amount which had created some tension between Bessy and him. Bessy had objected but after Tom told her that she was being unreasonable by not allowing an English gentleman to demonstrate age-old chivalry, she agreed. Bessy wasn't exactly sure what chivalry meant; however, she took the point and reminded herself to relax.

Whilst that was happening, Tom placed an advertisement in the Adelaide classifieds. He kept silent about it though. He'd thought about it overnight, knowing he was to be alone soon.

"I feel a bit awful about this," Paddo said, at the same time reminding Bessy they needed to be in front of the hostel in five minutes.

"Don't give it even a millisecond's thought," Tom said, already looking forward to a few days of privacy.

"Are you sure?" Bessy said.

"Hey look. We're not a family. We're not connected by leg chains. This is freedom," Tom reassured them. "Go for it."

"Are you going to stay here the whole time?" asked Paddo.

"I might. I haven't decided. It's cheap for what it is. I'll let you know."

Bessy gave him a kiss and a big hug. Tom felt good. He hadn't had a kiss and a hug from a female since he had left England. But even then, he couldn't remember when he had last received one, apart from his mother. Paddo shook his hand.

After they had left, Tom climbed into his bunk bed and examined the wording of his advertisement that was set to appear the next morning. He had paid for the paper and online version. He had decided he should stay in Adelaide for a week or even two. He wanted to place a bait to see if someone, somewhere, might be interested to take it, just for fun.

The advert read: *Practising private investigator. Willing to take on the unusual. Reasonable rates.*

He remained confused about 'practicing' and 'practising' but decided that when he had someone in his lair, if it ever arose, he would explain that he was in training and practising to be a PI but unlicensed and learning. And given he was unlicensed, his fees were in fact more than reasonable. He convinced himself that this first step in this new direction, just the advertisement itself, was rather silly yet educational on some level and would probably amount to nothing but a bill from the newspaper.

* * * *

Bessy and Paddo were excited. Bessy had never felt happier in her whole life. She felt like she was living in a dream where one day she would wake up and be handed a train ticket back to Melbourne, with a kiss and a wave after a quiet whisper in her ear that it had all been fun but now it was over. She thought about sharing this with Paddo as the small tour bus wound its way through the streets of Glenelg on its way to the

Barossa Valley. Instead, she looked at him and smiled. He smiled back, took her hand in his and rested both on his thigh.

The bus was small and comfortable, and the driver picked up two more people just outside of Glenelg, bringing the passengers to a total of twelve.

"Good afternoon everyone," said a fellow with a microphone at the front of the bus. "I know we met earlier. My name is David and I am your tour guide for the first two days. My colleague, Janet, will meet us in Clare and she will guide you for that leg of our tour. Firstly, a warm welcome to everyone. We now have everyone on board and I'm looking forward to getting to know you all. It's a beautiful afternoon as you can see. We will be in Nuriootpa this afternoon where we will start our tour and stay the night."

David spoke clearly and with a lovely tone to his voice. He wore jeans with sneakers and a beige jacket over a black tee-shirt. He explained that he had previously worked for one of the major wineries for more than a decade.

"Nuriootpa is 'meeting place' in Aboriginal," he continued. Paddo looked at Bessy and gave a sort of nod of approval and a raise of his eyebrows. "We like to start our journey there and allow everyone to meet each other. We have booked in at a lovely restaurant in the area and hope that we can all get to know each other at the start, which we find makes it a lot of fun."

Bessy looked around the bus. She counted another four men besides Paddo of varying ages and seven women, including herself. Three of the girls looked around her own age and seemed to know each other.

After a little over an hour, they arrived in the small town. David had arranged to 'hit the deck running' by visiting one of the cellar doors. First, they checked into their accommodation but were soon back on the bus. He explained they had a special arrangement with the winery, permitting them to visit after its public opening hours and this was exclusive to their tour. Paddo took mental note that this was clever as it made everyone on the tour immediately feel special. It was also the perfect time to enjoy a glass or two of wine. He said to Bessy that he was glad they had decided to leave the driving to someone else.

Bessy had heard of the winery. They tasted several wines and both felt a little intimidated by the sophisticated surrounds and formal atmosphere of the room. However, after a couple of glasses, they relaxed and offered some observations about the wine.

"This one has more, I don't know, body to it?" she said.

The lady behind the long, timber bar agreed. "It's one of our more complex Shiraz selections."

"I think it's lovely," said one of the girls standing next to Paddo and he nodded in agreement.

Someone asked how old the vines were. The lady serving said that some of the vines were over 120 years old. She talked knowledgably about 'ancestor vines' and that they were believed to be some of the oldest in production in the world.

People had already started to introduce themselves to others in the group. An older lady introduced herself to Bessy and made it very clear she was happy to be on her first ever winery tour after years of thinking about it. The group of three girls said they were German and travelling together. They spoke quietly to themselves and seemed to be making comments about the wines and noting the differences in each glass.

Paddo was hungry so was delighted when David announced it was time to get back on the bus and make their way back to the accommodation where they would be eating in the restaurant there.

Bessy was eager to have an early night.

David had mentioned something to them about matching food with wine to get the maximum pleasure out of the wine. This was something Paddo had heard of but had a suspicion was exaggerated. He mentioned as much to Bessy as he sat looking at the menu in the restaurant.

"No, David is right," she said. "It is well known."

Paddo read the label on the red-wine bottle that had been placed on the table. There were three tables of four people and each table had the same bottle. Tonight, the tour operator had chosen the wine, which was part of the package. The bottle was covered with a series of gold and silver round stamps, signifying awards and medals. A lady walked around to each table, pouring wine evenly into each of the larger than average glasses, then left the empty bottle on the table. Paddo had not quite digested each of the superlatives on the back label, so he picked the bottle up to read the description again. It said something about 'at its lush and prodigious peak with duck or game'. He studied the menu again. "I think I'll have the duck," he said.

"Yes, it does look good. It depends on how it's done. It can be a tad fatty," Bessy said. Eventually, she decided on the quail. Paddo thought this was a good choice, having read the label on the bottle.

The other couple at their table were on their honeymoon. They introduced themselves as Cynthia and John from Adelaide and said they had already been to Kangaroo Island for a week. Some chatting ensued about the island and some of the things to do there. The next stop for them would be Coffin Bay for a seafood festival the day after the tour finished.

Bessy had consumed half of her wine by the time her meal arrived. Paddo had left most of his so he could put the description on the back label to the test. Paddo waited until he was about a third of the way into the meal before taking another swallow of the wine. He had noticed people tossing the wine around in their mouth at the winery but decided that might be inappropriate in a restaurant.

When he mentioned this to Bessy, she said, "Good call."

Due to the generous size of his glass, Paddo was able to enjoy his experiment several times before reporting to the others, "Yes, this wine does go well, I think, with duck."

"It's a lovely wine," Cynthia said and her husband agreed.

Bessy achieved her desire for an early night by excusing Paddo and herself from dessert and coffee, saying they were both tired and looking forward to seeing everyone in the morning. They retired to their room. When Paddo asked if she was really tired she replied, "Of course not!"

CHAPTER EIGHTEEN

Tom was up early and decided to walk into town and get the newspaper and coffee. He wanted to keep the advertisement as a souvenir. The morning was clear and he could smell the ocean as he wandered down to the path and along the water's edge. He said good morning along the way to several people he passed walking their dogs. The joggers would not make eye contact. Too busy getting fit, he figured.

He bought the newspaper and returned to a seat overlooking the beach with a cup of long black. It took him a while to find the advertisement and the Saturday edition of the paper seemed filled with classifieds. After reading it, he looked out to the horizon, across Holdfast Bay. He took a sip on his coffee and decided after he finished it, he would take a longer walk, as far as he could, all along the edge of the bay. Just in case he got a call, which he knew was most unlikely, he checked his phone to make sure it was fully charged. He read some of the paper, mainly skimming through it, checking only a few headlines.

After finding a garbage bin, he disposed of the coffee cup and the newspaper, except for the page with the advertisement, which he neatly tore out, folded and placed into his back pocket. He then headed back in the direction he had come, passed the hostel and walked on for another hour, before turning back and coming into town again for a late breakfast and more coffee. After he finished his bacon and eggs, he decided to walk out on the jetty, which extended for a good way into the deep water of the bay. The sun was hot already and he watched children jumping off it into the water for a while.

Not having a hat and with the sun rapidly rising, he decided to go back and get one. By the time he arrived at the hostel, he decided to jump in the Troopy and go for a drive, not settling on any direction in particular. The gauge indicated there was very little diesel and at the first service station he saw, he filled up and checked the water and oil. Everything was fine and he was pleased the Troopy was justifying the money they had spent. He took a drive out to the marina and walked around and admired the boats. Half thinking about what to do next, as he paused and stood on the wharf for a moment while gazing into the water and watching small fish swim around a million dollar plus yacht, his phone rang. He expected it to be Paddo, no doubt, just making sure he was fine and reporting in, perhaps feeling a little guilty he had left him alone, yet again. But that was all fine.

"Hello," Tom said.

"I am ringing about the advert in the paper," said the voice on the other end.

He was shocked. "You are? I mean, yes," Tom said.

"Do I have the right person – Tom? The paper, the classified, said 'Tom.'"

"Most certainly, Sir. This is Tom."

"And you are an investigator?"

"That I am," he said, without thinking. *This is too surreal*, he thought, so he went with the flow.

"Can we meet then, perhaps today?"

"I don't see why not. And you are?"

"I would like to discuss details in person, if that would be alright."

"That's fine. Advisable, even," replied Tom.

"Where is your office? I am happy to come to you."

"I'm in Glenelg at the moment."

"That's fine. It's very convenient to me."

"If we meet here, then?"

"Can we meet in the open?"

"In the open?"

"I mean outside. Not inside."

Tom thought for a moment.

"That's a very good idea. But you will need to find me. I can suggest where. Perhaps, in front of the jetty. Do you know the jetty?"

"Yes, I know the jetty."

"I'm on the short side and have blond hair."

"I can be there in an hour."

"See you then."

Tom immediately felt like ringing Paddo but thought against it. Things were moving fast, all of a sudden. He needed to get back, park the Troopy and change his clothes. Something other than shorts, other than a tee-shirt and thongs. It was remarkable that the advertisement had worked, but he felt a little nervous as to where all this might lead. It now seemed like a stupid, deceptive thing to do, but he had an adrenalin rush that oddly felt good. *What have I just agreed to do?* He climbed up into the Troopy, his mind racing.

He went back to the hostel, still amazed that he had even received an enquiry, based on so little effort. A quick shower was essential. He was soon out and got into trousers, a collared shirt and shoes. He brushed his teeth and found his sunglasses. Ten minutes before the hour, he was sitting on the nearest bench to the jetty, thinking about timing a move closer to the structure and trying to look as casual but professional as he could muster.

He noticed several people he thought might be the man. *Why didn't I think to ask for a description*, he thought. *It probably wouldn't have been given anyway but what if he's really an undercover policeman? Or worse, a criminal?* A moment's trepidation almost overcame him as he tossed over in his mind what he was doing and whether he should just get up, go back to the hostel and lie on his bunk for the rest of the day and forget all about this ridiculous idea.

At precisely the hour – which was 12:30 pm – he walked to the front of the jetty and saw a man approach from the side.

"Are you Tom?" he said, in a clear but soft tone.

"Yes."

"Good. Can we walk?"

"Yes. Of course."

Tom noticed that the man wore a collar like a minister or priest. He felt relieved but then wondered if it was a disguise.

After they had walked a short distance, the man said, "My name is Father Draper. I'm a priest."

Tom took out his hat that he had folded into his pocket and put it on. "Nice to meet you, Father."

Father Draper was tall and thin, and looked about sixty-five years old. His face was quite wrinkled. He wore a wide-brimmed hat, sunglasses, black trousers and black shirt, and shiny black shoes. Even though it was hot, he also wore a black coat.

"You're surprised, aren't you? Though I expect in your industry you are not surprised with much." The priest looked ahead as he spoke.

Tom was surprised. "No, I'm not surprised. I never have any expectations."

"Good. You are awfully young."

"I just look young. My whole family look much younger than they really are."

"Lucky you."

Tom's natural walking pace was quick. He had to concentrate to slow down and match Father Draper's pace. He also reminded himself to slow down in general and just see what happened.

"Thank you for meeting me in person." Father Draper spoke much slower than on the phone.

"Do you have a parish nearby, Father?"

"Not far. I'd best tell you, I suppose."

"Whatever you think, Father. Only tell me what I need to know. It's much better that way."

"I will. Thank you."

They approached a bench. "Let's sit up here, shall we?" Father Draper said, as he angled slowly toward the bench. They sat down and watched the seagulls that immediately appeared in the hope of a free feed. Tom turned his gaze to the priest's face and could see the wheels of his mind turning something over.

"This is all confidential, of course," Father Draper said, crossing his legs.

Tom noticed the small gold cross on his lapel. "Of course," Tom said.

"And your rate?"

"Well, it depends, Father."

"It will be a one off, although you may need to do a little digging."

"Digging?"

"Finding something about her. About her, that I don't know."

"I see," Tom said.

The priest pulled out a packet of cigarettes from inside his coat pocket. "Do you mind?"

"Not at all."

He lit a cigarette and took a deep drag. "Look," he said, blowing a tube of smoke down towards the ground. "I've worked with this terrible woman for twenty years. Probably more, when I think of it. She's supposed to work for me but you wouldn't know it. She's a housekeeper at the presbytery. I am ashamed to say it, but I hate her. I can't stand her."

"Right," Tom said, wondering where this was all going.

Father Draper looked out to sea and tapped some ash off the end of his cigarette with the tip of his finger.

Tom decided to jump right in. "So this woman works for you at the monastery. Why haven't you just sacked her?"

"The presbytery. I am not the only priest. Three of us live in the presbytery. There is one senior to me. It's not up to me. I wish it was. She would have been long gone. He gets along with her. But she makes my life hell. Hell on Earth. I hope she goes to hell and someone pushes her in there tomorrow." Father took another deep drag.

Tom could see the agony on his face.

"I'm desperate. When I saw your ad this morning, I rang the number purely out of desperation. I get the paper to look at the horses, the form guide. But I always keep an eye on the classifieds. I really haven't … I came across your ad by accident. I was never, never going to contact a PI. But as I said, I'm desperate."

"Right," Tom said again. *Don't go fishing, unless you are prepared to catch a fish*, he thought, now regretting his decision to place the advertisement.

"I'm really after your expertise. I want you to find something out about her and embarrass her, or allow me to get to her, somehow, without her knowing it was me. This sounds dreadful for a priest, I know."

"It's fine, Father. We are all human."

"She's not."

"You said something about a 'one off'. What did you mean by that?"

"I don't really know. Look, I might be able to carry on if I know if she has a weakness. Or that she suffers something, or is made to suffer something. Nothing too serious. Just enough to … but just the once. I just need to punish her. Her time will come, but I need to know …"

"You don't mean violence, do you, Father?"

"Oh, God no! I'm not a criminal. Mind you, sometimes I think I would be happy to go to jail if …"

"Father, I'm sure I can help you."

"You can?"

"Most definitely."

"That's good."

"But I need some more information. And it can't be very serious, I mean, just something mild, surely."

"Of course. What do you need to know?"

"For one, what is it that she does that you hate, specifically? You say she is the housekeeper."

"She's okay at her job. Don't get me wrong. That's not it. She's just a bitch. She does things to annoy me deliberately. And she knows I know this. She makes appointments for me and doesn't tell me. Cooks only what the other priests want. Never irons my shirts. Always talks behind my back to the parishioners. If I ask her something simple, she argues with me. The list goes on."

"How many days does she work?"

"Every day except Monday. Let me tell you what she did last week. The hide of the woman."

"Yes, please do," said Tom, not convinced Father Draper was exactly justifying his vehemency.

"Every couple of years I go on retreat. All of the priests in the arch-diocese do. It goes for two days. Not long."

"Right."

"I told her not to disturb me during the retreat. Not to ring me."

"And she did," Tom said.

"No, she didn't!"

"She didn't?"

"No. That's just it."

"I'm not following."

"Look, it's supposed to be a non-talking retreat. We spend the days mostly in silence, praying. I spent it praying that she would … I won't tell what I prayed. Anyway, she knows it's a non-talking retreat. One of the priests told her once, under no circumstances was she to ring him. I never told her 'under no circumstances'."

"You wanted her to call you?"

"Yes!"

Tom looked around to see if anyone had heard Father Draper's raised voice. "Why?"

"An old friend of mine, a lady I've known for many, many years, dropped by the presbytery. She sometimes does this, unannounced. She lives interstate. Coral has met her before, when she has visited me. Anyway, my friend couldn't reach me on the phone as we had to switch the things off. But Coral could have passed on a message. All she had to do was ring the retreat. Messages are checked every few hours. Other priests get messages, despite all the silly nonsense about it being non-talking."

"Coral is the housekeeper? Coral not Carol?"

"Coral. Anyway, I get back and days pass and I get a call from my friend. I didn't even know she had been to see me. She said she had been in Adelaide for a week but had gone back to Perth. And she hadn't been able to contact me. When I asked Coral about my friend's visit, she said she had dropped in on the morning I left for the retreat. About an hour after I had left. Coral reminded me that I'd said not to call under any circumstances. That I mustn't be disturbed as it was a non-talking retreat. I never told her that. She just made that up as an excuse. She told my friend I could not be contacted and never said I would be back in a few days. She did it just to spite me, knowing I would have been back in time."

"Ah, that's frustrating."

"I only see my friend once in a blue moon. I can't tell you how frustrating it is." He stubbed his cigarette out under his foot, then picked the butt up and dropped it in a bin nearby.

"I need to know the address of the monastery, Father."

"The presbytery. Here it is." He handed Tom a piece of paper. "It's got my phone number on it as well."

"What does Coral look like? And her surname as well, Father."

"A little dumpy, medium height, I guess. Mousy-coloured hair … and glasses, like the bottom of a bottle. Coral Norma Quigley."

"Thank you, Father. I'll get onto the case straight away. When I know a little bit more, I will call you with a price. I am thinking it will not be more than $600.00. Would that be alright?"

"Thank you, Tom."

They shook hands.

"I'm going that way," Father Draper said.

"I'll sit here until you're out of sight."

* * * *

By mid-afternoon on the next day of their tour, Bessy and Paddo had got to know the German girls. The girls were all from Munich and they kept them amused with stories of beer festivals. Two of the girls were older than Bessy and one was younger.

The winery they visited that afternoon was very large so there were plenty of tasting opportunities. The cellar door provided an expansive counter space that allowed for a variety of experiences. Over the course of an hour, Bessy and Paddo moved separately from space to space and only came together occasionally to swap comments. Hanna, the younger German girl, and Bessy spent most of their time together.

By late afternoon, everyone on the tour had checked into new accommodation. There was a large spa which Paddo and Bessy and the German girls shared, over a glass of sparkling red that they had brought back from the winery.

"You are so spoiled," Bessy said to Paddo.

He smiled and raised his glass. Life couldn't be better.

* * * *

Tom had packed a mid-range telephoto lens that simply wasn't going to be good enough. But he wasn't thinking photographs would be crucial when it came to Coral. He needed to devise a plan. *Keep it simple*, he thought, realising he had no resources to do otherwise. He looked at his watch. It was 4 pm. Best get on the road and go and knock on the presbytery door.

He was there by 4:30 pm. He parked the Troopy in the church car park. He looked around to see where other cars belonging to the priests or Coral might be parked. No other cars were visible, although there was a gated driveway that looked like it could have a space for cars. He needed to lay eyes on Coral. He knocked on the big, heavy door of the presbytery and waited. He hoped Coral would answer the door, not one of the priests.

The door opened and a lady wearing a large apron greeted him. "Can I help you?"

"Um, yes. Good afternoon," he said, pleased that it appeared to be Coral, based upon the description. "My name is Peterson. Roald Peterson. I'm with Direct Food Marketers SA Incorporated. How are you this afternoon?"

"I'm fine, thanks." She held the door two thirds ajar and Tom noticed a trail of perspiration running across her brow.

He held his hand out to shake hers. "And you are?"

The woman fluttered her eyelids and for a moment didn't seem to be able to open them. She reluctantly removed her hand from the door and extended it, moving her foot to prop open the heavy door. Tom noticed she wore heavy, cream-coloured shoes with scuff marks.

"Coral," she said, with an upside-down smile.

"Lovely to meet you, Coral. Listen, I won't keep you. As I said, I'm from Direct Food Marketers and we specialise in home deliveries. All food and grocery items direct to your door. I'm just finishing up my shift at the moment and I have run out of brochures but I was wondering if I could make an appointment to come back and see you?"

"Oh, I don't think so." She shook her head.

"Are you sure? It's all no obligation, you know."

She had returned her arm to the door.

"I do the shopping," she said.

"And I'm sure you do a wonderful job. But it's such hard work these days."

"It's not that hard."

"For a capable woman like you, I am sure."

"Look, I really don't have time for this. And I'm not interested. I'm just about to finish my own shift so you will have to excuse me," she said.

"Absolutely. I am sorry to disturb you. Please, have a lovely evening and if there is anything …"

She slammed the door quickly and firmly before he could finish or take a step back.

He pivoted on his heels and returned to the Troopy. He moved it out of the car park and across the street so that he had a view of the gated driveway. At 5:05 pm, the gate automatically opened and Coral drove out in a small, light-blue Corolla. Tom started up the Troopy and followed her.

After about ten minutes, he saw her pull into a garage and assumed it was her residence. He felt a little awkward and dishonest but he agreed with Father Draper, she seemed to be not the nicest person in the world. He was now determined to justify this nonsense in his own mind by using it to test himself whether he had it in him to ever become a private investigator.

Tom parked a little up the street and realised he didn't know what to do next. He decided to wait for a while and think. Twenty minutes later,

Coral was back on the road. He had almost missed her leave. The Troopy didn't start up straight away and he had to catch up to her before he lost her. Luckily, she was a very slow driver. Once he'd caught up with her, he made sure there were at least three cars between hers and the Troopy. After about another five minutes, she pulled into what looked like another church. But on closer view, it was some type of hall or meeting space. She turned into a car park and as Tom drove by, he saw Coral heading inside. He parked the Troopy down the street, swapped his shirt and tie for an old shirt that he found in the back seat and donned his hat which he pulled down low over his forehead.

He sauntered past the car park, trying to see what was going on in the hall but couldn't make out any detail. He decided the best thing was just to walk straight up to the front entrance, quickly but not so hurried as to attract attention, and see what he could see. He knew there were people inside. He only had one chance so he needed to be efficient. As he approached, he noticed a sign on the door. The door had a small panel of clear glass in it, so he would have to be careful not to be seen peering in. The sign said, *Meeting here tonight and Monday night: All welcome – The Slimmer Winners.*

He was gone in a flash and was sure he hadn't been seen. And if he had, well, as the sign said, everyone was welcome, anyway. He had enough to think about, for now.

* * * *

"I am telling you she is going to something like a weight watchers program," Tom said to Father Draper later that night on the phone.

"Really? She's always been a bit of a porker."

"Well, that's what I found out today."

"Good work, young man. What's next?" Father Draper seemed to be slurring his words a little.

"Father, have you been drinking?"

"I might have had a few. Anyway, that's good, what you've found out."

"It's probably not a secret, Father. They're respectable groups and quite common."

"Oh, I know that. But she won't like me knowing it, though. I want to think about this a little. I will call you tomorrow."

When Father Draper called the next day, Tom was hardly out of bed.

"I need to leave it to you, I've decided. I want you to embarrass her, somehow, and tell me all about it."

"Father, that's a little tough."

"You said you could help me. Well, that would help me. Look, she eats like a horse. Do this for me, somehow. She's not nice, Tom. I can assure you of that! She steals from the poor box. She has a key. I didn't tell you that, did I!"

Not long after, Tom's phone rang again.

"Paddo! How's it going?" Tom felt like his head was spinning.

"Fantastic! We are off to Clare today. Bessy is having a great time. The Barossa is very pretty. You'd love it."

"That's good to hear."

"What have you been up to?" asked Paddo.

"Oh, not much. Been walking a bit. Some other stuff, but I will tell you when you get back. You're back tomorrow, aren't you?"

"I think so, yes. We'll bring you some wine. It won't be altar wine, not that you need altering. It will be the good stuff."

"Very good. Well, I'll see you both then."

As he hung up, Tom thought he knew where he could certainly get some altar wine and who might need altering in the city of churches.

CHAPTER NINETEEN

Tom stretched out on his bunk, thinking through the issues. A priest for a client! Why should he question, even for a moment, the morality of what he was contemplating? Coral wasn't very pleasant it seemed but he didn't really know if she was as nasty as Father Draper was making out. Maybe she deserved something. But what? And how? And when? Paddo and Bessy would be back on Monday. He could hear Paddo's voice already, "You did what?"

But a challenge was not something he could easily dismiss, especially one brought about by his own hand. He felt he was chained now to this one. Besides, he could do with the money, and none of it was going to be placed in the poor box at the church. He'd give some money later, not now. This was too difficult a job. He told himself he would deserve every cent for what he was about to do for this man of the cloth.

By Monday morning, he had settled on a strategy. It would involve an explanation to Paddo and Bessy, as he had to use the Troopy.

Paddo and Bessy returned soon after midday and they met Tom at the hostel. They were very keen to tell him all the details of their tour.

"Oh, Tom. You would have loved the last place we went. It was run by a group of old monks or priests or something. They were so lovely," Bessy said.

Tom just smiled.

Paddo thought he seemed unusually quiet. "Are you sick?" he asked.

"No. I'm fine. I've just been busy."

"Doing what? Busy swimming? On the beach?" Paddo said.

"Various."

"Ah, the old various and sundry. That'll wear you out."

"Paddo, he hasn't been on a holiday within a holiday, like us. You should be nice to him," Bessy said.

"I am nice to him. Here, this is for you." He handed him a bottle of Shiraz.

"Thank you, old son, how awfully decent of you." Tom took the bottle and put it on the floor.

"Why don't we have it tonight? Right here?" Paddo said.

"I can't, tonight."

"Have you got a date?"

"No, I just have a commitment."

"A commitment?" This time it was Bessy who was surprised. "Where?"

"Over the other side of town. I'll need the Troopy for a couple of hours." Tom avoided looking at them.

Paddo looked at Bessy. "What have you been up to?" Paddo said slowly, looking back at Tom.

"I'll tell you everything later. Tomorrow in fact."

Tom told them he'd see them later tonight, after dinner sometime, and left the room.

The plan Tom had in mind would only work if Coral attended the Monday night meeting of the Slimmer Winners. There was no back-up plan but he would need one if she wasn't there. He could always pay her a visit at her house but he felt a little uneasy about that. He was kicking himself now for placing the advertisement and would rather be drinking wine and hearing about how to drink it properly.

He returned to his parking spot in Coral's street by 5 pm. As it was a Monday, he knew she was not working at the presbytery. He noticed her car was parked in the driveway. Shortly before 5:30 pm, she pulled out and headed in the same direction as before. He hoped she was going to pull into the hall's car park where the meeting was to take place. She stopped at a chemist on the way and he had difficulty finding a park. He considered he had no choice but to pull into a space reserved for disabled people, which added to his feeling of guilt. He attempted to excuse himself by noting he was not getting out of the Troopy. When he saw a police officer he wondered if he was going to be booked. Coral returned to her car with a package and continued in the direction of the hall.

Tom was relieved when she pulled into the car park near the hall and he saw her go inside. He continued on to a supermarket around the corner where he parked, then crossed the road to a pizza parlour. He ordered a family size pizza with the lot. Then he went back to the supermarket, bought some flowers, a card, a small box of chocolates and a large chocolate donut. Back at the car, he placed his shopping on the front seat and climbed into the driver's seat. He found a pen in the dash compartment. *From your secret admirer*, he wrote on the card. *I don't care about your weight. I think you are lovely, just the way you are.* He then drew some hearts and crosses. He winced – stealing from the poor box, he reminded himself.

Tom looked at his watch, then returned to the pizza shop to collect his order. He moved the Troopy into a car space near the hall but out of view. The sun was fading but he put his sunglasses on, placed his hat on his head and stuck on a false moustache. He also slipped into some other trousers. With his hands full with the pizza box, flowers and other items, he moved quickly towards the door of the hall. He peered through the glass panel and saw a group of ten or so women all seated in a circle. He opened the door by pushing it with his foot and feeling like a fool, calmly swaggered over to the group. "A special delivery for one! Coral?" he said in a poor attempt at a Spanish accent and with a big smile plastered on his face.

The women looked at him and each other in horror. One lady opened her mouth and held it open in shock. The smell of the pizza quickly filled the air. Tom placed the pizza box gently on Coral's lap with the card on top. In his eagerness to commit the deed and get out, he forgot to wait for Coral to be identified. "These are a for you … the lucky … or should I say, lovely one." Dressed in white flared trousers he had bought from a second-hand store and with his fake moustache, he felt like a skinny, short Spanish Elvis.

"Donta forget the goodies here." He placed them on the floor next to her. "I bid you farewell. It's nota from me ..." he said as he half skipped, half-danced out the door.

No one spoke. Coral opened the card. She looked inside the pizza box. Then at the flowers and the chocolates and the donut. She reached in and grabbed a massive slice of pizza.

One of the ladies said, "Oh Coral, don't. Please don't."

But Coral didn't seem to hear her. She lifted the slice to her mouth. One of the women gasped. Another said she couldn't watch.

"I don't care," Coral said. I haven't had a pizza for three years."

The group leader ran her hands over her face.

* * * *

Outside, Tom got back into the Troopy and drove back to the hostel. He couldn't wait to get out of the flares. He could have easily changed back into his trousers in the Troopy but his mind was focused on whether the deed had worked and what he would tell Draper.

"What the hell are you wearing those pants for?" Paddo said, who had been reading in their room and watched him rush in.

"I'll tell you later. Right now, I have to go and make a confession to a priest."

When he got to the presbytery, Father Draper answered the door. "I don't think it's a good idea we meet here."

"Let me in Father. It's not a problem."

He took Tom to the study and they sat down. After hearing what Tom had to say, he nodded and said calmly, "That's fine. It will put all those pounds back on her. I'm satisfied. Thank you." Tom had expected something more, but that was it.

He opened a tin box in a drawer and took out $600 cash in $50 notes. "Be sure to place some in the poor box in the church on your way out. I changed the locks today," he said, handing it over.

"Are you going to confess this to one of your colleagues, Father, and ask forgiveness?" asked Tom.

"One day. There's no rush. I have to feel sorry, first."

Tom thought about putting $50 in the poor box but couldn't guarantee that old Draper wouldn't take it down to the bottle shop. He resolved to find a way to make his own peace with the dreadful thing he had done for this man of God.

On the drive back, Tom realised he had done this task without properly thinking it through, just to honour his ridiculous commitment to Draper. Even the money didn't make him feel better.

Paddo wasn't at the hostel, so Tom walked into town and went to a pub for dinner. The beer made him feel sleepy and he was in bed by 9:30 pm that night.

* * * *

Bessy was in Tom's dorm by 7 am the next day.

"Wake up. You're coming to breakfast," she said, giving him a shake.

"I am?"

"Yes, you are."

"Can I have a shower?"

"If you must."

Tom jumped out of bed, got his towel and headed for the showers.

Paddo was grooming himself in the mirror. "Do you think we should stay in Adelaide?" Paddo asked Bessy.

"I think we should discuss it this morning with Tom," Bessy replied.

"We have a lot to discuss," noted Paddo.

They found a café in the main street and ordered breakfast.

"There are many unresolved questions in this universe, Tom. None more significant than why you were wearing white flares last night," Paddo said.

"I wish I'd seen them," added Bessy.

"No, you don't," Paddo said.

"It hardly matters what I was wearing, it's what I was doing while I was wearing them."

"And what was that, Tom, are we allowed to know now?" asked Bessy.

So Tom told them the whole story. By the time breakfast was finished and after numerous 'you're having us on' and similar comments, Bessy said, "I didn't think you were at all serious when you mentioned you wanted to be a PI."

"Well, I hope you've learnt something," Paddo said.

"Like what?" asked Tom.

"Something about yourself," Paddo said.

Tom nodded and sipped on his second cup of coffee. He knew that was a good answer.

"What about the confidentiality stuff? You've told us," Bessy said.

"Like every rule that ever existed, there are a number of qualifications and exceptions," Tom said.

"Is that right?" Paddo said, sarcastically.

"Yes. That *is* right. In this case, I am playing the duty to my travelling colleagues exception. The duty to explain. Normally, a PI doesn't have that duty. A PI is not subject to the same stuff as a doctor, anyway. There are some bendables in the PI handbook."

"Sounds like you've written it," Paddo remarked.

"Not yet."

"That poor woman," Bessy said. "That's awful for her. How could you do such a nasty thing, Tom?"

"Don't remind me, please. But in truth, she may never know. It may help her to like herself more," replied Tom. But he was feeling low and that justification wasn't cutting it.

"Based on a lie, Tom," Bessy added.

"If Father Draper lets on, it will be bad. I don't think he will. He's sick but perhaps not that sick."

"Paddo and I wanted to get your feelings on whether we should stay in Adelaide," Bessy said, changing the subject.

"I'm happy to leave before I get another bloody phone call, to be honest," Tom replied, draining the last of his coffee.

Bessy looked at Paddo.

"I'm happy to go," he said.

"The city of churches hasn't quite been what I expected," Tom said. "What do you want to do, Bess?" This was the first time Tom had called her Bess.

"I'm ready to leave but where will we go?"

Paddo expelled some air, as if some big task was before him. And it was. "We're a fair distance from everywhere else by car which is a problem."

"That's true, Paddo," Tom said.

"This means we have decisions to make. If we go further west, if and when we return to the east, it's even further away. If we head east, it's a bloody long way by car." Paddo was uncertain what he wanted to do.

"If we head east and break it into small chunks, then it's not so bad," offered Bessy.

"That's true, as well," Tom said.

"Where do we want to land?" asked Paddo, not necessarily to anyone.

"Well, I think we should go back to the hostel, split up and do some research, then get together this afternoon, drink Tom's bottle of Shiraz and eat cheese by the beach, compare notes and decide." Bessy thought someone had to take the lead.

"That's a good idea," Tom said.

"It must be your turn for a good idea, Tom," Paddo said.

"That's true," said Tom.

Paddo shook his head.

* * * *

By 10 am the next day, they were back on the road, heading east. They decided to try to make it to Broken Hill by early evening and then continue on to Bourke the next day. From there, they aimed to pass through Moree on their way to Boggabilla, drive across to Warwick and then to Brisbane. They debated about stopping at Goondiwindi but decided to see how they were feeling at the time. Tom suggested that the Great Barrier Reef was the ultimate place to land so they set a goal for the southern-most tip within two weeks.

Bessy noticed that the two boys had given scant regard to the heart of the outback. "You Pommies are just thinking about getting to our destination, not the highlights on the way. You're not taking it all in." She had grown in confidence since the start of the trip. Paddo's devotion to her helped but it wasn't just that. She felt more assertive and at ease with herself. It helped that the boys were allowing her every bit of equal input, even when it came to the most trivial of things. She was living in the moment and going with the flow like she had never done before.

"Bess, would you like to take the wheel on the way to Bourke?" asked Tom.

Paddo was surprised when she agreed.

This was to be a lengthy drive and it would be a test to their patience and compatibility. They all agreed there would be no night driving and there would be compulsory stops every two hours. "No matter what!" Bessy was the voice of reason. Paddo and Tom were happy to oblige.

About an hour out of Broken Hill, the conversation ultimately got around to Paddo who was now driving. "I know what I don't want to do more than what I want to do."

"What don't you want to do, Paddo?"

"I don't want work to dominate my life. I don't want working to be my sole purpose. I want more balance."

"Balance with what?" The questions started coming from both Bessy and Tom.

"Other things than work."

"Like what?"

"Interests, people, places, the natural environment, I guess. Kids, maybe."

"Maybe?"

"Yeah, maybe."

"Sometimes you need money, lots of it, to do these things. Kids cost hundreds of thousands of dollars," Tom said.

"They do cost money, I know that. My parents spent so much damn money on my schooling. But I would have been just the same if they hadn't."

"You think that but you have no way of knowing."

"I think I know."

"I don't think you sound very ambitious," Tom said.

"Maybe I'm not. I'm not ambitious like my father. I don't want his life and to have this huge, all-consuming life in business. I'd rather be working in the natural environment, maybe a park ranger. I was actually envious that you got to play tour guide with those Danish girls in the national park. I want to work in a place like that. I'm ambitious for a happy life."

The evening approached with its palette of colours. The sky moved from blue to red then grey before turning black.

"When I went to India, it made me think," Paddo continued eventually. "The people there were happy. I've never seen so many happy people. They weren't losing sleep about the stock market or their insurance, that's for sure. They were living. I'd like to be like that."

"What do you think your parents expect, Paddo?" asked Bessy.

"They know I'm not like Roger. But there is pressure to be like Dad. He is hard working and Roger is just like him. I suppose I have been lazy, compared to Dad. Sometimes I feel guilty I haven't gone into the family business side of things. They are more ... I don't know ... into the trophies of life: the flash car, the big house. I think that's fine, if that's what you want. The irony is that it's not enough for me. Less is more. It leaves more room for other things that aren't just things, I guess."

"If I knew the difference, I could add to this conversation," Bessy said.

"We're all the same in a way. It's just that, if you think about it, we like different things. And that's fine. But I get a bit peeved when people have every material possession they want, yet it's still not enough."

"That's human nature, Paddo," Tom said. "The grass is always greener ..."

"I know. It's almost an illness ... a disease I don't want to catch."

"People get great happiness from possessions, Paddo," Tom said.

"I know they do. It might be a watch or something given or earned. I do know that." He talked slowly as he reflected.

Bessy showed the boys the ring her mother had given her. She told them it gave her happiness.

CHAPTER TWENTY

Broken Hill, NSW

"It's only half past six Tom. We have plenty of time," Paddo said, as they got out of the Troopy. It was really half an hour earlier. Paddo had already changed his watch to New South Wales time.

"It's actually six. Look at the clock over there," Bessy said, pointing to a large old clock on the façade of a building, as she stepped onto the pavement.

"What time is it, aren't we in New South Wales?" asked Paddo, confused.

"Yes, but we are still on Adelaide time here. Broken Hill is in New South Wales but it's half an hour behind the rest of New South Wales." Bessy almost added that some say Broken Hill is behind the rest of the state in other ways, but she was never one to disparage a regional area, not when she was used to such patronising and uninformed views from big city folk.

"We still have plenty of time to find a place to stay. Let's stay in a pub, that way we don't have to move." Paddo had driven the last two hours and was thirsty and tired. "I need a beer to pick me up." Paddo pointed to a pub as he stood on the curb side. "I like that one. Let's get a beer there and stay. I'm really not fussed about scouting around for something better."

"I like a man who knows what he wants," Tom said to Bessy, as he put his arm around her shoulders and they wandered across the road.

They checked into the rooms immediately, then came downstairs for drinks. The pub was full of historical photos and there was a small local crowd of tradesmen and other regulars. Most of the patrons were used to seeing the occasional tourist come in and could easily identify the three of them as out-of-towners.

"Do you like your room, Tom?" asked Paddo, as he sat on a stool nearest the bar.

"Bargain. And yours?"

"It'll do."

After a few beers Tom said, "I'm feeling a bit crap over what I did to Coral. I guess it was a pretty low thing to do."

"So you should," Paddo said.

"It wasn't very nice of you at all, Tom. She may have had her faults but that was truly awful," added Bessy.

"I know," Tom said. "You don't have to mention it again. I don't know what I was thinking. It happened all too quickly. The last thing I expected was to encounter someone like Draper. I don't think he will be feeling sorry for anyone but himself."

"Well, I hope you will make it up somehow. I want to see you do something nice, soon," she said.

"I will. In fact, I had a soft spot for Coral, in a way," Tom said, draining the last of his glass of beer.

"Really?" Paddo said.

"Yep. I just can't mention where that particular soft spot is. It refuses to be anything but soft, whenever I think of her."

Paddo gave Bessy that all too familiar look, shook his head and said he would go and get some menus.

"Are you serious about making up for it, Tom? Or are you just going to wise crack about it?" Bessy looked at Tom with an expression that told him to be very careful with his response.

"I'm sorry, Bessy. I will make up for it."

"Will you? I think you need to grow up a bit! If you want to become a private investigator, you'll need to show a little bit more respect for people," she said.

They were on the road by 8 am the next morning, Broken Hill time, with Bessy at the wheel. The boys were impressed with her confidence. Tom had stayed downstairs after Paddo and Bessy had retreated to their room and didn't get to bed until closing time, after several more schooners of beer and conversations with the locals. He fell asleep in the back of the Troopy somewhere between Wilcannia and Cubba, sprawled out in the rear seat in a deep slumber and didn't wake until they pulled into Cobar.

Paddo and Bessy chatted quietly so they didn't disturb him. Paddo told her more about Norwich and she felt pangs to travel overseas, although she held back saying so. He asked her about her brother and sisters and she told him what she could remember. As she did so, she realised that the only memories she could share were becoming ever more distant, fading into the past.

They made it to Bourke at 5 pm. Tom, refreshed and eager to make progress, had taken the wheel for the last two hours. They managed to narrowly miss hitting a huge kangaroo about half an hour before town and Bessy said she was very glad she wasn't driving. The Troopy was very dusty and dirty inside and out. By the time they got into town it looked like it was home to stay and ready to be given a good wash down. But it wasn't a priority.

The sting of the sun had gone and they stretched their legs by the Darling River. Paddo paused to read a sign that said the river was the main transport link from Bourke to Adelaide in the 1800s when paddle steamers were the means of travel. For the first time in a while, they split up, wandering the town separately, taking the opportunity to give each other space. Paddo took interest in some information he found in a café about Gundabooka National Park. Bessy met him in the same café and found some information about Professor Hollows and his commitment to an Aboriginal eye health program. She told Paddo that he was regarded as a hero in Australia for his passionate and caring work for people who had difficulty accessing basic eye care and she was surprised to find out he was buried in Bourke. They chatted about that for a little while on a bench outside the café until they spotted Tom wandering on the other side of the street, and then checked into a budget motel for the night.

* * * *

Boggabilla 6:10 am, two days later

"Mum, Mum, is that you?"

"Yes. Is now a good time to talk?"

"Oh, um, okay. How are you? Yes. It's fine."

"I'm alright. I've been thinking of you. How are you doing?"

"I'm good. Sorry, I just woke up. The phone woke me up."

"Where are you?"

"Ah, where are we, um, at Boggabilla."

"Where's that?"

"A few hundred miles from Brisbane, I think. We're heading there."

"With your friend, Tom?"

"Yes."

"It's early there, isn't it? I hope you don't mind me calling. I never know when to call."

"It's fine, Mum. I'm awake. It's good to hear your voice."

"Are you looking after yourself?"

"Yes. I'm good."

"Well, I wanted to talk to you about Dad."

"Dad. Okay. How is he? Is he alright?"

"Oh, I hope so, Patrick. He's been ill."

"What do you mean?"

"We had to take him to the hospital last week for some tests."

"What sort of tests?"

"Lots of things. Blood tests and liver, mainly. He was feeling unwell for about a week before that. And he just got worse. Dr Taylor said he should have some tests."

"Is he okay?"

"He said he feels a bit better. He's got very little energy. I have told him he works too hard. That he has to slow down. Retire, basically. But you know what he's like."

"I do. Where is he? Is he at home?"

"Yes. The doctor said he should rest. He is taking that advice, thankfully."

"Well, you give him my love. Has he got any results?"

"No. But the doctor wants us to make an appointment in about a week."

"Right."

"Are you having a good time?"

"It's been great, Mum."

"Well that's lovely, darling. I will call you in about a week."

"I can call you."

"No, no. I am in and out, at the moment. I will call you."

"Okay."

"Love you, and take care. Patrick, please look after yourself."

"I will, Mum. Love you, too. Say hi to Dad."

* * * *

Goondiwindi, three hours later

"It's the resting place of the birds, Paddo, in case you wanted to know," Tom said, sitting on a park bench.

"What is?"

"This town. The Aboriginal word means that."

"Oh, right."

"What's that horse statue thing over there?" asked Bessy. They wandered over to it and read that it commemorated Gunsynd, a race horse that won the 1972 Cox Plate and came third in the Melbourne Cup and was known as the 'Goondiwindi Grey'. Paddo was still distracted from the call from his mother and Tom, as usual, was hungry. They were still 350 kilometres from Brisbane.

"I could eat a horse," Tom said. He then convinced them that they should all eat now, and then make "a dash" for Brisbane. Paddo said he didn't care and Bessy said she could eat, as she'd had very little breakfast. After a hamburger with beetroot, yet again, Tom took charge of the Troopy. He stuck to the speed limit as he went through the outskirts of town but put his foot down and tested the limits of the vehicle once he hit the highway. They only stopped momentarily at Toowoomba for a bathroom stop and found themselves in Brisbane at 3:30 pm, very satisfied with their journey. Bessy had rung ahead and booked cheap but, what she figured, good accommodation in West End.

Tom was happy to have a separate room. "Very good of you," Bessy said.

By this stage, Tom had complained a little, half joking but with a touch of truth, about being the odd one out. But he was more than happy to have his personal space and to be in his position. He suggested that after their massive car trip they should have an 'absence of direction' for the next few days. When this directive elicited no response, he took that as agreement. Bessy felt it was probably meaningless anyway and spontaneity would rule the day in any event. Tom was prone to changing his mind at the drop of a hat.

The accommodation would not break their bank accounts, although Bessy was starting to keep a closer eye on her funds. She had insisted on paying all of her own way, mostly. Paddo continually offered to pay but she would generally have none of that.

That first night, Bessy mentioned to Paddo that he hadn't spoken at all about the call he had received from his mother that morning. He was much quieter than usual and she had noticed he wasn't talking much at all. When she had asked him if he was feeling okay, he had just nodded. When Tom had asked him about his preference for something, he said he didn't care. Apart from helping with directions in Brisbane, he had virtually said nothing since Goondiwindi. Tom had raved on in the car about the races at Ascot, horses still on his mind, and then wanted to play a sort of trivia question and answer game. But he asked too many questions about sport and Paddo did not participate. Bessy switched to the simplicity of 'I spy with my little eye' with Tom for a good hour. Paddo stared out the window most of the time.

"Is everything alright with your mum?" she asked eventually. Paddo had just got out of the shower.

"Yes, she's fine."

He didn't seem to want to elaborate. Bessy had heard something about his dad when he was talking on the phone but she had been under the covers. She didn't let on she had been woken by the call and didn't want to press him for information. Bessy had not seen him so distant before. She wondered whether this distance was due to the space between him and his home, thousands of miles away.

They were both reading, tired out after their journey. Bessy had bought a book in Melbourne some time ago. Paddo read a book about Aboriginal Dreamtime that he'd bought in Bourke. Bessy attempted to make small talk during pauses between the pages, largely to no avail.

CHAPTER TWENTY-ONE

The Town of 1770, almost three weeks later

As they got out of the Troopy, the salty smell of the ocean and the feel of sand underfoot were familiar to Paddo and Tom. Bundaberg and the bustle of Brisbane had been left behind and this southern tip of the Great Barrier Reef was most definitely where they wanted to land. The smoothness in which their plan had been executed pleased them immensely. Bessy's face showed it. She was in love, on holiday, and seemingly, without a care in the world. The weeks in Brisbane and then several days in Bundaberg had gone by in a carefree way.

As if by providence they found a spot to pitch their tents right on the grass adjacent to the sand leading down to the water's edge. A row of tents along the strip allowed for two more and they were able to back the Troopy up next to their site. Tom had suggested one of the backpacker hostels but as soon as he saw the view across the shimmering water, he was overjoyed Bessy had convinced him it was time to camp once more.

They had decided to stay at 1770 because it was a far shorter drive than to the central and northern end of the reef, and there were no deadly marine stingers or crocodiles.

The weather promised to be dry and warm, and they found themselves spoilt for choice as to what to do. A priority was a day trip to Lady Musgrave Island, a small coral cay not far off shore. Snorkelling would be a first for each and they were excited to be able to swim the reefs around the island.

Paddo had long since returned to his usual self. He was quick to point out that Lady Musgrave Island was actually known as 'Wallaginji' by the local Aboriginal tribes and that it meant 'beautiful reef'. "I refuse to call it 'Lady Musgrave'."

In the last week in Brisbane, Tom had been sick for a few days with a stomach bug. As they set up camp, he told Paddo he was back to feeling himself again. "I'm okay, now. That was a nasty little bug. I'm glad I didn't give it to you. I'm sorry it slowed us down."

"It didn't help that you hit the bars in West End insanely hard and had a lot of late nights. You weren't looking after yourself," Paddo said, as he hammered a tent peg into the sand.

"Those craft beers were too good to pass up. You had a few yourself, I noticed, son." Tom snapped photos as the others worked.

"Yes. But I didn't overdo it. You tend to hit it too hard sometimes. You burn the candle at both ends and wonder why you end up in the dark."

"Well, as I say. I'm feeling myself again. I know that's not something *you* have to worry about."

"What?"

"Feeling yourself. Unlike me, you have someone to do that for you."

"Bessy, can you throw this nutcase in the water? Or better still, let's forget to pick him up on the boat on the way back tomorrow."

"Righto. Deal," Bessy said, as she set up the camp stove.

Paddo hadn't heard from his mother until a few days before they had got on the road again from Brisbane, and before they had reached Bundaberg. She told him that his father's test results were inconclusive but he seemed to be a little better. The enforced rest had certainly helped. Roger had come home for a while and taken some leave from work. Henry was expected to join them shortly and they were all going to take a few days break at their holiday house in Exmoor National Park in Somerset. Paddo thought that was a fabulous idea. It was a perfect retreat, tucked away in a small valley below the beautiful, rolling moors.

"What time do we have to be at the wharf tomorrow?" Paddo asked Bessy, as he draped the top layer over her tent.

"7:30."

"That's early."

"We can walk from here. We might want to go into town and get some food this afternoon. Something to eat for the morning."

"Do they supply lunch?"

"I think so. We're back before dinner."

After they had erected both tents and unpacked the Troopy, they decided to take a drive to Agnes Water, the neighbouring town, for supplies.

"I'd like to go for a swim. We haven't been swimming for ages," Tom said as soon as he got in the Troopy.

On the way, Bessy told them that Agnes Water is the northern most surfing beach along the entire east coast and that further north, the Great Barrier Reef prevents surfing beaches. "That's part of the reason they call it a barrier," she added. "So, now is your last opportunity to surf, unless we go south."

When they got to the beach, the conditions were calm with hardly any waves at all. They sunbathed for almost an hour before swimming. Tom produced a kite that he had bought in Brisbane but gave up on it after unsuccessful attempts to get it to stay in the air. Bessy suggested he try later in the week as it would be windy then. After getting some provisions at the local supermarket, they took a drive around the town before heading back to the site.

The next day they were up and cooking breakfast by 6 am. Bessy took charge of the small stove and washing up, while Paddo was allocated the minor task of packing one small bag for all of them with hats, sunscreen, extra tee-shirts and towels. Tom strolled along the water's edge and took more photos. When he returned just before they had to leave to catch the boat, Bessy gave him a mild blast for being lazy.

The crew called the passengers to board just before 7:30 and soon they were on their way for what would be almost an hour and a half trip to the island. Bessy handed two ginger lozenges to Paddo then placed the packet in front of Tom, telling him to take a couple. He smiled and shook his head. "I'm good. It's a bit early for sweets."

"They're not lollies, Tom. They're ginger tablets. They can help quell sea sickness."

"No thanks. I'll be right, matey." He gave her a smile and a wink.

Bessy put two in her mouth and Paddo said he'd give them a go.

The sky was blue and the water a gorgeous darker blue that varied in patches to clearer shades of turquoise, aqua and light blue. Bessy was so excited, she grabbed Paddo's upper arm, pulled him close and kissed him. Her hair blew around her face as they sat on the top deck. She thought how handsome and tanned he looked. Her mind sometimes wandered back to her flat in Flinders Street but now, it seemed like she was in another universe.

After about thirty minutes, the wind had picked up and the ride got somewhat rougher. Tom, who had been sitting in the seats just near them, got up and started to walk around, pacing up and down. Bessy didn't notice at first but then she thought he looked paler than usual. After about five minutes, he quickened his pace and darted out of sight, down the stairs.

"Where's the bathroom?" he asked one of the male attendants, with a tone of urgency to his voice. He pointed to where they were. Tom didn't have time to say thanks and went into a cold sweat when he saw they all had red occupied signs displayed.

A lady attendant came by and asked if he was feeling alright.

He could hardly speak. "Not really."

"Feeling a bit sick?"

"Yes."

"You will be okay. It's not normally as windy as this," she said. He felt anything but normal.

A toilet door opened. "Excuse me," Tom managed to say, pushing past a man almost before he had exited. Five minutes later he emerged, the pallor of his face evident to the lady attendant who returned to him.

"Sometimes we find if you stay stationary and look out at the horizon, it helps. We'll be there soon."

"Thanks."

"I'll get you some ginger tablets, if you like. Some say they help as well."

"Thank you. My friend has some. I think I'll go back on the top deck."

"Good idea. Let me know if I can help."

"Where're those bloody ginger tablets?" he said to Bessy. She reached into the bag and before she could say anything, he told her to give him three. By the time the island had come into sight, he felt better but his neck felt stiff from holding a constant, steady gaze at the horizon. Once the boat came to a complete stop and the motors were turned off, he felt relieved and had fully recovered.

"She's not just a pretty face, you know, Tom. You should know that by now. I took some tablets," Paddo said, with a smirk.

"Yes, well, it was too early for me to be thinking clearly."

"We don't want any burly in the water. People are going to be swimming there soon."

"Can you please give it a break!"

A male tour operator made some announcements and gave everyone on board a run-down of what would be involved over the course of the next five hours. Lunch would be provided at 12:30 pm and they might want to plan their day based upon the period before and after that.

Tom decided to pay extra for scuba diving off the boat. He was accompanied by three others but most people, including Paddo and Bessy, were content to snorkel. A few on board opted to catch reef fish instead on a separate, smaller boat. Another small boat would run trips to and from the island and the operator encouraged everyone to take the opportunity to wander around it, so long as they were back by 3 pm.

Tom listened to his final instructions for scuba diving. As he entered the crystal-clear water, a family of long tom fish swam by.

Bessy floated on top of spectacular coral formations, her face a mere few inches away from clown fish. Paddo hovered above giant sea turtles resting on the bottom only a couple of metres down. He motioned her over and they held hands, floating above the huge shelled creatures.

Separating, each ventured around the various edges of the coral, closer to the island.

Bessy returned to the boat a few times to rest, only to re-enter the water after a brief period. Everyone seemed to be having the time of their lives. As she sat on the deck, a woman told Bessy it was the best day of her life.

It was tempting to try and swim to the island but instead Paddo and Bessy took the small boat ride to conserve energy. Once on land, they wandered around the edges picking up shells and crushed, tiny bits of old dead coral, letting it run through their fingers. Tom soon appeared and took their photo.

After half an hour, they returned to the boat for lunch, enjoying fresh fruit, salads, cold meats and bread, all set out in a buffet style. Bessy and Paddo relaxed inside out of the midday sun. She stretched her legs out over him while he read brochures about the history of the island. Tom took the opportunity to snorkel, exploring the reefs not far from the edge of the island. Each dozed off on the way back before agreeing it was an absolute highlight of their journey thus far.

They were all asleep not long after the setting of the sun.

* * * *

Over the course of the next three days, they returned to Agnes Water for a swim more than once. Tom got to fly his kite. Paddo managed to body surf. Bessy read some more of her book and they all ate some delicious local seafood. On the third night, they enjoyed cocktails in a little bar in the town before strolling along the sand, stopping occasionally to lie down and gaze at the stars.

On the fourth day, the Troopy's rugged capabilities came in handy once again, when they visited Eurimbula National Park. A walking track led them to Ganoonga Noonga lookout, affording views across the swamps to the coast. As best as Paddo could work out, the name meant low grounds. In the course of the day, they came across stunning free spots to camp but of course, they had left all their gear behind.

By the next day, they knew it was time to decide on their next move. It would be a simple case of north or south. After a lazy morning and a big breakfast cooked at the camp, they reached a consensus to head south to the Sunshine Coast with the possibility of going even further to the Gold Coast. The glorious weather had contributed to their enjoyment so far. They hadn't seen rain for almost a month. Sunshine dwelled in each of their lives in more ways than one. Their thoughts were now influenced by the anticipation of where the next part of their road trip might lead them.

It was about 3 pm that afternoon when Paddo's phone rang from where it sat on the floor of the back of the Troopy. He was driving south and Bessy, who was asleep on the back seat, was awoken by it. Instinctively, she picked it up and answered it for him.

"Yes. This is Patrick's phone. Who's calling?" There was a pause and Bessy said, "Oh, yes. Hello. I'm sorry, he's just driving at the moment. Paddo …"

Paddo pulled over by the side of the road.

"He's just pulling over now," she said, clearing her hair from her face. "Here he is now. It's your mother," she said, handing him the phone. Bessy thought she could detect a sense of urgency in his mother's tone. She listened to the one-sided conversation.

"Hello, Mum … I'm fine. How are you?"

Paddo listened then for quite some time. He reached down and switched the ignition off.

He said, "Okay," three times, with sizeable gaps between each.

He looked straight ahead, blinking and thinking, as he listened.

Eventually came, "When?" and then, "Since when?" and, after a moment, "What did he say?" and "Are you sure?" and "I …." and then, "How is he?"

After more listening, he said, "How long did he say?" And then, "Mum, that's … Oh …" letting out a deep sigh.

Then came, "Mum, I know …" and then, "Yes, yes, of course. Yes. Of course. I will."

After another long pause, "I will let you know. We're in Queensland. Heading back towards Brisbane. Yes. Yes. I know. I'm sorry, too, not for me, of course. Please tell him… I don't want you to worry …"

Paddo was still staring straight ahead.

"I will have to call you back, probably in the morning. In the morning, your time. We're on the road. I love you, too." And he hung up.

He placed the phone on the dash and held the back of his hand to his mouth, slowly passing it across his lips. "That was my mum." He forgot Bessy already knew this and continued staring straight ahead.

Tom looked at him but resisted saying anything. He sensed Paddo was going to speak.

"He's got cancer. My Dad. It's bad. The doctors have given him three months."

For a moment, no one spoke. A semi-trailer whistled by and the whole Troopy shook.

"Can I get in the front, Tom?" Bessy said.

"Don't get out here!" Paddo said abruptly.

He started up the Troopy.

"Paddo!" Tom said.

"I'm not going to drive, relax would you! I'm just going to pull up here."

"Let's go back into town. I don't want us driving now," Bessy said.

Paddo didn't respond. He pulled up and switched the engine off. He got out and started walking in the direction they were going but then stopped about twenty metres away. They were all out of the car now.

Bessy followed Paddo who was staring at the road. She held him but he didn't hold her back at first. He felt rigid and cold so she grabbed his hand. Finally he relaxed. And then he held her. He didn't say anything. He started to cry but he quickly wiped some tears away and she could see he was trying to pull himself together. She led him back to the car.

Tom did a u-turn and they were back in Maryborough in five minutes. He pulled up in front of the very first motel he saw, went in and checked them all in. They only had the one room with three beds. Bessy, who had stayed in the car with Paddo, said that was fine.

Paddo stretched out on the bed and Bessy took his shoes off. Tom left, saying he would be back in ten minutes.

Bessy sat beside Paddo and ran her hands through his hair slowly.

"What did your mum say?" she said softly. "It's alright, if you don't want to talk."

"I can talk."

"That's terrible news, Paddo, I am so sorry," she said.

"Yep."

She waited and did not want to press him for details. His eyes were elsewhere.

"He, ah, he got sick, again, when they went to Exmoor, apparently. The holiday house. Quite badly. He didn't last a day and they had to come back. He was jaundiced the week before but felt okay." He got up and got a drink of water. After a sip, he sat on the edge of the bed. "It then turned into vomiting apparently and other things. He had already lost weight."

"Didn't you say he had some tests?"

"Yes, but when he was back in Norwich they followed it with an MRI and something else, I think she said, like an angiogram. The cancer has grown quickly and spread through vital blood vessels, apparently. I don't think my mother has or knows all the details. I don't know."

"Oh, Paddo. That's awful."

"Yes."

"Did she say what type it is? The cancer?"

"Pancreatic."

Bessy got some water and sat back on the bed. "How is your mother holding up?"

"It's hard to tell. She is heavily reliant upon my father and dotes on him. It's a tragedy for her, let alone my father."

"And your brother?"

"She didn't mention Roger. I didn't think to ask."

"It will come as a shock, for everyone."

"It will."

"Is your father in pain?"

"I think, a bit. But he's tough."

They sat together without saying too much more and eventually Tom returned. He had some snacks, a big bottle of water and a newspaper. He opened some peanuts and gave Paddo a hug.

"I'm sorry, old son," he said.

"Thanks."

Tom asked if he could turn the TV on and Paddo said of course. They watched the news and then flicked the channel to a game show and answered some of the questions. Tom eventually offered to go and get some takeaway Chinese but Bessy and Paddo said they weren't hungry. He was gone for about an hour.

By the time he got back, they were asleep in their beds.

* * * *

The weather was overcast the next morning and cooler. They didn't discuss any plans, other than what time everyone was happy to check out.

"Whenever," came Paddo's response, striking a familiar chord to how his mood had been some weeks back.

Tom started the Troopy without a word about where they were heading. Bessy and Tom had both silently concluded they should stick to the plan to go south to the Sunshine Coast. Exactly where had never been decided. By the time they reached Gympie, Paddo hadn't said a word, other than that he was feeling "alright". From the back, Bessy chatted to Tom about whether he had any ideas where to stay on the Sunshine Coast.

"Do you think we should stop at Noosa or Mooloolaba?" asked Bessy.

"I'd be happy to just stop at a bar," he replied, trying to lighten the air.

"We can do both, can't we?" replied Bessy. "What do you reckon, Paddo?"

"It doesn't bother me."

It stayed that way until near the Noosa turn off.

"It's executive decision time, folks. Who is going to be the executive, Paddo?" Tom said.

"I told you, I don't give a shit!"

"Paddo!" Bessy said.

"I'm sorry," he said after a while, staring out the window.

The exit passed and Tom said, "I didn't want to go there anyway. Too crowded, I reckon."

Tom and Bessy concluded almost telepathically that it was best they make the decisions with as minimal fuss as possible. When Tom drove into Mooloolaba, he headed straight for the beachside caravan park, hoping a camp site was available. He was very pleased to be informed by the kindly lady in the office they had the choice of two back-row sites and Tom told her they would be happy with either. She told him to drive down and take the one they preferred.

"This one seems fine," Bessy said and they set up two small tents close together within the space allocated.

"It's beautiful here," Paddo said softly, not long into the set-up. Bessy was pleased just to hear something remotely positive come out his mouth.

The overcast sky had dissolved into blue but the beach was windy and not many people were in the water. Tom decided to go for a walk and headed off in the direction of the Esplanade to check out the cafés and shops.

Bessy led Paddo around to the river and along the wharf precinct. She tried to make him laugh by saying it was really windy and told him her father used to say, "It is so windy it would blow a dog off a chain." But then she cursed herself under her breath for mentioning her father at this sad time.

They strolled slowly and fairly aimlessly through a candy store, a bag shop and a tourist shop. Bessy tried on a few hats and laughed but Paddo said, "Let's keep moving."

When Bessy spotted a pub on the river at the far end of the wharfed area, she said she was thirsty and she grabbed his hand and picked up her pace. His arm was loose and his hand felt cold and lifeless. Leading him to a table, she then went to the bar and brought back two beers. They sat overlooking the river.

Paddo asked Bessy what the date was. She told him, then asked, "Why do you want to know?"

He took the top off the beer and sighed, peering out across the shimmering water. "I told Mum I would come home." He turned to Bessy, looking at her closely now.

Bessy felt like he had been looking through her since late yesterday. But this look was different. She nodded and took a sip as well. "That's understandable," she said, after a while. She felt a little scared and her voice quivered a fraction when she said it. *Now is not the time to think of yourself,* she thought.

"She asked me."

"Of course, she would. She needs you; you're her son."

"It's not urgent. Well, I guess in some ways it is."

"You said they gave him three months. Sounds urgent to me."

"It could be longer."

"You can't risk these things, Paddo. You'd never forgive yourself."

"I know."

"Family is the most important thing." Bessy was feeling good she was able to be there for him. But she now wondered how long they had together.

"I know. But you have become important to me, too," he said. Tears welled in his eyes.

She reached out and put her hand on his. "I understand if you need to go. Of course, I do. It's very important."

"I want to go but I don't want to go."

"You have to do what's right. Right in your heart."

"That means …" He shook his head, removed his hand from hers, unable to finish saying what he was thinking. He rubbed his sore, blood-shot eyes.

Bessy started to cry but gathered herself.

"I didn't sleep last night," he said. "I couldn't stop thinking."

"You need to rest."

"I need to decide."

"You need to go."

"I don't want to lose you," he said.

She smiled. "Paddo, you won't lose me."

"I might and ... I don't want that ... no matter what. No matter what." He started to choke up.

"We can work this out. The two of us."

"You don't understand." He shook his head. "I feel like ... like I've let my father down. I've been so selfish." He could hardly get the words out, holding back the tears.

"No. No you haven't," she said.

"Yes I have! I haven't told you, but he asked me to think about helping him. Helping him with his work, when I got back." He burst into uncontrollable crying now. "Now it's too bloody late," he said, turning away.

"Paddo ..."

"No, Bessy." He looked at her again. "I've been doing *nothing* with my life for years except trying to have a good time, thinking of myself the whole time. And he told me he was getting tired. I have made a mistake by not helping him earlier."

"Don't do this to yourself, Paddo."

He stopped talking and held his hand against his forehead, face down, his elbow on the small round table propping up his head. He breathed heavily in and out and sniffed, slowly trying to recover.

She sat in silence for the moment, giving him the space to deal with his grief.

When he went to wipe his dripping nose, his arm bumped his beer and it fell, crashing to the boardwalk below. "Christ!" he said, utter despair returning to his face.

"It doesn't matter," she said, "Don't worry about it!"

He couldn't move at all now, as if he had given up. The young lady behind the bar soon appeared and cleaned it up and asked if she could deliver another.

When he seemed unable to answer, Bessy said, "Thank you so much," and smiled at her.

The beer was delivered to the table and they sat in silence again for a moment, watching rowers on the river paddling in the sun. He sipped his beer slowly now.

"I love you," he said.

She wasn't scared any more. "I love you too."

CHAPTER TWENTY-TWO

Paddo was woken by the chirping of the birds shortly after sunrise. He quietly arose, put on his swimmers, grabbed a towel, unzipped the tent and went outside.

"Where are you going?" Bessy called from inside the tent. He crouched down and put his head inside.

"Just for a swim." Bessy still had her head on the pillow. He zipped the tent back up and she heard him wander off. Tom was sleeping in Bessy's single tent.

It was a still morning and yesterday's wind had completely vanished. He went down to the sand and laid his towel out and sat for a while. *A brand new day*, he thought, and what would it bring? He resolved not to think too much but he knew the time for more thinking had arrived. He walked down to the edge of the water which felt cool but not cold, so he waded in and swam out a good distance. The water was flat with only a few gentle waves breaking on the edge of the sand. It was clean and refreshing, and felt good on his skin. He looked back toward the beach where the sunlight was slowly hitting the tips of the trees that lined the shore. Hardly anyone was around. *What a beautiful place to live*, he thought. But then he thought of Norwich.

When he got out he started a slow jog up the beach. He headed in the direction of the breakwater and walked out over the rocks and on top to see the view of the river mouth. The water was a beautiful colour and the tide was gently rising. A group of young boys fishing off the rocks on the riverside said hello. A fishing trawler was making its way out of the mouth and out to sea.

Then he jogged in the opposite direction for a good distance before jogging back and slowing to a walk as he headed up the beach to his towel. He was glad that his head felt lighter than yesterday. He sat on his towel and stared at the fishing trawler on the horizon, until he could no longer see it. By the time he got up and shook the sand off his towel, he had made some decisions.

Tom was up cooking breakfast. "Morning, son," he said, as Paddo arrived back at camp. "How was the water?"

"Brilliant."

"Good. Bacon?"

"Why not. Thanks."

He went into the tent and found Bessy still asleep. He snuggled up to her.

"Good morning," he said. She could smell the salt water on his skin and in his hair.

She rolled over. "What time is it?" she said, in a sleepy voice.

"I don't really know," he replied. He jumped up and said it was a beautiful day.

"Oh, that's good," she said. She was awake enough to notice he seemed happier.

Paddo poured some fresh water into a billy can and put it on the burner. The smell of the bacon cooking drew Bessy from the tent. Although Tom didn't cook much, he did a good job when he did. "Will praising you make you cook for us more often, Tom?" Bessy asked when they sat down to eat.

"I can't promise anything, my dear, except to be at your humble service as my time may allow. Keeping the compliments flowing will only assist the cause."

"Right."

"Any plans for today, Paddo?" asked Tom, feeling in a risky, if not bold mood, as he dished out. He thought he would test the water, given Paddo had been in the water and seemed refreshed as a result.

"Um, maybe. I'm open to ideas. Maybe we could head up to Noosa for the day. I'd like to see it; what do you think?"

"Sure," Tom said. "We could leave the set-up here. I don't fancy packing up."

"Bessy?" Paddo said.

"I'm happy to do that. It sounds like a fun place. I used to have a friend at school who went on a holiday there once. But it was a long time ago."

After securing the tents as best they could and cleaning up, they climbed into the Troopy. When Tom paid the lady at the office on the way out, he said they would like to stay at least one more night. She mentioned they might want to visit the Eumundi Markets as well. She said it wasn't far from Noosa and he thanked her for the tip.

Tom continued his driving stint while Paddo sat in the back and looked at his phone. Soon they were at Noosa and as it was still early, they had little trouble finding a parking spot. They had no expectations, as other things had occupied their minds. Noosa felt very laid back, something they had all picked up on as soon as they hit the street.

"The Eumundi Markets sound good from what I've read online but they close early afternoon," Paddo said. They had a look at the beach and decided Mooloolaba was better.

They walked to the river mouth, then went back to the Troopy so they could drive to the development around the river and see the beautiful big houses. "What a place to live," Bessy said. "Wow."

The thought of doing some clothes shopping crossed Bessy's mind but Tom suggested, somewhat sensibly, they might want to wait for the markets. "Smart thinking," Bessy said. "It looks a little exy here."

As time was at a premium if they were to make the markets, they decided to drive up to the headland instead of heading back to the main street to take the seaside boardwalk, although it looked very tempting. They chose the shortest of the walks through the rainforest and relegated the longer walks to another time, if they ever made it back. Tom took photos of some huge trees with Paddo and Bessy standing in front. He snapped a whole series of photos of the scenic views of the coast and seemed very pleased with his efforts.

By the time they arrived at Eumundi, some of the stallholders looked like they were packing up but most of the market was still in full swing.

"What a quaint, cute little town," Bessy said. "I love it."

There were big fig trees and historic timber buildings, many of which embodied the distinctive Queenslander style with colonial-themed architecture and iron roofing. Paddo commented on the artistic feel the town and the market itself conveyed, and on the combination of alternative culture, Aboriginal heritage and farming themes.

Tom's first priority was eating and he enjoyed some Malay food with sweet chilli noodles as he wandered separately from stall to stall. Paddo noticed a small framed piece of Aboriginal art in the form of an original painting. He thought he could fit it in his bag so he bought it.

Bessy tried on several hats before settling for one that was a dusty grey-blue colour and which flopped to the side but held its shape. This time Paddo was willing to stop and let her try on hats before deciding on the one she wanted. They spent time looking at the bangles and local hand-crafted jewellery. Paddo bought her a rose-gold bangle. He bought himself a tee-shirt that had 'Eumundi Markets' on it and a thin, dark-brown leather bracelet tie for his wrist that looked good on his tanned arm. Bessy held a matching necklace up to him. "It says here on the label it is thought to give protection against evil, danger and disease, in the tradition of an ancient amulet."

"I'll take ten of them, then," he said jokingly.

Soon they ran into Tom. He had a small paper bag. "What did you get?" asked Bessy.

He showed them a small wooden bowl. "Feel how light it is."

Bessy turned it upside down and admired its smoothness and simple shape.

"What's the wood?" Paddo said.

"Australian red cedar. *Toona Australis.*"

"Beautiful. It's a glorious colour. You've already eaten, haven't you?" Bessy asked him.

"Just a snack. I can eat again."

"You can always eat again. Where on earth do you put it?"

"Don't answer that question," Paddo said.

They headed into the main street and had a counter lunch at a pub. Bessy said she would drive back if the boys wanted to have a few beers and they took up her generous offer. Tom wanted to try the local Eumundi lager – maybe several – if it was any good. He found it was very refreshing and convinced Bessy to try the Eumundi light.

The late lunch turned into a relaxing afternoon and they sat and chatted about Noosa and the markets and Mooloolaba. It was late afternoon by the time they got back to the camp site. Tom immediately took off and went for a swim.

Paddo suggested he and Bessy have a nap in the tent but it was too hot and stuffy. Instead, they sat in the camp chairs and Paddo boiled the billy to make them both tea.

"Have you thought any more about what we talked about yesterday?" Bessy asked.

"You mean going back to Norwich?"

"Yes." She waited.

He took a sip of his tea. "I want you to come with me."

She hadn't known what to expect but it certainly wasn't that. All day she had been trying to put the whole thing out of her head. She was only partially successful. "I don't think I can."

"You don't want to?"

"No. I mean, yes I do. Of course I do. I mean, I don't think I can."

"Why not?"

"Well, I don't have that much money left, for one."

"I have money. That's not an issue."

"It's an issue for me. That's not the only thing."

"Tell me."

"Well, I've got the flat, remember. The lease. I can't just walk away from that."

"Did you renew the lease? Is it within term?"

"It's got a month to run. Hang on." She thought for a moment and checked the calendar on her phone. "It expires in three weeks, I think."

"That's fine, then. That's not a problem."

"Paddo, have you thought this through? You have had some bad news. Maybe you should take the time to think a bit more."

"I know I love you, Bessy."

"That's why we can't let emotion take control over rationality. There's more to decide than things that just affect us, isn't there?" she asked.

He put the tea down on the sand and scratched his head. "You mean Tom?"

"Well, yes. And the Troopy and that I have to get back to Melbourne, at some point."

"Hmm," he said, half nodding in acknowledgement.

"Have you spoken with Tom?"

"Not really."

"You probably should," she said, feeling compelled to be wise, but she felt just as torn and was forcing herself to be the necessary voice of reason.

"Yes. I guess I should."

"What do you think he will want to do?"

"About staying?"

"Yes."

"I'm not sure. But he will be upfront with me. He's a pretty decisive guy, and flexible."

"I think you should talk to him soon. Tonight, even."

"You're right."

"Did you tell your mother when you will be back?"

"I said I would call her, when I knew."

"If we went back to Brisbane, you could fly out from there. I could fly to Melbourne."

"What about Tom?"

"That's why you should talk to him."

"If you are not going to come with me, I'll have to come back and get you. You know that?"

"Let's discuss that after you talk to Tom."

"Where the hell is he?"

"Patience, Paddo. Patience."

When Tom returned, Bessy went and had a shower. She wanted to wash her hair. There would be no rush in returning to the camp. Paddo had decided they should all go to the surf club for dinner but she fully expected he would want to talk to Tom before that.

"How was the water?" Paddo asked.

"Beautiful," replied Tom, towelling his hair. "This is a top spot. I love that beach. It's my favourite, so far."

"We've seen some good beaches, that's for sure."

"Oh yeah. Beats the crap out of Brighton."

"I reckon we go to the surf club for dinner."

"Great. I could eat the crotch out of a low-flying crow."

Paddo sat down in the camp chair. "Look Tom, I've been thinking—"

"Didn't I tell you not to do that? It's dangerous." Tom placed his towel over the tent rope.

"Yes, well. I don't always take your advice."

"I've noticed."

Tom sat down in the other chair. He grabbed a bottle of water.

"I think I need to go back to Norwich. I told my mother I would."

"Sounds like you should."

"I don't know how long, well, they said three months."

"Whether it's three months or three years, Paddo, your dad's unwell. Man, you need to see him."

"That's what I'm thinking."

"How soon can you get a flight?"

"I haven't looked. But I thought if we head back to Brisbane, tomorrow, maybe, I could get on the next flight out."

"You gotta go, son. There is no question about that."

"But what about you?"

"What do you mean, what about me?"

"Well, I feel a bit bad about it."

"What are talking about? We've had a smashing time, you and me. And Bessy. It's her, son, not me, you should think about."

"She's fine. I think. I've asked her to come but she can't."

"That's right, I would have thought. She had a life before you."

"I know. Bessy has mentioned a few things I should be aware of."

"She's a magnificent girl, son. I'm envious to tell you the truth. You can't take her but whatever you do, and I mean *whatever* you do, don't let her go. You'll be lucky to ever find another like her."

"Thanks. I know. It's not how I want it."

"Be grateful for what you have. That you're young, you know. You need to handle this shit sandwich for now."

"What will you do?"

"Run amuck, I expect. Catch a flight to South America."

"Seriously."

"I am being serious."

"You can keep the Troopy."

"I can sell it. You're entitled to half. Although, I could forfeit your share for early desertion."

"The money's not important."

"I'll make a decision after you've gone. You leave it to me. You don't need to be concerned about it."

"Whatever you want to do is fine by me."

"Actually, I might go to New Zealand. Be a shame to miss it when I'm down this far already. Or Tasmania. In that case, I will sell the Troopy. We've given it a good bashing you know."

"Sounds great." Paddo was very relieved Tom was taking it all so well.

"I'm going to get a six-pack from the bottlo," Tom said. He'd picked up the term 'bottlo' some time back and was adapting to the 'lingo' nicely by now. "I'll be back in a jiffy, mate. We can have a few stubbies in this bonza spot before dinner. What do you think?"

"Yep. Sounds good. I'll shout you some more beers at dinner."

After Paddo had a shower, he filled Bessy in about his conversation with Tom who arrived shortly after with the beers. They sat and chatted while they had a drink.

"Do you have a passport, Bessy?" asked Tom.

"No."

"Best apply for one soon, I reckon," he said.

"I will," she said. "When I get back to Melbourne."

They all had a sense that this may be the last night of their journey together. Tomorrow would see new directional tasks and events to arrange. As they walked to the surf club, there seemed to be an unspoken understanding to make no more mention of anything significant. Anything 'serious' was somehow off the agenda, at least for the moment.

They took their time before ordering food. The surf club walls were adorned with photos of past surfing greats and an impressive display of long Malibu-style surfboards. They sat on the outside deck overlooking the ocean and drank their beers until they thought it was wise to eat something.

After their meals, they went to a cocktail bar on the Esplanade and got seriously happy.

* * * *

It wasn't until 11 am the next day when their eyelids opened, and only then because of the sun beating down on the tent. It meant they had to pay the full charge for the night, which was a minor inconvenience in comparison to the impossibility of an early departure. Their actions of the night before caused memory loss and headaches but there were absolutely no regrets.

They hit Brisbane by 3:30 pm. Incapable of making a decision about where to stay, they relied on what they knew and stayed in the same place as before, in West End.

CHAPTER TWENTY-THREE

"Hello. Mum?"

"Patrick?"

"Hello. How are you?"

"I'm good."

"How is Dad?"

"He's sleeping."

"How has he been?"

"The doctor was here this morning. He's very tired. Not talking very much. He was quite ill yesterday. He's having trouble keeping anything down."

"What did the doctor say?"

"Not a lot. That he should rest. He's been telling me about some drugs but I'm not taking it all in. I'm picking some prescriptions up tomorrow."

"Is he in pain?"

"I think he is at times. It upsets me."

"Look, Mum. I'm booked on a flight tomorrow night. It's out of Brisbane. That puts me at Heathrow, Tuesday morning, your time."

"Oh, that's wonderful. Thank you, so much. I will let your father know. Hopefully, that news will lift him."

"Yes. I hope so, too."

"Do you want me to pick you up?"

"No. You stay with Dad. The train is fine. It's easy. You don't need to worry about anything. I will just see you at the house when I get there. It'll be in the afternoon."

"Oh, I can't wait to give you a hug. I've missed you. We all have."

"I've missed you too, Mum."

"Well, I'm sorry you have to cut your trip short, Patrick."

"Mum, it's fine."

"Call me from the airport when you arrive. So I know."

"Okay. Will do. Give my love to Dad. And tell him I'll be there soon."

"Bye. Love you."

Bessy had decided to fly to Melbourne the morning after Paddo's flight. It would be her first time on a plane but she was not looking forward to it. Tom had decided he wouldn't be boarding any planes until well after the other two had gone.

"When I get to England, I'm going to assess the situation with Dad. I want to return here if I can and bring you back with me," Paddo said to Bessy, soon after he got off the phone.

"That doesn't make sense."

"I don't care. It doesn't have to make sense, unless you don't want to come. Then, I agree."

"I do want to."

"Then, just let me do what I want to do."

"But Paddo, your mother will want and need you there. Your father may be too ill for you to leave."

"I'm not coming back to stay. I'm coming back to make sure ..."

"Why don't I just come later? Or don't you think I'm capable of coming over by myself?"

"That's not it."

"I would feel guilty bringing you out here again. I'm not a child."

In the afternoon, Paddo went for a long walk. He needed to clear his mind and do some more thinking. He walked around the streets of the city's inner west until he almost got lost. Bessy cleaned out her bag, all the while tossing things over in her mind. When Paddo returned, he asked her if she would like to go out for dinner. Tom stayed in the hostel.

A Greek restaurant was the nearest of an array of dining options and it was an easy and quick choice. Paddo put on the best clothes he had. Bessy wore one of the two dresses she had with her and her best shoes. He ordered a bottle of red wine, finding one on the drinks menu from a vineyard they had visited in South Australia. "What a long time ago that seems now," he said.

He extended his hand across the table and held her fingers. He touched the ring her mother gave her.

"We have had a lot on our minds," he said.

"Yes, we have."

"I want to ask you a question, if you don't mind," he said.

"Why would I mind?"

"I've been thinking about what's important. About everything, really. About us. About our future. About what's sensible and what's right. Everything you've said."

"Sounds like a lot," she said and smiled.

He paused.

"Will you, Bessy O'Halloran, marry me?"

Bessy smiled again and tilted her head. She'd had an inkling that he might say this at some point but not now.

"You don't mean now, do you?"

"No. When we are ready. When *you* are ready."

"Then, yes. I will, Patrick."

His hand was still on hers. He picked it up and kissed it. They laughed. Then she cried.

After dinner they left before finishing the bottle of wine, returned to their room at the hostel and made love, holding each other, knowing distance was soon to enter their lives.

* * * *

The next morning, Tom asked what time he needed to drop Paddo at the airport.

"If we leave here at 4, that should be plenty of time," Paddo said.

"I'll do the same for you tomorrow as well, Bessy. What time?"

"The flight is at 11:30 am," replied Bessy.

"Tom, there is one other favour I want to ask before I leave. But you don't have to do it, until later," said Paddo.

"What's that, son?"

"I'd like you to be best man at our wedding."

"At *our* wedding? I can't be both best man and groom. I don't remember you asking me to marry you."

"At Bessy's and my wedding, you fool!"

"Oh, yes. Of course. It would be an honour. Congratulations, fools!" He kissed Bessy and shook Paddo's hand. "Where are the cigars? Oh, that's for children, isn't it? Babies, and all that. Wow! You know, Bessy. I told him not to fall in love. But, that's before I knew you. Hey, that's brilliant news! Good on you!"

"Thanks Tom," Bessy said.

They went back to the other room and Bessy helped Paddo with the final stages of his packing.

"What's your mother going to say? She hasn't met me. Does she know I even exist?"

"She's about to find out," he replied, fiddling with his shaving bag and tossing in a few items.

"The first thing she's going to ask is how long have you known her. And then she'll say, that's not long enough," Bessy said.

"It's not up to her. We may not have known each other all that long but we've gotten to know each other very well and long enough to know. And that's what I'll be telling her."

"The poor woman. She has a lot on her plate."

"She needs some good news."

"Well, I hope she takes it like that."

Paddo stopped what he was doing for a moment like he'd had a revelation. "You know what? She will because my father will. It will make him happy – that I'm happy. That I have met someone who makes me happy. That I can share this news with him. It will give him a reason to carry on. I want him to meet you."

"I will need to get lots of things done."

"When I get home, I will send you the money." He returned to something in his bag.

"What money?"

"Well, I'm thinking you're right about coming over by yourself. It does make more sense. I will send the money for the flight."

"You don't have to."

"I thought you said you were running short."

"I should get the money back from my bond on the flat."

"You're going to need the money sooner than that, Bessy."

"Maybe."

"Bess, money is not an issue. I have had a trust fund set up for my benefit since I was a kid. I don't get any choice. I get money from that, whether I want it or not. Just let me do it. I have never spent much of it because I've never really found much I wanted to spend it on, until now. What's the time?"

"It's 3:30."

He squeezed some final things into his bag then unfolded some paper details of the flight.

"I'm sorry I haven't given you a ring."

"Don't be silly."

"When you come to Norwich, we will get one then. That's something to look forward to. You can take your time, then. And choose." He gave her a kiss on the forehead. Bessy hit the point where she knew she was going to spend the next few hours in tears. She felt a lump in her throat emerging and tried to control it.

"Let's go," he said.

The drive to the airport took just under forty minutes. They discussed the ins and outs of parking or just dropping Paddo off, and Paddo insisted that there was simply no point in everyone going to the terminal.

"I agree," Tom said. "A quick goodbye is a good goodbye."

It was only Bessy who found that decision hard. But she was choked up and things were moving far too quickly. She could not offer proper resistance. Before she knew it, Tom had pulled up in the drop-off zone. Bessy was annoyed he had been so incredibly efficient.

"Better make it quick, Bess," Tom said, glancing at her in the back seat. He shook Paddo's hand. "I'll see you on the flip side of the globe.

Safe travels, son," he said. They gave each other a hug in the front seats before Paddo stepped onto the curb side.

Bessy got out. She put her arms around him and stood on her tippy toes and squeezed him hard.

"I've got to go, darling," he said.

She let go and nodded, wiping away the tears.

"I love you. I will call you," he said.

He moved away after getting his bags out of the back. She ran to him and kissed him again. Tom looked on and smiled. Paddo went through the glass doors and Bessy got back in the front seat.

Tom had left the motor running and she said, "Thanks, Tom," and grabbed a tissue while he manoeuvred the Troopy back into the traffic.

* * * *

The next day, Tom told Bessy he would park the car at the domestic airport car park.

"Why? You don't need to go to that trouble, Tom."

"We'll get you out there early. You've never been on a flight before and I want to be there, just in case you have any questions."

"That's nice of you, Tom."

"Besides, you told me you wanted to see me do something nice and I believe charity begins at home."

"Have you spent that $600 the priest gave you yet?"

"You made me think when you said I had to grow up. I'm going to post a bank cheque for the lot back to Draper with a letter saying give it to Coral as a bonus and see if that helps the relationship. It will make him think. It's been troubling me."

"Good to hear, Tom."

Soon they were at the airport. Tom had already run through the pitfalls of security and what she could take in carry-on luggage and, after helping her print the boarding pass and self-checking the cabin baggage, all he had to do was point her in the direction of the scanners.

"Thank you for being such a wonderful friend, Tom, and a brilliant travelling companion. You mean the world to me."

"Don't give it a second thought. It's been fabulous fun, Bess. We were just very, very lucky to have met you."

"Oh, thank you. But I'm the lucky one."

Tom kissed her on the cheek and they hugged.

"I will see you next in your country," Bessy said.

"You will," he said.

Tom had got her there in good time and she lined up to go through security. She waved at him with an excited smile as he left.

She felt like a child at her first day at school in some ways and she was soon in the air, reading the in-flight magazine. Allowing herself the space to enjoy the journey without tossing over in her head everything that had happened, she knew there would be time for that later. The next flight would be to England but that seemed a fantasy. It was true, she reminded herself, not fantasy, and it was time to embrace it. In the first time in a long time, she was by herself but this time it was different. This time, she did not feel alone.

The flight arrived at Tullamarine on time. Bag collection went smoothly and she was at her apartment shortly before 5 pm. The place smelled musty. She put a chair against the front door to let some air in while she emptied her bag on the floor.

She grabbed her phone and sat on the floor in the lounge room, near the front door.

"Hello."

"Ah yes, ah."

"Is that you, you old girl?"

"Whosa calling me old?"

"Who indeed?"

"Bessy. Is thata you? Oh, my God! I don't know, I never hear from you."

"Ha! How are you, Abriana?"

"I'm a good. But whata you do, where are you?"

"I'm home."

"Home?"

"In Melbourne. I got in this afternoon. I flew from Brisbane."

"You flew. Oh, that's wonderful."

"You're good?"

"So, so. The business, she's okay."

"That's good."

"Where did you go?"

"A few places. We ended up in Queensland. Swimming with fish."

"Oh, you lucky! You must be happy."

"I am."

"Is your boy there?"

"No."

"No?"

"He's gone back to England."

"Oh, so soon?"

"His father is ill. He's not long found out."

"Oh, that'sa bad news. Sorry to hear."

"Yes. It is sad. But he's a good man, Abriana."

"Yes. Yes."

"He left yesterday."

"Okay. What is you do, what happens now, for you? Do you need work?"

"I don't think so."

"You know you can come back to us."

"I have some news for you!"

"News?"

"Yes. He asked me to marry him."

"No!"

Bessy laughed. "Yes. And I said, yes."

"Ah, my dear, is a too good a news. I can't a believe it! Oh, I must see you."

"Yes, I will call you again soon."

"But he's a gone, to his home?"

"Yes. His mother needs him too."

"Ah, what an angel."

"I said I would meet him, in England."

"Okay. When you go?"

"I don't know exactly. Maybe three weeks."

"Lovely. Lovely."

"I will call you, before I go."

"You do, please. Oh, I am so happy for you."

"Thanks. Say hi to Lino."

"Yes. Yes. I will. Bye."

* * * *

"Dad," Paddo said softly again. It was so quiet. The sun was streaming in through the window, filling the room with a soft, yellow light. He could hear the second hand on the clock on the wall ticking over. "Dad," he said again. Nothing. "Mum, we should just leave him."

"The doctor said to wake him, if he sleeps too long."

"I thought he said he should rest."

"Yes. But not all the time. He needs to eat and drink. Lachlan. Lachlan, dear. Patrick is here."

He half opened one eye. Then the other.

"Hello, Dad."

A smile. He tried to manoeuvre himself up higher on the pillow.

"Here," said Miriam trying to help him.

"Leave it, I can do it," he said a little sharply.

She pulled away, reluctantly accepting his wish and shook her head.

"Hey. How was your trip to Australia?"

"Brilliant. Just brilliant."

"Oh, that's good. I knew you would like it."

He started to cough and raised his head. He had trouble clearing his throat. Paddo noticed a bucket beside the bed.

"Do you need the bucket, darling?"

"No."

He rested his head back on the pillow.

"It's a bit of a shit sight to come back to. Sorry about that."

"I'm just glad to see you, Dad."

"I'm glad to see you, too. Tell me about it. Your trip."

"Ah, well, we got around a bit. It's a big country, you know. We got to Sydney, Melbourne, we went to Adelaide, Brisbane, a lot of places in between. A bit of the outback, the reef."

"That sounds really good."

"We bought a car. Got quite a bit of use in the end. In fact, my friend Tom still has it, unless he's sold it by now."

Paddo could see that his father was dying. He had prepared himself for this, but nothing could prepare him for the harsh reality of looking into his father's eyes. He didn't know what to say next. He didn't want to talk about doctors or anything like that. There was no good news there. His father had diverted his eyes, almost as if he was looking at the clock on the wall.

"I have some news for you both. It's good news." He looked at his mother. Lachlan didn't move his head but his eyes moved back to Paddo.

"What is it?" asked Miriam.

"I met a girl in Australia. And I love her. I've asked her to marry me."

Lachlan smiled. His eyes widened.

"What? Why didn't you tell me?" asked Miriam.

"I'm telling you now, Mum. I wanted to wait and tell you and Dad at the same time."

"That's wonderful, Patrick, really wonderful," Lachlan said.

Miriam scratched her head. "What does she do?" she asked.

Paddo looked at his father. "Thanks, Dad. I'm very happy. She's a lovely girl."

"When can I meet her?" asked Lachlan.

"Soon. I hope. She's gone back to Melbourne to get some things sorted out. She's going to fly over in a few weeks."

"Oh, my boy. I'm proud of you!"

Paddo was amazed at how much weight his father had lost and how much he had aged. But he was so pleased that his news made him happy.

"What's her name?" asked Miriam.

"Bessy. Her full name is Beatrice O'Halloran."

"How long have you known her?"

"Long enough for us to know we want to get married. We travelled together."

"I thought you were travelling with Tom."

"The three of us travelled together." He could tell she either disapproved or didn't understand or both, just by the look on her face.

"I think your father needs to rest now."

"I'm fine," Lachlan protested.

He coughed and then he asked for a glass of water which Miriam went into the kitchen to fetch. Lachlan placed his hand inside Paddo's hand. He looked at his son. "Thank you for coming back," he said.

"Dad, I got here as quick as I could."

"I know and I appreciate it. You show me this girl. That's what I want."

Paddo wiped tears from his own eyes.

"The doctors have given me no chance. I told them not to bullshit me. Or I'd sack them. The lot of them. There's plenty of money. You won't have to worry."

"I don't care about the money."

"I know you don't. Don't lose that. But hey," he poked him in the ribs, "don't lose the money, either."

Miriam returned and passed him the water. "Thank you, love."

"Have you discussed a date?" Miriam asked Paddo.

"Not yet."

"But she is coming here?"

"Yes."

"You will live here?"

"I expect so. She doesn't really have a lot to hold her in Australia."

"What about her parents?"

"They died some time ago, Mum."

"Oh." She began to say something but then stopped herself, her mind still processing her son's news and whether it was indeed good.

"She has some sisters and a brother. But they are much older. She doesn't keep in contact. Well, they don't keep in contact with her."

"Why?"

"You can ask her when you get to know her."

Miriam got up and drew the window shut. "It's getting cold in here," she said.

CHAPTER TWENTY-FOUR

Tom had thought about staying in Brisbane but decided against it. The news about Paddo's father made him think there was plenty of time for work in his life and his focus now should be relaxing and enjoying the rest of his trip. Besides, he wasn't qualified as a private investigator and his recent experience had exposed him to the reality that he truly had no idea what was involved. The only thing he was qualified to do was to take photos. Best focus on that, he told himself. When he got back to England, there would be time to explore what it would take to become a licensed PI.

It didn't take him long to settle on the South Island of New Zealand as his preferred next port of call. His research had shown him that it was indeed possible to take the Troopy across Bass Strait to Tasmania but he figured that driving it by himself back to the southern tip of Australia was simply out of the question. It might have been different if it wasn't going over ground he'd already covered.

One place he hadn't already seen was the Gold Coast, not far south of Brisbane. He was more than pleased to discover that not only did it have some great beaches but it had a vibrant nightlife, plenty of other 'touristy' things to do and an airport that had flights direct to New Zealand. It ticked off so many boxes that he soon headed down the South-east Freeway thinking about the land of the long white cloud and the best way to sell the Troopy.

At about this time, Bessy was on the phone to Paddo.

"I'm so glad I came home," he said. "Dad is a lot worse than I expected. I think Mum may have been holding back a little. He seems to be going downhill rapidly."

"That's very sad, Paddo. Was he happy to see you?"

"Yes. That's the good thing out of all this. That I'm here in time."

"Well, that's something."

"He's looking forward to meeting you."

"You have told them about us, then?"

"Yes."

"And was it a shock?"

"It was a good shock."

"I have a lot to do before I can be with you."

"That's the thing, Bess. I'm not certain how much time we have. Dr Taylor was here the other day and he said the cancer is the most aggressive he has seen. He reckons Dad must have been quiet about his symptoms for quite a while. That makes sense. I can't remember my dad ever complaining about being sick, ever. He could well have experienced a lot of symptoms when he was overseas working and we would never have known."

"That's dreadful. Poor man. How is your mum holding up? I bet she was glad to see you."

"She's okay. Have you applied for the passport yet?"

"I'm going to organise it tomorrow."

"The thing is, you might want to ask for an emergency application. They can usually cater for that, if you have good reason. Not only do I really want you here but obviously, with Dad, it seems the sooner the better."

"Okay. I have to go to the real estate agent tomorrow as well."

"I forgot about that."

Paddo asked for her bank account details. "I'm going to deposit several thousand pounds into your account. That should be enough, but if it's not, ring me. Be sure to let me know. I also want you to book business class, when you book the flight."

"Oh Paddo, that's lovely but do you think that's necessary? I know you want to, but I feel a bit bad," Bessy said.

"Listen, we're getting married. You know the bit about 'what's yours is mine and what's mine is yours'? You're just going to have to get used to it. It's just money. Think of it as a tool. Something I can give you to help things along. I don't want you to stress about it. That's all."

"I guess, but what do I have that I can give you?"

"You have given me something I intend to keep for the rest of my life. Your love."

"Oh, you are so sweet. How did I end up deserving you?"

"Ha." Paddo chuckled. "Are you ready for this journey, this big risk you are taking?"

"I've already started the journey, Paddo. Yes, I'm ready."

"Good. I'll call you in a few days and see how things are. I love you, Bess."

"I love you, too."

* * * *

The weather continued to remain dry and hot for Tom at the Gold Coast. He thought it might be hard to sell the Troopy privately and quickly. He had researched long-stay parking fees at the airport but ruled that off the list of options as it was only putting off the inevitable and would cost a lot of money. However, he was expecting to take a hit on the sale price.

He took the Troopy to a car wash and spent some time sprucing it up for the intended sale. The vacuum kept cutting out. *Maybe it's just sucking too much dirt*, he thought, *or it just plain sucks*. Either way, it was nearly impossible to get every grain of sand out of the corners of the floor and the road grime off the sides.

Finally, he was satisfied and took the car to a dealer he had spotted in a suburban back street. The sign said 'Wholesale' and 'Quality' and looked to have a range of older second-hand vehicles and four-wheel drives. Some even seemed older than the Troopy. After waiting in the lot for a couple of minutes, a short, older man with a large pot belly approached him somewhat unenthusiastically.

"That's my one over there," Tom said, pointing to where he had parked in front of the dealership.

There were no other customers and it was obvious that the man had seen Tom pull up and was now ready with his approach. At first, he didn't say anything – didn't even introduce himself. He just walked slowly over to the Troopy.

Tom noted he wore shorts, thongs and a tee-shirt that he had possibly owned since he was a boy. He had brown, leathery skin like he had spent decades being exposed to the hot sun while wandering around car yards with no shade. Tom assumed he should tag along behind. "I'm interested in off-loading it," he said. "I'm in no rush. Just beginning to think about it. I don't want to do a trade; I don't need another car."

"Right," the man said.

"Oh, you *can* talk," Tom said under his breath.

"What did you say?"

"Nothing."

After peering under the passenger side, the car dealer said, "Pop the bonnet."

Tom jumped up into the Troopy to do as he asked, then hopped out leaving the door open.

"Close the door," the man said. He peered under the bonnet and poked around.

Tom had no idea about engine parts, except for the radiator, the oil stick, where the oil went and what looked like the engine. The dealer got in the driver's side, then walked around the back and looked underneath. He was shorter than Tom and didn't have to bend down far.

"It's seen a lot of k's."

"K's?"

"Too many."

"You mean kilometres," Tom said, working it out. "I don't think it has any rust."

"All cars have rust. This is no exception."

Silence. But after a few more seconds, the dealer said, "I reckon you've got a leak in that front passenger side. Enough to get a wet foot."

"Only in the heaviest of rain. It's not bad." Tom was amazed how he had picked that up. His thoughts turned dark thinking about how Big Albert had ripped them off.

"I don't think I'm interested to tell you the truth."

Tom wondered exactly how many times a day this fellow told the truth. He might know his stuff about cars but he felt he would probably say anything for a deal.

"Why not?"

"It's got New South Wales plates for one and there is not much interest in this type of thing. I don't want it sitting in the lot for six months or more. I'd have to get it to my other lot."

"Where's that?" But the man didn't answer. "Surely, it can be easily changed to Queensland registration. You must have customers from New South Wales; it's just down the road."

The dealer scratched the back of his neck, squinted, then reached further down his back, causing his tee-shirt to rise and expose his hairy belly hanging over his flimsy shorts. Tom waited, wondering whether his itchy back was really the main priority for the moment.

"Look," the man said, "If you're desperate …"

"I told you, I'm in no rush." Tom was getting quite annoyed now.

"If you're in a rush, I reckon …" He paused and gave his back another thorough scratch. "Do the windscreen wipers work? They can be a pain in the arse."

"They're fine."

"$3,000."

"Nope." Tom was regretting stepping foot inside the lot at all now.

The dealer smiled and shook his head. "You could push me to $4,000 but that's it. I gotta make something on it and I gotta spend some money on it, first."

"I'll think about it. Thanks for your time." Tom walked out of the lot with no intention of thinking about it, other than thinking about what a waste of time.

* * * *

Bessy was assured at the post office that her passport should be ready for collection in five business days. She said that her fiancé's father was seriously ill and was not expected to live much longer. It was the first time she had used this word to describe Paddo and it dawned on her what a momentous decision she had made. But it pleased her immensely to say it – as the lady at the counter could tell.

"They're usually efficient when it comes to these sort of things," the lady said. "The last one I had came back in less than five days."

"Oh, I hope so. It would be a big relief," Bessy said.

"When are you getting married?" the lady asked.

"We haven't set a date yet. Probably next year but perhaps a little longer. Our first priority is being with family in England."

"I hope it's all okay. You will get a phone call when it's ready to collect."

"Thank you so much."

The real estate agent asked her to sign some papers and told her an inspection of her flat would be arranged the day of her departure. Exactly fourteen days from now. Next she went to a travel agent and discussed all flight options. A flight via Singapore would be leaving at 9.30 pm the day after she was vacating the apartment. The agent said she could hold the booking for two days. Usually, she would require a copy of a passport prior to booking, but due to Bessy's circumstances, she told her they would permit it.

Bessy returned the next day and booked the flight with the money from Paddo that had already hit her account.

* * * *

Tom visited another dealer the next day. It was a much bigger dealership and the fellow who greeted him wore a tie. He was a little older than Tom, perhaps in his early thirties. Whilst he was friendlier than the other dealer, Tom was disappointed his offer was only $250 more and Tom decided to go to the beach and think about it. As he sat on the sand he considered calling Paddo and discussing it but decided there was no use in stating the obvious, and Paddo didn't need to be distracted when he needed to be doing more important things. He recalled Paddo's words about just leaving it up to him. Besides, he could pay Paddo the difference as to what they might have got if he'd sold it privately. He knew Paddo would refuse to take it anyway. By the time he was dry and walking back to his budget motel, he had decided to go back to the second dealer and sell the Troopy. He would then book a flight to Christchurch. Later he would decide how long he would stay and whether he would come back to Australia or fly home from New Zealand.

Over a cup of tea in his room, he decided that he had seen enough of Australia, at least this time around. There were plenty of things he hadn't done, like the top end and the red centre. But he'd gotten used to travelling with Paddo and later, Bessy. He missed them already; it just wasn't the same. But as a last hurrah, he thought he would do a solo stint in New Zealand. He may never get the opportunity again. At that moment, he had a strange feeling that he'd never felt before – a sense of maturity combined with a clearness of mind.

Later that afternoon, he went to a travel agent and booked into a tour with a group that had one spot remaining. It was ready to depart in two days and if he was prepared to pay on the spot, he could fill the last spot based on a 30 per cent discount. It was an under-35's bus tour with a party of fifteen people. He would fly into Queenstown and the price included all accommodation and most meals. It would take in Queenstown, Wanaka, Fox Glacier and Mount Cook. He took it and booked his flight to England from Christchurch, via connections in Sydney and Dubai.

He sold the Troopy the following morning.

CHAPTER TWENTY-FIVE

Norwich, seven days later

After a late breakfast, Miriam sat at the table knitting while Paddo washed up.

"Bessy will be here in a little over a week now, Mum."

"What day does she get in?"

"It's a Sunday. The 12th."

"I will have to make up the spare room," Miriam said.

"I can do that."

"If Roger comes, he can stay in the other room."

"The one with the single bed?"

"Yes."

"When are you expecting him?"

"Soon. He's been very busy. He's already taken a lot of time off, you know."

"I know. I spoke to him the other day."

"I'm so worried, Patrick." Her knitting needles flew through the scarf she was knitting as if it needed to be finished in a hurry.

"We all are."

From the kitchen window, they could see Lachlan pottering around the garden in his dressing gown and slippers, watering the plants.

"He seems to have picked up quite a bit, do you think?" Paddo asked.

Miriam didn't take her eyes off the knitting. "I just can't help but feel it's all too hard. It's too hard for me to see him this way."

"It's hard for all of us, Mum. It's harder for him."

"I know it is!"

"Worrying is not going to do anything for Dad. You, Roger and I need to think about what he wants to do with the rest of his time. Have you talked to him about anything like that?"

"No. Not really. I'm still coming to grips with it."

"I think he's already come to grips with it."

"How can you tell?"

"He's always been a realist."

"I don't know what he wants. I haven't known for years."

Paddo could hear bitterness in her tone.

"If I knew," she continued, "I'd give it to him. But …"

"Sometimes it's not a case of giving."

"What do you mean?"

"Maybe try to find out what *he* wants. He's not going to ask. So let him tell us what he wants. I think he wants our love. We can give him that at least."

"Of course. Don't you think I know that? I've let him do whatever he wants for thirty years. More! I have never stopped him travelling. Never asked him not to do something! It's been whatever *he* has wanted."

"I know. And I know it's been hard on you at times. I know when we were kids, you could have used his help more." He put the last of the dishes in the rack by the sink and sat down.

"It never bothered me." But Paddo knew this wasn't true.

"I want to try and talk to him. See what he wants," he said.

"He can't travel, you know. Dr Taylor said he can't. He was cranky as hell with me that I took him to Exmoor. What a disaster that turned out to be. It was horrible."

"I thought that was a good idea. You had no way of knowing things were going to develop the way they did."

Lachlan appeared in the kitchen. "Can't you talk about something other than me? I'm really not that interesting," he said with a smile as he shuffled past the fridge.

"Lachlan, you shouldn't be wearing those slippers outside!" Miriam said.

"You can throw them out soon," he said without looking at her.

Miriam continued knitting at a furious pace.

"How are you feeling today, Dad?"

"Up to shit." He continued down the hallway to the bedroom.

"Are you hungry?" Miriam called after him.

"No."

They both heard the sound of the bedroom door close shut.

"He'll sleep now for hours," Miriam said.

She put her knitting down and went into the bedroom to tuck him in. She gave him a kiss on his forehead. "Just sing out if you want anything."

Paddo called out that he was going for a ride on his bike. He needed to escape the sadness for a while.

* * * *

"You look so tanned. I like it."

Bessy and Abriana were tucked up in a café in Little Bourke Street.

"It will fade as soon as I get to England, I expect. Paddo said the days are getting shorter every day and they only get a couple of hours of sun."

"I'm a so excited for you! Let me see those photos."

Bessy had printed three photos. One was of the three of them standing in front of the old museum in Jeparit. Another was of Paddo and her sitting on a large rock by a creek, and one was just of Paddo, setting up the tent in the Town of 1770.

"Ah, he's a so handsome! The little blond fellow, he's a funny looking."

Bessy laughed. "Yes. He's lovely, too."

"Have you set date?"

"No. There are other priorities at the moment, what with his dad."

"It's a so sad."

"Whenever it is, I want you to come. You and Lino. Do you think you might be able to make it to England?"

"She depends. I'd love to. Lino, ha! I can't a get him to go to dinner, let alone UK."

"You will come then?"

"We shall see. I could visit my mother, I suppose. She is in Florence. I need to see her. It's been too long for me."

"Perfect."

Abriana had to get to work. They kissed and hugged goodbye.

Bessy spent the next few days slowly getting her bag together and arranging with her neighbours to take some of her furniture and white goods.

* * * *

In the meantime, Tom was entertaining his companions on the bus with stories of England and his adventures in Australia. The highlight so far for him had been Fox Glacier. He had walked to the edge and taken some artistic photos from various angles. He thought it was simply incredible that you could hike through a rainforest to get to a glacier. "What a weird little planet we inhabit," he said to some girls from Perth who were on the tour.

In Queenstown, he'd managed to get to know one of the girls a little better than the others. Both Tom and this girl understood it was a holiday romance. "What a weird little man you are," she said, then added, "but, you're kind of cute."

Finally, it was time for Tom to make his way to England. He bought a book to read and set his mind for the long flight ahead. He had chosen a flight that had a three-hour stop in Dubai. The stopover in Sydney would be even less. It would still take well over a whole day to get to London.

* * * *

For Bessy, travelling via Singapore, it would take twenty-two hours. She would be ready to depart two days after Tom had left.

Paddo missed Bessy but time seemed to be passing quickly. He had made virtually no effort to catch up with his friends since he was back and spent as much time with his father as he could. He sat with him in the largest room in the house, where Lachlan had his favourite chair, books, and art work on the walls.

"Bessy will be here in a couple of days, Dad. She's looking forward to meeting you, you know."

"That's great news, Patrick. And me, her."

"Dad, Mum and I were thinking that you might want to do something. Get out of the house, maybe?"

"It's hard for me to travel. Even harder for others, in my state. I won't put people through that again. It doesn't bother me to stay right here. I like this house. I don't need to go anywhere."

"Are you feeling a bit better today?"

"Marginally. Where's your mother?"

"She went to town."

"Good. Get me a Scotch please. You'll find the bottle over there." He pointed towards a set of drawers.

"Dad. Do you think you should?"

"Are you my wife?"

Paddo grinned and shook his head. He retrieved a half-full bottle of Cardhu single malt from the drawer.

"Get yourself a glass, if you want," Lachlan said.

Paddo checked his watch. 11:34 am. He picked up two glasses. "Ice?"

"Not for me."

Paddo poured the Scotch. "Put a bit more in," Lachlan said.

Paddo sat down next to his father. "Cheers," he said as he passed the other glass to Lachlan.

"Cheers, indeed." His father took a sip and then another, draining the glass. "Here, fill it up."

Paddo obliged.

"When are you getting married?" he asked.

"We haven't decided. I haven't had a chance to really work that out. When Bessy gets here, we can talk about it."

"I see."

"I haven't even bought her a ring yet."

"You better get to that, then, when she gets here."

"I intend to."

"And don't skimp. Spend some bloody money!"

"I won't Dad. I mean, I will. I don't know much about rings, though."

"Ask your mother. Believe me, she does."

Paddo took a sip. "This is quite good."

"It's been my favourite."

They sat in silence while Paddo tried to think of something that might enthuse his father. A walk by the river, maybe?

"Do you mind if I come to your wedding?" Lachlan's voice suddenly interrupted Paddo's thoughts.

Paddo shook his head, shocked and confused by the question. "*Mind?* I ... that's a bit of a silly question, isn't it? Why would you say that?"

"Think, Patrick. Think!" He paused. "It's not silly. You haven't set a date."

He held his father's gaze for a moment, thinking. He'd been asked by his father to think before, while he was in Australia, about coming back and helping him. There was no time now for more regret. He knew he couldn't let him down again.

Lachlan took another sip of his Scotch and stared at the carpet. His eyes held a dark, vacant look. "Look. I know it may not be possible. I might die tomorrow, for all I know."

"Dad, don't say that sort of stuff."

"But I don't think I will. I think Taylor and that other barrel of laughs, the specialist from London, is right about the three months thing. That gives me what, a good – sorry – *manageable* six weeks from now. Do you think you could set a date within that time? I can pay any fee anyone wants to charge. It would mean ..." His voice broke. Tears gathered in the corners of his eyes.

"Yes, of course. Yes! We don't need much time. I should have suggested it."

Lachlan set his glass down on the table next to his chair, pulled himself together and cleared his throat. "I want to have a word with the Canon down at the cathedral."

"The cathedral?"

"Yes. You'll get married there, won't you?"

"I never thought about it."

"Think about it now."

Paddo got up and poured himself another Scotch. He sat down again and frowned.

"Well, what's your answer?"

"The cathedral is beautiful, Dad, but …"

"But what?"

"I'd rather somewhere smaller. There's a lot of beautiful little churches in Norwich. The cathedral is incredible, but it's so big!"

"My son deserves incredible."

"I'd prefer smaller, Dad. More intimate. I think Bessy would too. I think something smaller, to be honest."

Lachlan sighed. "Okay. I want you to be happy, Patrick. I want to see happiness before I go." He drained his glass. "Here, pour me another one before your mother comes home. And tell her what *we've* decided later. After I've passed out."

CHAPTER TWENTY-SIX

When Tom called Paddo and told him he was back in Norwich, Paddo said that was fantastic news. Tom said he thought he might be happy about it but expressed surprise that he was *that* pleased. "Have you been drinking?" asked Tom.

"No. I'll tell you later why I'm so pleased. In fact, I need to see you soon."

"You sound desperate. Won't Bessy be able to look after your needs for you? I can't do everything for you, as capable as I am."

"Settle down. I'm meeting Bessy at Paddington Station tomorrow."

"Why don't you pick her up from the airport?"

"That's what everyone else said. Dad said I could take the Range Rover but I've already arranged to catch the train with her. It's easy and I think it's fun."

"Are you nuts? For God sake, man! Pick her up in the Range. It's a beautiful car! I don't think it's fun on the train. Come to your senses, son."

"Yes, well you're not me, are you?"

"No, thankfully," replied Tom. "I couldn't live with myself."

"I'll take her for a drive later, probably to the coast or something."

"Okay. Well, you call me when you want me to come around."

"It'll be soon. You're not going anywhere, are you?"

"Not unless you mean to the pub."

"Good. Stick to that plan, can you, for a while. Until we talk."

"That'll be tough. But, okay."

Miriam had gone out to get her hair done. Paddo and Lachlan were alone in the house. Lachlan always picked up when Miriam announced she was going to town.

"Climb up on that shelf," Lachlan told Paddo after he got off the phone. "That one. Run your hand across the top."

Paddo pulled down an unopened bottle of Scotch. "You know what to do," his father said. "Don't worry, I'm only going to have one."

A Scotch was the last thing that Paddo felt like but once again he sat down with his father.

"I know I haven't been the best father to you and Roger," he said.

"It's fine, Dad. Both Roger and I are … we're grateful for what you and Mum have done for us. You shouldn't worry."

"I'm not worried. I just thought I could have been there more. And I'm pissed off I've realised too late."

"Roger and I both know, we've always known you wanted to, Dad. But no one expects … what's happened is not what you expected."

"I won't be here to see your kids. Are you going to have children?"

"I think so. Bessy loves children and would be a wonderful mother."

"That's good. It makes me happy to hear that. I would like you to learn from my mistakes."

"Dad …"

"No, listen to me. I never told you I loved you. I never told Roger." Tears again welled up in his eyes.

"You didn't have to. We know, we knew." Paddo fought his own urge to cry.

"Well, I do. Now pour me another."

"Dad, I wanted to tell you something. I *did* think about what you asked me to think about, when I was in Australia. I was going to come back and tell you that I wanted to study environmental management and become a park ranger, if I can. I feel, well, I wasted some years and I should have helped you with the business in that time. I'm sorry and I wanted to say …"

"Don't you worry about that nonsense now!"

"I wanted to say I am sorry I wasn't more of the son you wanted me to be."

"I'm proud of your decision. It's what you want to do. That's the most important thing. You will be very good at it."

When Miriam returned, she seemed to be in a state because Paddo insisted on catching the train to meet Bessy.

"Mum. It's easy. She catches the express to Paddington, then I'll be there to meet her. Simple. Easy."

"You're upsetting your father! It's not right, Patrick. He wants you to take the car."

Paddo decided it wasn't worth arguing about. There would be plenty of things to organise soon with his mother and he had better pick his battles. He couldn't reach Bessy so he rang the airline. No problem at all, they said, they could pass the message on. The business class hotline helped.

* * * *

Bessy sat at the gate at Singapore trying to find her boarding pass. She was in a mild panic that she had lost it and was trying to remember whether she was ever given it in Melbourne or whether she needed to get it now. She looked at her watch and realised the flight was due to board in twenty minutes. Then she heard her name called out over the speaker, twice in quick succession, telling her to approach the counter. *I've really stuffed up now*, she thought.

"Yes. Hello. I'm Beatrice O'Halloran."

"Ah Miss O'Halloran, we have a message here from a Mr Paddington-Smythe. He will pick you up and meet you at the airport. Here, I've written it down for you."

"Oh. Thank you."

Bessy soon found her boarding pass.

* * * *

Paddo had to get up early the next morning. He expected things to move quickly when he returned to Norwich but it was all a little overwhelming.

On the drive to Heathrow, he tossed ideas around about how he would tell Bessy. He grew philosophical as the miles clicked over, telling himself that the shorter the build up to the wedding the better. He was hoping that Bessy would understand.

The plane was on time and he stood in a position at the exit where she would easily see him. He was looking forward to hearing the details about her last days in Melbourne and how the inspection of the flat went. There were so many things to talk about now.

He saw her before she saw him. Bessy dropped her bag and he lifted her off her feet as he kissed her, enfolding her in his strong arms. She felt like she was dreaming again. At that moment, it was like no one else existed, only them. A woman pushed past them shaking her head but they didn't notice and wouldn't have cared anyway.

"It's a short walk; best follow me," Paddo said at last. "Are you tired? You don't look it."

"I slept really well on the plane. Not to Singapore but to London."

"That's great."

Soon they arrived at the car. "Is this your car?" Bessy said. "It's beautiful."

"No. It's Dad's. He wanted me to pick you up in it."

She climbed into the front seat. "Wow. It's like a lounge room. How gorgeous!"

"It's a little different from the Troopy. To be honest, I prefer the Troopy," he said.

"What happened to the Troopy?"

"Tom sold it. He said he's too embarrassed to tell me what he got for it. I don't care."

It took them a little while to get out of the airport traffic.

"We have a bit of a drive. Not too long. Are you hungry?"

"No. Not really. We got breakfast on the plane."

"I expect that was several hours ago, now. We can stop before we get to Norwich."

Bessy told him all about her last days in Melbourne, how she had seen Abriana, and that she'd had to pay to steam clean the carpets, but she expected all her bond to be in her account by now. "It took me days to cull what I wasn't going to take and then to pack." Her suitcase was massive.

Paddo had decided that he had no option but to tell Bessy everything. Otherwise she would hear it from his mother as soon as they got to Norwich, albeit indirectly. After an hour of chatting about Tom's trip to New Zealand, the cooler weather in England, and his father's poor health, he felt he should begin.

"My father is not going to live much longer."

"Have the doctors revised his prognosis?"

"No, but he thinks the three months they gave him some time back is correct. From what we can see, he's probably right. But who knows, really."

"I'm so sorry, Paddo."

"It's very sad. But he has come to terms with it. Well, at least for the moment. I can't say the same for my mother. But it's understandably affected her in lots of ways. It's not going to be the easiest house to live in for a while."

"Well, it's good that your dad has come to terms with it. It must be so hard. I'm pretty nervous about being there. I don't want to be in the way or a burden to your mother."

"You won't be a burden. To the contrary. You may have to have patience with her, though. Since I got back, I've just been around the house which means Mum's had a bit of free time from looking after Dad. We've spent a lot of time just chatting."

"That's wonderful."

"I was hoping we could do something special for him in the time he has left. I asked him if there was anything he wanted to do. Travelling is not an option but he does have a dying wish."

"He has? That's good, isn't it?"

"He wants to come to our wedding. To see his son married. Soon." He turned and smiled at her, wanting to see her face.

"Soon?"

"Soon."

"How soon?"

"I'm sorry. I want to apologise in advance."

"Apologise? What for?"

"For what I'm about to tell you."

"What?"

"Would you mind – you can say no of course – if we got married in six weeks? We've already made some arrangements for the wedding and given Dad's health ..."

"Six weeks!" She sat for a moment, looking at the road and the traffic whizzing past in the other direction. "Paddo, I think ..." She paused, reflecting on yet more powerful emotions now flooding into her mind and sat more upright in her seat. "Wow! That's kind of ... I guess. It's not what I was expecting."

"I know. When you agreed to marry me, it was when *you* were ready. There would be no rush." His nerves made it difficult to concentrate on the road, and he desperately wanted to hold her now and reassure her that it was indeed her decision, above everything. "I'm so worried about Dad, but I can explain to him ..."

It was love at the foremost in her mind above everything else, including the love of her fiancé for his father. She turned to him before he could say more and said, "Yes – let's do it!"

"Are you sure?" Paddo beamed. "When I got back to Norwich, I was thinking we'd wait for say six months at least. Not six weeks!"

"I know. I don't know if it's enough time to plan a wedding but if it's what your father wants, then we should at least try. It's not as if you and I are uncertain. Are we?"

"I've never been so certain in my life," Paddo said, turning to her again.

"Me either. Then, I don't see a problem. Do you? I don't see any reason to wait. But, what if six weeks is too long – for your dad, I mean?"

"Well, we haven't got much choice. It takes time to fulfil the legal requirements. We could get married sooner, but the law makes people wait. It's also not a given that we can do it in six weeks. The Home Office can even extend the time, apparently. But Dad will have his team of lawyers working on it. He has already called them, actually."

"But what happens if we don't get approval?"

"It'll happen. Dad will make it happen. Actually, did you bring your birth certificate? Dad mentioned we will need it after he made enquiries yesterday."

"Yep. My whole life's in that bag in the back."

"You don't even have a ring, a diamond, yet."

"Oh, Paddo. Don't worry about that. That's nothing."

"We are definitely going to the jeweller's tomorrow. My mother may want to come. Wow! What a family you're marrying into."

"She can come. It would be lovely."

"She'll want to educate us both about diamond rings. We'll have to humour her but the choice will be yours, of course. You mustn't let her dominate you. I won't have it."

"Will it be a small wedding?"

"I'll show you some churches this week. I've no idea about anything else. But my mother is one of these super organised people. She means well, but she can be a toe treader."

"I don't care. I'm just glad we're together again. You can take me on whatever ride you want. I could get used to riding in *this* car, though."

Paddo laughed. "I'm bloody lucky, you know," he said.

"I'll remind you that you said that later." She grabbed his hand and held it until they stopped for a drink and a small bite to eat.

When they arrived at the house, Bessy felt more nervous than she could ever remember. Paddo pushed the door open with his foot, holding both her bags. She kept a cautious distance behind him. He turned around and said, "I'll just leave the bags here for the moment. Come in."

Bessy felt underdressed. *I feel like 'a dag,'* she thought, being fresh off a plane but not by any means feeling fresh. The house was far more elaborate and beautiful than she had imagined. The front garden was in exquisite condition, full of deep colours of purple and red.

Miriam and Lachlan were in the sitting room. Lachlan had put on his favourite tweed jacket and tie. Miriam wore a patterned woollen skirt and silk top, with a wool cardigan, all of which she had purchased in Harrods last year but had not worn since.

"Mum, Dad, please meet Bessy."

Bessy suddenly realised she didn't know how to address them so resorted to being polite. "Hello Mrs Paddington-Smythe. Sir, so pleased to meet you," she said and held out her hand.

"Call me Lachlan," Lachlan said as he shook her hand and smiled.

"Sit down, dear. You must be exhausted," Miriam said. "Patrick, can you bring the jug of water from the refrigerator? And some glasses."

"Thank you," Bessy said.

"I understand you've had a wonderful time with the boys," Miriam said.

"Oh, yes. It was fabulous," she replied, then glanced around the room. "You have a lovely house, here. Paddo has told me a lot about it."

Paddo returned and poured water for everyone. His father winked at him but he pretended not to notice as he and Bessy sat down together.

"It's lovely to meet you, Bessy," Lachlan said. "Patrick hasn't had many girlfriends, you know."

"That's not what you told me, Paddo," Bessy said and Lachlan laughed.

"Tell me, dear. You're from Melbourne?" asked Miriam.

"Well, yes. But I grew up in country Victoria. A little place called Jeparit. It only has about six hundred people."

"That's a tiny town. You must be glad you moved, although I suppose it was probably quaint, was it?" Miriam said.

"I actually loved it," Bessy said and smiled at Paddo who smiled back.

"How was the drive, Patrick?" Miriam asked. "I'm glad you took the car."

"I think it was fine. Don't you think?" he said, turning to Bessy.

"Felt like we were here in no time," she said.

"I don't like this water," Lachlan said.

"It's perfectly good water, darling. You have been drinking it for years."

"It tastes funny."

"You must be ready for a bath or a shower," Miriam said to Bessy.

"That would be lovely."

"Come with me and I'll show you where everything is." Miriam took Bessy's hand.

As soon as they were out of sight, Lachlan produced the Cardhu. "Right, my boy! Pass me your glass," he said.

"Dad!" Paddo said. "Mum will have a fit."

"I've been waiting all day for you to get here. I'm not waiting any longer. Now that Bessy's here, your mother won't say boo, you'll see."

Paddo figured his father was probably right.

"Besides, it helps me sleep."

Dinner that night was a three-course meal. It consisted of vegetable soup, roast beef and vegetables, with Yorkshire pudding, and a dessert of chocolate truffle, strawberries and brandy cream.

"This is wonderful," Bessy said, halfway through the main course. "You're a very good cook, Miriam."

"Thank you, dear. But the thanks must go to the maid I'm afraid. But I'll pass it on."

"Please do," Bessy said. Paddo smiled.

Lachlan excused himself shortly into the meal. "I'm sorry, lass. I'm not much fun," he said, as he pushed the chair out from underneath him and got up slowly. Miriam started to get up but he said sharply, "Sit down!"

After Lachlan went to his bedroom, Miriam asked Bessy more questions, mostly about where she had worked. When she described The Gourmet Pheasant, Miriam said, "Patrick spent so much time working in a similar job, not earning very much of course."

Bessy answered her other questions politely. She had grown full quickly but felt obliged to finish her meal. She had a small portion of dessert.

"Mum, I'm sure Bessy's tired. Maybe best if we all get an early night. She can fill you in about everything after she's had a good night's sleep."

"Good idea, Patrick, it's been a very big day," she agreed. "Just leave the dishes for our maid," she added.

An hour later, Bessy was snuggled up to Paddo in bed.

"I feel like I'm still on the plane. Up in the air."

"It'll be gone by the morning."

"I don't care. I'm just happy to be here."

"There'll be a few other things up in the air still in the morning," Paddo said.

"I don't care." And she fell asleep in his arms with her head on his chest.

CHAPTER TWENTY-SEVEN

In the next few weeks, everyone in the house did their best to ignore the red tape that cast a shadow over the wedding plans. Miriam turned her attention to the pink lace that the maid of honour would wear and forged ahead with the plans regardless. By the third week, the tension increased when they learned that it could even be seventy days or more before the marriage could legally occur.

That afternoon, Bessy had heard Lachlan yell in pain from the other end of the house. When she expressed her outrage at the situation, Paddo soothed her. "I suppose the government have to do their job; the rules are there for the common good."

She thought of Jeparit and how death was on the doorstep again. "Can't the doctors do anything?" she asked.

"He refused treatment, Bess. He said all it would have done was prolong his agony. Dr Taylor thought it wouldn't have helped much anyway. And Dad doesn't want to be knocked out with drugs yet."

"It's not right, Paddo. Making us wait. He's a dying man."

"It'll be okay."

He didn't let on the wedding was more up in the air than she realised, for the lawyers had expressed concern that as a foreigner, not having any marriage or special visa, and immigration control becoming increasingly spoken of, a certificate of approval was hardly a given. Couples could be refused permission – even required to leave the country, establish bona fides, made to wait longer. There was talk of laws changing and a lot of paperwork had to be sent off.

Miriam had surprised Paddo with her patience and grace under pressure. He put this partly down to Bessy's presence. Bessy spent a good deal of time each day with Miriam, discussing the plans, offering suggestions, even doing some housework, despite being told to leave it for the maid.

Paddo made enquiries about enrolling in a course in environmental management and wondered if he could combine it with a study of Indigenous peoples. Tom dropped by the house frequently, something that Paddo encouraged him to do, if for nothing more than to break the tension with his upbeat spirit and usual good cheer. Tom got to know Lachlan in the process and would sit and tell him about their trip to Australia, trying to make him laugh. He pretended to like Scotch and would bounce in saying, "Good morning Mrs P-S. How are we today?" Some afternoons, he would sit and ask Lachlan about his travels and some of his business deals, and was interested to hear everything he had the energy to tell him.

Roger came to Norwich but could only stay a short while. He spent a lot of the time sitting with Lachlan and reading by his bedside while his father slept. Bessy and Roger got to know each other a little during his stay. He offered suggestions about the wedding and helped arrange a marquee. He assured Paddo that he should go ahead with the plans. He thought there was little chance the government would require more time. He referred Bessy to a lawyer friend who specialised in immigration. Bessy and Paddo took a trip to London to see him and they stayed overnight. They needed some space after the intensity of the last few weeks and Paddo took Bessy to see the usual sights. They both felt a lot better after they had seen Roger's friend. This time, they took the train. Bessy told Paddo it was fun.

Bessy contacted Abriana and told her the date they were aiming for, which was now a little over two weeks away. She was very honest with Abriana and apologised that she had left it so late due to the uncertainty, but she wanted her to be her only bridesmaid.

"I'll be there. I would not miss it for the world," she told Bessy. "Is a no problem at all."

"But what if we have to cancel it? This is possible."

"Ah, so what. I visit my mother, anyway. I need to see her. You make me think about it, with Mr Lachlan and all this happening. Is no good for me to not see her."

Lino wouldn't be able to make it on such short notice. "I prefer to come by myself, anyway," she said with a laugh.

Bessy told her she would book her accommodation in Norwich and gave her instructions about how to get the train from London. On the day she arrived, they would visit the dressmaker for a final fitting.

"I want to see that rock on your finger and meet this prince," Abriana said. They agreed they would next speak when she was in England.

Everyone decided there was little choice but to keep the guest list down. If flexibility was the key, then it made sense to have a manageable number. It would be confined to family and only the closest of friends. Lachlan's brother and his wife, who Lachlan had not seen in almost ten years, would be coming. They lived in Wales on an estate with their adult daughter, who would not be able to make it. Paddo had only met her once, when he was fourteen, and he'd only seen his uncle a few times in his whole life.

In the end, the guest list still totalled thirty-five people. Miriam's best friend had offered her manicured grounds for the reception. She lived on acreage almost ten miles outside of Norwich and had a large formal garden. The marquee was to be set up several days before. It would be cold but elaborate heating would be arranged at considerable expense. Miriam's friend had a friend who ran a catering business and Bessy was introduced to both ladies when she accompanied Miriam to see the property. After a stroll around the gardens, they had a cup of tea and Bessy chose the menu.

"I insist that you make every choice," Miriam said.

No one discussed how much it was all going to cost. Paddo had told Bessy it was best not to mention it. He said that he and Tom would select the wine and she should try, as much as possible, to relax and take it all in as best she could.

She told him about her trip to see the reception venue, how lovely the other ladies were, and how his mother was being so nice to her. It occurred to him that it was not just Bessy who was having an impact on harmony. It was his father's wish, for everything to work out and for everyone to simply be happy, coming true. He never expected to see his family all working together and respecting each other. He felt very proud of his family and, that in the most heartbreaking circumstances, Bessy was able to see them at their very best.

But with less than a week to go before the big day, Dr Taylor was called to the house. Earlier, everyone had been overjoyed to hear that the Home Office had notified Paddo that there would be no extension of investigations. "Our marriage won't be a sham after all, Bess" he said jokingly, relieved that after jumping through so many hoops and formalities, things had worked out. But by the afternoon, their relief had turned to worry.

Dr Taylor told Miriam he would consult with Lachlan on his own. "Let me see him first, then I'll come out and talk to you after that."

Miriam, Paddo and Bessy sat in the kitchen and waited. Lachlan had eaten and drunk very little in the last few days. His usual walks around the garden had become less frequent. When the doctor emerged, he sat down with them.

"We are awfully worried, John," Miriam said.

"Well, he is too. He's not worried about dying. He is worried about when. You have the wedding coming up, soon, I believe?"

"It's next Saturday," Paddo said.

"He'll be there, I think. He is a determined man. I find him frustrating. But determined, he is. But, can you hide the Scotch? That is not something he should be having now." He smiled.

"Oh, yes! Of course. I've told him so many times. Patrick, go and get that Scotch and pour it down the sink!" Miriam said.

"Wait, my boy. That's not called for. Put it in my bag, if you must, but never pour good Scotch down the sink," Dr Taylor said, as he smiled at Bessy.

Miriam rolled her eyes.

"Look," Doctor Taylor continued. "He's in the stage before the final stage in my view. It's a really evil, aggressive form of cancer. He's very unlucky."

"Is he in a lot of pain, Doctor?" asked Paddo.

"At times. I've given him something for that. Miriam, I've written down something else he can take. I want you to go and pick it up for him. I could give him stronger medication but that will dope him up too much. He wants to be with it for a while yet."

"Can we do anything else?" asked Miriam.

"Just continue on the way you are. If he thinks you are giving up, he may well too. Make sure he can see what you are doing. Mornings seem better for him than afternoons. Talk to him about next Saturday. If you are religious, pray. He's going to need some help. Have a plan in place, if on the day, he is too weak to attend."

"Thank you, John." Miriam had known and trusted him for many years.

"I will come back and see him after the wedding. You can call me of course, beforehand, if need be."

The next day, Erica the caterer told Miriam that she couldn't get the special French canapes by Saturday. Miriam burst into tears. When Paddo heard the dreadful news, he said sarcastically, "Dad's going to be devastated, Mum. Not to mention Bessy." Immediately, he knew he'd said the wrong thing – had been insensitive.

"Oh, stop it, Patrick," she said, then blew her nose. "It's the little touches that count."

He gave her a hug. "I'm sorry, Mum. I was just trying to switch to the big picture. We have all been under a lot of stress. Don't worry about those little things. It's fine, you have done your best, let it go." He held her as she cried and they felt closer than ever.

Before dark, Paddo and Bessy took a bike ride into town and met Tom. They went to the café where Paddo used to work so he could show it to Bessy.

"I'm a bit nervous about seeing Henry. Is he still with Roger?" asked Tom.

"Oh, yes. More than ever. They will be arriving a couple of days before the wedding."

"Does he know what I look like?"

"He knows who you are, Tom, and has probably already planned his revenge."

"Now I'm nervous and scared."

"What did you do to Henry, Tom?"

"You don't want to know, Bessy," Paddo said, replying on Tom's behalf.

"Tom?" she said.

"Nothing, really. I just sent him on a wild goose chase, of sorts. It was ages ago."

"It will come out in the fullness of time," Paddo said.

Tom was excited to share some news of his own with them. "I'm officially enrolled in a private investigator's course!"

"That's wonderful, Tom," Bessy said.

"It's going to take a while to get my licence but I'm having fun already."

Bessy told the two boys she would get serious about nursing after the honeymoon.

"The honeymoon. Ah yes, where are you going?" asked Tom.

"Exmoor National Park. The house. It's very cool there. You should come for a day and stay overnight," Paddo said, looking at Bessy.

"You're inviting your mate on your honeymoon!"

"It was Bessy's suggestion."

"Really, you like me that much?"

"We said a day, Tom. We were hoping you'd think it's too far to drive for a day, so yes we like you but, you know …"

"I see. I think I'll leave you to go on your own bushwalks."

"It will be walks over the moors, Tom, and looking out over the ocean. The moors roll to the shore, in parts. It's really beautiful. You can see Wales from there on a clear day," Paddo said, exaggerating a little.

"I've never seen a whale," Bessy said.

Tom and Paddo laughed.

"What are you laughing at?"

* * * *

On the evening before the wedding, Miriam, Bessy and Abriana shared a bottle of wine in the kitchen.

"I am so happy, you donta know how much, thank you," Abriana said, as her glass of wine was filled up for the third or fourth time. Her head bobbed like a buoy in a bay. Her dark hair was pulled up high and tight underneath a complicated wrap that swirled to a mysterious knot somewhere on the crown of her head.

"I think we should all make this our last," Miriam said. "We have such a big day tomorrow." She was slightly tipsy as they all were. It had been a long journey but it was not quite over.

Tom had collected Paddo two nights prior and they had absconded directly to the pub and then to another. Bessy was now in a 'no communication' zone with him.

For a fleeting moment, Miriam had forgotten about Lachlan and his illness.

He emerged and paraded in front of the three women in his suit and his tie. "Will this do?" he said.

"Oh, darling! You look wonderful."

"You look a stunning, Mr Lachlan," Abriana said, her accent even thicker with the wine.

"Thanks. You don't look too bad yourself," he said. He hadn't had a drink for a week.

After dinner, Bessy called a taxi for Abriana and gave her a final run-down of the next day. "Be sure to go straight to bed. I will see you at the hairdressing salon, where I told you, at 9 am sharp."

Abriana gave Bessy a sloppy kiss and a big hug. "You will."

Bessy had a cup of tea with Miriam before bed and they discussed everything they could think of that could go wrong. Miriam had two friends arriving early in the morning to help while she was at the hairdressers with Bessy and Abriana. Their main task was to make sure Lachlan was looked after but also to help control the ensuing madness.

The family's concerns about Lachlan had dissipated and he was in fine spirits. Miriam climbed into bed and held Lachlan close to her.

As her head rested on the pillow, Bessy felt her shoulders relax. She thought briefly about Australia, about Jeparit and her mother, then about how her father would not be walking her down the aisle tomorrow. In her dream that night, she thought she saw his face.

* * * *

The next morning, Bessy opened her eyes and realised she hadn't moved all night. Through the window, she could see the soft sunlight outside. It was expected to be cold with only a small chance of rain but she didn't care. The weather was not important. Today she would see Paddo again. And he would become her husband.

Miriam and Bessy met Abriana at the hairdressers as planned. "How did you sleep?" Miriam asked Abriana as they were being seated in the salon.

"The usual way. Ona my back."

Bessy laughed and soon they were all talking about hairstyles.

Meanwhile, Tom and Paddo were having breakfast at Tom's place.

"What time do we have to be at the church again?" asked Tom.

"I have told you three times, Tom. 2 pm. The ceremony is at 2:30 pm. Bessy will arrive with my father in the Rolls at 2:15 but we have to be in the church."

"Right. What time again did you say we have to be there then?"

Paddo shook his head and told him to quit it.

"How are we getting there?" asked Tom.

"Aren't you supposed to be organising all of this? Isn't that what a best man does?"

"I don't know. I haven't been a best man before."

"I will not be giving you a reference. Although I could say, 'Nice guy but falls short of best man material.' Actually, I think I'd leave the 'nice guy' bit out, as well."

"I'd probably be better as the photographer," Tom said, sipping his coffee. "I'll ask Mum if she can drop us there."

At that moment, Tom's mother entered the dining room and caught the end of their conversation. "Sorry, I can't," she said. "But I've asked Rebecca to take you." Rebecca was Tom's sister.

"That would be good."

"Good morning, Mrs Greer," Paddo said.

"Good morning, Paddo. Are you nervous?"

"No, I'm fine. Well, maybe a little."

"You'll be fine. You have a good day for it."

"Seems to be."

"How is your father?"

"I spoke to Mum last night and she said he's fine. Well, not fine but he seems okay."

"That's good. I'm going to get some washing on while this sun is out. I expect I'll see you before you go."

"You will, Mum," Tom said.

Paddo finished his coffee and placed his cup in the sink. "We have to pick up the suits and the flowers this morning, Tom. I'll need your help and a car."

"You can take Rebecca's car, Tom," said Mrs Greer on her way to the laundry.

"What flowers?" asked Tom

"The mini-carnations for the lapels."

"Oh, right."

"Now, you have the rings, don't you?"

"What rings?" Tom jabbed him in the ribs. It hurt.

"Get in the bloody car," Paddo said.

They weren't early enough to beat the usual Saturday morning crowds. After another cup of coffee, they went to the tailor shop, then they picked up the flowers. The lady was very helpful and would not let them leave without showing them how to place the flowers exactly right on the lapels. "Put the flowers in the fridge when you get home, in their little boxes and take them out an hour before you put them on," she instructed them.

Outside the florist, they ran into some mutual friends and were delayed another fifteen minutes chatting to them. They finally arrived back at the house by 11:30 and decided to have an early lunch and relax before heading to the church. "I'd like to get there a little earlier if we can," Paddo said.

"Good idea," Tom agreed.

Time seemed to drag at first and Paddo was excited. His butterflies were flapping. Then suddenly it was time to get dressed. The suits were traditional black with a white shirt and bow tie. They had both bought new shiny black shoes. Before they had too much time to preen, Rebecca arrived, the car keys dangling from her hand.

"Ready to go, boys? Wow, you both scrubbed up alright! Have you got the rings, Tom?"

"Yes. Do you remember your vows, Paddo?"

"Yes."

"*Will* you remember your vows, Paddo?"

"I most certainly will, now get in the car."

They were at the church in very good time. It was a small but exquisitely beautiful old Norwich church, one that Paddo had admired from the outside for as long as he could remember. They looked inside and wandered the small grounds. The priest made an appearance and they chatted for a moment. At 2 pm a car pulled up, parked in front and Roger and Henry emerged. Tom looked on nervously, as they both walked up to greet them.

"Tom, you remember my brother, Roger." They shook hands.

"Of course. Lovely to see you again."

"And this is Henry."

"Hi," Tom said.

Henry nodded and gave a tiny forced smile.

"Well, it's a brilliant day," Roger said. "You must be pleased with that?"

Paddo smiled and said yes.

Tom looked at the matching lapel pins on Roger and Henry's suits. "Oh, no. I've screwed up!"

"What is it?" Paddo said.

"I forgot the bloody flowers! For our lapels."

Paddo looked down at his naked lapel.

"Uh-oh. What time is it?" Until now, they had managed to avoid any panic but now it was time to panic.

"We will have to go back for them!" Tom said.

"Where are they? I don't remember seeing them since we picked them up," Paddo said, trying not to chew Tom's head off but feeling a desperate need to do so.

"Um," Tom said. "I think … let me think … I must have left them in the car. My sister's car. I forgot to get them out when we took the suits into the house, damn it."

"You were supposed to put them in the bloody fridge. Are you sure they're not in the fridge?"

"They're not in the fridge. I … let me think. We hung the suits up in the car on the handles … and I think I put the flowers in the glove box."

"What the … why would you do that?"

"I don't know. I didn't want to put them on the floor!"

Roger and Henry looked on as the exchange was unfolding.

"Bloody hell, Tom! You're hopeless." Paddo was furious but equally upset with himself. At last he calmed down enough to wonder if the lapel flowers were really necessary. "Roger. What about if you or Henry went back to the house and got them?"

"Why don't you ring Rebecca? Didn't Tom say they were in her car?" replied Roger.

"Yes, that's a better idea. Tom, ring her and see if she can get here!"

Tom grabbed his phone and they waited for Rebecca to answer. "We've left the suit flowers in your car," Tom yelled without even a hello.

While Tom talked to his sister, Paddo was thinking about how much trouble he'd be in with his mother, and rightly so, if this solution didn't work. Then he heard Tom say, "We'll have someone there in three minutes."

Tom hung up. "Good news! She's downtown but she's working. Someone will have to meet her at work, get her keys and grab them out of the car. Then take the keys back."

"What! All in twenty minutes?" Roger said.

"It's do-able. One of you should go," Tom said, now belatedly taking charge and looking at Roger and Henry.

Roger turned to Henry. "Can you go? I can't risk not being here. Life will not be worth living if Mum arrives and I'm not here."

Henry frowned. "Well, I guess so. Where do I have to go?"

With a sense of deja vu, Tom realised he was once again giving Henry instructions about how to pick something up. To save time, he walked with Henry to his car, pointing down the street in the direction he needed to go. "Take a right at the next street, then continue until the third left."

Henry listened carefully to Tom's instructions before climbing into the car. Tom stood on the curb and opened the passenger side door. He leaned in and said, "At least they will definitely smell better than the last thing I asked you to pick up."

"Smart arse," Henry said as he started the car.

"Cheers," Tom said and he swung the door closed.

It wasn't until they were at the altar with music playing softly and almost everyone gathered inside the church, except Abriana, Lachlan and Bessy, that Henry arrived, slightly out of breath, with the slightly wilted flowers.

"Thanks, Henry," Tom said. "I appreciate it. Do you know how to put them on?"

"Of course I do," he said, carefully positioning it and then pricking Tom with the pin, before securing it.

"Ouch!" Tom said, hopping backwards.

Henry grinned and stepped around him to pin on Paddo's flower.

Paddo turned and looked at his mother who gave a frown and then a half smile out of the corner of her mouth, as Henry, also smiling, quickly took his seat.

The music increased in volume and everyone but Paddo turned around to see Abriana making her way down the aisle. She was dressed in a pale-yellow dress with pink lace. After Abriana took her place at the altar, Bessy and Lachlan started down the aisle. Bessy wore her hair out with a pretty crown of small red, pink and yellow flowers. Her dress was a traditional white wedding dress that was cut low around her neck and had a small train. She looked stunning. She had instructed Paddo not to look at her until she arrived next to him. Lachlan was dressed in a dark-grey pin-striped suit with coat tails and grey top hat. He looked every bit the proud father-in-law to be.

Paddo and Bessy's vows were short and simple. They placed the rings on each other's fingers and kissed. The congregation clapped and cheered. Paddo and Bessy turned and looked at Lachlan and they could see, even from where they stood, that he had tears in his eyes.

Outside, after more kisses and hugs, Bessy and Paddo stepped into the vintage Rolls Royce and left for the reception. Tom and Abriana followed in the shiny black Range Rover. He gave her a kiss on the cheek. "You look beautiful," he said.

"And you look very handsome."

The marquee was gorgeous and the rest of the estate was exquisitely decorated. A bottle of French white wine was placed on each table, together with a bottle of red wine from the Barossa Valley, Australia.

After dinner and some short speeches, everyone partied well into the night. Bessy danced with Lachlan for a good while but at about 8 pm she noticed his energy was starting to fade. She called Roger and Henry over.

"Would you like to go now, Dad?" asked Roger.

"I want to go now," he said.

Paddo chatted with Lachlan's brother towards the end of the night and thanked him for coming from Wales. "I hear your friend Tom is becoming a private investigator," he said. "I think he might be very good one day. I've given him a little job to practise on. I think he's had a little too much to drink, but he made me laugh when I needed to laugh." There was a tear in his uncle's eye and Paddo gave him a hug and said he would visit him soon.

A sprinkle of rain fell, as Bessy and Paddo got into the car near on midnight. Tom kissed Bessy and Miriam kissed them both. The day was ending. As they pulled out of the estate, Bessy said, "I want this day to last forever. Can't we stop time, just for a while?"

* * * *

Five days later, the phone call came.

Paddo and Bessy donned rain jackets and jumpers. High on the moor, the wind blew with some force and the sky was big and grey. The view to the coast was partly obscured by the clouds, but they could still see the water. The sky curved from one horizon to another, making it look like the roundness of the Earth could be viewed from where they stood. The ground was dressed in shades of green with tufts of brown and yellow, and a dusting of winter white. Exmoor was in one of its many and varied moods, and Bessy marvelled at its beauty as she started to walk, holding tightly on to her grieving husband's hand. "He's in a better place, now."

Paddo stopped and tried to look out over the ocean. Bessy watched his tears fall down his cheeks.

"I'm sorry it's not a clearer day," he said. "That you can't see Wales across the water. But I know it's there." He paused then said, "I want to visit my uncle soon. I want to get to know him."

"I will take you to visit him. We will journey to Wales together," she said.

They turned and continued to walk, the silence broken only by the swirling gusts. The only person they could see was a farmer, tending his sheep, way off in the distance. Strands of Bessy's hair flicked around her face underneath the edges of her woollen beanie. She realised she could help Paddo with his grief. Her own losses had strengthened her and she knew she could give him something even more than her love in his time of pain.

ACKNOWLEDGEMENTS

Thanks to Michael Charlwood for his cover artwork and to Patrice Shaw from PS Editing and Kirsty Ogden from Epiphany Editing & Publishing, Brisbane.

ABOUT THE AUTHOR

Carl Spence is 53 and lives in regional New South Wales with his wife. *The Girl from Jeparit* is the first in a three-part series, although each book is a standalone story. This novel is Carl's first foray into fiction writing and he hopes to have novels two and three available in the not too distant future.

www.ingramcontent.com/pod-product-compliance
Lightning Source LLC
Chambersburg PA
CBHW021417110726
47901CB00008B/2198